ONLY THE TRUTH

ADAM CROFT

**BLACK CANNON
PUBLISHING**

First published in Great Britain in 2017.

Previously published by Thomas & Mercer, Seattle.

This edition published in 2021 by Black Cannon Publishing.

ISBN: 978-1-912599-69-1

A CIP catalogue record for this book is available from the British Library.

Printed and bound in Great Britain by Clays Ltd, Elcograf S.p.A.

MORE BOOKS BY ADAM CROFT

RUTLAND CRIME SERIES

KNIGHT & CULVERHOUSE CRIME THRILLERS

PSYCHOLOGICAL THRILLERS

- Only The Truth
- In Her Image
- Tell Me I'm Wrong
- The Perfect Lie
- Closer To You

KEMPSTON HARDWICK MYSTERIES

1. Exit Stage Left
2. The Westerlea House Mystery
3. Death Under the Sun
4. The Thirteenth Room
5. The Wrong Man

All titles are available to order from all good book shops.

Signed and personalised books available at adamcroft.net/shop

EBOOK-ONLY SHORT STORIES

- Gone
- The Harder They Fall
- Love You To Death
- The Defender

To find out more, visit adamcroft.net

To someone very small, who I've not yet met, and doesn't yet know it, but is about to change my life forever.

This job has its perks. One of the best ones is lying next to me right now, giggling as she catches her breath.

'Sounds like you need to exercise more often,' I tease.

She punches my arm – gently, playfully – and tells me she's more than happy with the workout she's just had. 'It's gone three,' she says, padding at my shoulder. 'I've got to get back downstairs. That reception won't run itself. And you're going to need to get some dinner before you risk turning into an Adonis yourself.'

She's got a point – I've got a bit of a beer belly, but it's hardly noticeable when I'm lying down. And, let's face it, that's the position she's mostly seen me in since I came to stay here almost a week ago. Like I said, the job has its perks.

'Jesus, look at the state of my make-up,' she says, standing up and glancing in the mirror at the other end of the room. As she leans to the side, the faded scar below her belly button becomes slightly more pronounced. Just another small thing that makes Jess unique. She pulls her face in all sorts of odd directions, as if that's going to fix her make-up. That's one of the things I like best about her – she's got that remarkable vain streak in a personality that otherwise doesn't give a shit. I've only known her a few days, but she intrigues me more than almost any woman I've met.

And I've met a lot. This job takes me all over the country – and further, sometimes. It's a nice way to separate life from reality, giving you a sense of adventure whilst earning an honest crust. Not many people are able to say that. I'm lucky. You only need to mention to women that you work in TV, and you're golden. Even when you elaborate and tell them you just supply and help erect lighting rigs, all they want to know is which celebrities you've met and what film sets you've worked on. I don't mind; it's a means to an end.

'You know,' she says, finally relenting and climbing back into bed, 'I really should fix that telly for you one day.'

'I've only got a day and a half left here. It'd be a shame to waste it.' I plant a long kiss on her lips.

I've always been quite good at telling when a woman is interested in me, and I'd judged from her body language when I arrived at the hotel a few days ago that things might be promising. You can just tell. I'm rarely wrong. I'd gone up to my room, left it a few minutes, then came back down to tell her the TV wasn't working. Right on cue, she offered to take a look herself. Since then, the ruse of 'fixing the TV' had taken on a whole new meaning altogether.

She leans her head on my chest and plays with the hairs around my navel. 'I can hear your heart beating,' she says.

'Always a good sign,' I reply, running my hands through her hair. It feels so soft and light. Carefree. Just like her.

She giggles and taps me on the chest. 'At least it shows you're alive. That's a start.'

'I often thought I wasn't.'

'Oooh, deep,' she says. 'Far too deep.'

I laugh. 'Nah, seriously. My dad was a doctor and I remember him trying to teach me basic first-aid stuff when I was younger. The usual stuff: how to put someone in the recovery position, how to tie a tourniquet. He used to get really short-tempered when I couldn't find pulses. I was terrible at it. I could just about find one on the wrist some-times, but for some reason I couldn't do it from the neck. It used to drive him mad. He told me I'd be a terrible doctor.'

'That doesn't sound very nice.'

'He was right, though,' I say, laughing. 'The human body's not really my area of expertise.'

'Oh, I don't know,' she says impishly. 'You seem to know your way around pretty well. Tell me about your family.'

This takes me a little by surprise. 'Sorry?'

'You mentioned your dad. Tell me more about them.'

I'm never really one for talking about my family or my childhood, nor do I see why I should make an exception for a girl I barely know, but she seems genuinely interested. Very few people are genuinely interested in me.

'They were good people,' I say. 'Very good people.'

'Is that it?'

'What more do you want to know? He was a doctor; she was a legal secretary.'

'Was?'

I swallow. 'Yeah. They're dead now.'

'I'm sorry.'

'Don't be,' I reply. 'And before you ask, cancer. Got them both within eighteen months. Mum's was bowel, Dad's was lung. Ironic for a man who spent his life telling people to stop smoking and who knew all the signs to look out for.'

'What kind of doctor?'

'Just a GP,' I say, as if this is some sort of ignoble choice of profession. 'He had his own practice by the time he retired. Then he was dead within four months. Mum followed soon after.'

'So now you're a poor little orphan boy?' she says, lightly and teasingly, although the comment stings me more than it has any right to.

'Yeah. Something like that.'

She kisses me on the lips, more gently this time, then slides back out of the bed and bends down to pick up her underwear. I can't help but admire the light curves. She's small, petite, but perfectly formed. It's almost as if it gives her a charm and innocence – something which is quite a big turn-on, seeing as I know she's far from innocent.

'I must say, I'm quite enjoying having a broken TV,' I say, changing the subject. 'It's certainly got its advantages.'

'Well, yeah, not having Channels 4 or 5 is definitely an advantage,' she says, winking at me in the mirror as she starts to touch up her make-up.

'I dunno. I quite like to spend my mid-afternoons watching *Countdown*. I've not had any better offers recently.'

She picks up my boxer shorts and throws them at me, the soft fabric landing on my chest. 'If you're not careful, I'll fix your damn telly and you can watch as much *Countdown* as you like. Now, you'd better go down to the restaurant. Dinner's included in your room cost, you know.'

'I know. Good job, too, as I doubt many people would actually pay for it.'

'Harsh,' she says. 'But true.'

'I'm going to take a shower,' I say, standing and tossing the boxer shorts onto the chair beside the bed. 'Probably best I don't follow you straight downstairs. People might start talking.'

'Well, we wouldn't want that, now, would we, Dan?' she says, with a slow wink which gets me hard again.

She kisses me again at the door and leaves, somehow managing to look just as flawless as she did twenty minutes ago. And, once again, I'm on my own.

2

The water from the shower feels softer, lighter than usual. It always does when I'm by the coast. I know there's likely no rhyme or reason for it. I don't know if it's something to do with hard-water and soft-water areas – I don't even know whether I live in a hard-water or a soft-water area anyway. Water's just water, surely? It's probably all in my mind. But it's got to be said – showers feel better in Herne Bay than they do in East Grinstead. As a matter of fact, most things feel better in Herne Bay than they do in East Grinstead. The women certainly do.

I rinse the lather from my body, switch off the shower and towel myself down. It's weird – showering's such a private thing, yet I wonder how many people have had a shower in here, how many have used this towel, slept in that bed, sat on that toilet. People could have even died in here, for all I know. If you think about how many rooms are in a hotel and how many people stay there each week, it must happen pretty regularly. It's one of those odd unspoken truths about hotels, and for some reason none of us seem to mind. It's a case of having to deal with it, I think. You play the hand you're dealt. It's all you can do. Another job, another hotel. That's the way it is in this industry.

We've been working on the set of a period drama. A few big names, but it's still a load of bollocks. These things always are. Junk-viewing for the masses. If you starve people for long enough, they'll happily eat shit. Seven days here, then we're done and back to sunny Sussex. It's easy enough work – very early starts, but then we're usually off the set by 2 p.m. I say that, but in reality I'm barely on it other than when a rig needs moving or taking down. It's almost like being on a paid holiday, except you do need to do a few hours' work every now and again. Not that I can really call it work. There's a lot of standing around, followed by a lot of frantic construction and dismantling, followed by a lot more standing around. They say working in TV is glamorous, but it's actually really very boring.

One of the big benefits is being able to see a lot of the country, and other countries too from time to time. The production company I work for tends to do UK-based dramas, but on the rare occasion when I get to go abroad, it's always an extra bonus. There aren't many jobs where you get to sit in a deckchair in Marrakech, for example, watching some of TV's biggest stars do their thing. To be perfectly honest, it's far from being the worst job in the world. But the grass is always greener, isn't it?

Herne Bay's not quite Marrakech, I must admit. It's a

pretty little coastal town, not somewhere I've been before, but there are certainly some very nice sights around. And yes, Jessica's one of them. The beauty of it all is that she knows nothing long-term's going to happen. She's a receptionist at a hotel, and I live seventy miles away – when I'm even home – with my wife. Okay, so she doesn't know about that last bit, but why should she? It'd do no-one any good to start rocking the boat now. It's not an act of deception. Not really. Lisa knows I'm an independent sort of person. She knows I've got history and that it's no use trying to put shackles on me because then I fight harder. I'm not the perfect husband, but who is? We've all got our faults and our weaknesses. Mine is other women. It could certainly be much worse.

Lisa and I are very different people. We live almost completely separate lives, apart from the odd few days a month when I'm actually home for any decent period of time. She's always been into physical jobs, too, from farm work to delivery driving. That's not to say she hasn't got an academic brain – she certainly has – but she gets far more pleasure out of physical work, which I can appreciate. It's one of the only similarities we have, apart from the unspoken truth that we're never going to have kids. It's never something that's been mentioned, but we both know the other doesn't want them and we're both fine with that. I guess deep down we're both free spirits trapped in the same rat race and faceless world as everyone else.

These are the sorts of things that tend to go through my mind while I take a shower. Other people sing; I philosophise. Usually about the strange disconnect I have between my two deep desires: firstly, to pack in all this travelling around anonymous and impersonal hotels and stay at home; secondly, to just up sticks and disappear somewhere, embracing my inner being. I think that's the constant state of suspension most people are in at some point in their lives. It's human nature at its very simplest level. It's fight or flight.

Although I don't mind being away from home, I miss my creature comforts. After what I went through in my childhood, I don't take anything for granted. I'm perfectly used to not having them most of the time – I went for years with nothing but my own company – but that doesn't mean I don't miss life's little luxuries. Things like food. I like my own cooking, and always have. I wouldn't say I'm fussy about food, but I know what I like and I know what I don't like. Unfortunately, as glamorous as working in television might sound, the truth is you're usually put up in the same bland orange chain hotels with the same bland orange walls and the same bland orange food. 'You always know what you're getting' is their big selling point. For me, that's half the problem.

I prefer charm, personality. I like something a bit different and out of the ordinary. I guess that's one of the things that attracted me to Jess. Her slightly alternative look is something that appeals. It speaks of a woman who can control herself, who knows what she likes and isn't afraid to go out there and get it. I think most men would find it hard not to be turned on by those qualities in a woman.

You need a bit of variety and spice when you're working in a job like this. It's far more boring than people think, but it's all I know. It didn't require any fancy degrees or A Levels – just a keen eye for detail and the ability to work really strange hours whilst drinking your body weight in coffee every day. All things I excel at.

When I come to think of it, this job is just as faceless as the hotel they've put me up in. Far too many people are pretending they like each other and telling everyone how talented they are, when really they're just in it for themselves. I'm not going to lie – I'm exactly the same. That's the truth. Only the truth hurts sometimes.

3

There's writing on the wall. It's illegible, but there's an arrow going from it, pointing to a crude drawing of what looks like a penguin. It's been there ever since he's had this bed, and he knows its every line and angle. Every last piece of graphite dust. He doesn't know what the picture means, but that's irrelevant. It's a distraction. It's something for him to look at, something for the mind to concentrate on while he tries to block out the sobs of Teddy Tomlin. Even at his age, he knows what those sobs mean. He's heard them many times before and he'll hear them many times again.

He knows what it's like. He's been there himself, not so long ago. They have to show you who's in charge, have to make it perfectly clear that they're doing you a favour and giving you food, warmth and an occasional smattering of comforts. And they're doing it because no-one else will. Because you've got no other option. Because your parents didn't love you enough to keep you. Because you're a bastard *child. Because your mummy and daddy were too selfish to stay alive.*

The whitewashed brick walls should be cold, firm, unloving. But to Daniel they're the warmest part of this whole place. They feel so warm because they signify the outside; the big wide world that he's going to be allowed out into in just a few years' time. They won't let him out now, because he's only seven years, three months and fourteen days old. Tomorrow he'll be seven years, three months and fifteen days old. One day nearer his sixteenth birthday.

Even though this is all he's ever really known, he's certain that the outside world will be kinder to him. It'll present opportunities, direction. It'll be free from early-morning bell calls, free from nuns floating innocently down corridors, free from whitewashed walls.

He doesn't remember much from before. Nothing, really. He thinks it's because he was very young at the time, but the Mother Superior says it's because God is protecting him. He isn't sure if he believes in God, but he doesn't have a choice in a place like this.

It's very odd, he thinks, how he's being told that he's here because he's godless, because God has punished him, yet God is protecting him. He's a funny bloke, God. A strange mix of anger, benevolence and whimsy. It reminds him rather of Mr Duggan, who comes to visit the home occasionally. The Mother Superior tells the boys Mr Duggan is a very important man, but he's not sure how. Whenever Mr Duggan comes to visit, a couple of the boys are sent to see him. Sometimes they go one at a time, sometimes in pairs. The boys are never very happy when they come back from seeing Mr Duggan. Some of them are quiet; some of them cry. Some of them have faces filled with hurt and anger. Most of them seem confused.

Daniel's been lucky. He's never been sent to see Mr Duggan. He's not quite sure why, because some boys have been sent twice, three times. They're the ones who are quiet when they return. They don't look angry or hurt. They just look empty. They're the ones who have given up.

It's Thursday tomorrow. Thursday means games. It means getting outside in the fresh air and running around for an hour or two. It means letting off some steam. It builds up and starts to eat away at you from the inside if you're not careful. That's why you need things to look forward to. Like games. Like your sixteenth birthday. Eight years, eight months and fifteen days. November the sixteenth is the next big milestone. His eighth birthday. He'll be exactly halfway there. Halfway to the first day of his life.

Teddy Tomlin's sobbing has quietened down a bit. Daniel daren't ask him why he's crying. He knows why he's crying. It's the same reason boys throughout Pendleton House are crying right now. Even in his formative years, he knows that the most painful truths are truths unspoken. Truths that everybody knows but nobody dares speak.

He pulls Percy, his stuffed bear, closer to him. Percy's his only link to before. He's the only thing Daniel came here with. The bear's starting to get a little scruffy around the edges, some cotton threads starting to fray and come loose. Much like Daniel himself. But he's going to keep on hugging

Percy every night, well aware that this comforting act will put more pressure on the bear's fraying threads and loose seams, helping the inner stuffing ooze out through the gaps.

The moonlight coming in through the window is a pretty shade of blue. It gives some colour to the wall and the pencilled penguin. It won't last long – the light will move to the other side of the room by dawn and Teddy Tomlin will be greeted by the warm morning's sun on his face. It's the way it's always been, and it's the way it always will be for another eight years, eight months and fifteen days. But he doesn't mind that. He's counting down.

The radiators clatter and gurgle as the central heating winds down for the night. Not that it does a particularly good job of heating Pendleton House when it's on, but its daily death rattle signifies the end of another day and the impending dawn of another day closer to the big day.

In the silence, he registers that Teddy Tomlin's sobs have become a gentle snore. He rolls over as quietly as he can and squints against the moonlight. The reflection from the white-washed walls allows him to see the dried tears on Teddy Tomlin's cheeks, belying his peaceful, sleeping face.

Daniel decides to close his eyes and do the same.

4

It's the dreadful, bland food I'm not especially looking forward to as I get dressed and head downstairs to the restaurant. There's no-one on reception as I walk through, which is nothing new, and I wonder where Jess might be.

Despite it being fairly early, there are still two families in the restaurant with screaming bloody kids. It's almost like they're trying to outdo each other. I say restaurant, but it's more like a cross between a McDonald's and a farm. Another put-you-up identikit gastropub designed to make hotel guests feel at home wherever they are. If home happens to be an abattoir, that is.

The barman tries to engage me in conversation. He asks me if I'm staying here for business or pleasure. *Both,* I want to tell him. *I'm screwing that little receptionist you've probably had your eye on for the past couple of months.* 'Business,' I say. 'I work in TV.' I immediately regret saying it, as those two letters inevitably draw people into conversation.

'Oh cool!' he says, his voice rising an octave as his shoulders bob and he tucks a long strand of hair behind his ear. 'My brother's a runner on that programme. The one that's on in the mornings.'

'*This Morning?*' I ask, more than a hint of sarcasm in my voice.

'Yeah, that's the one. He wants to get into presenting at some point. That's how quite a lot of them get started, apparently.'

'Apparently.'

'So what do you do?' He leans forward on the bar, and I realise I'm in for the long haul.

'Nothing very exciting,' I say. 'I design and put up lighting rigs on location sets.'

'Oh cool!' he says again. 'Do you get to meet lots of big stars?'

'I see them occasionally. They don't tend to engage with the likes of us, though. They're too busy trying to remember the three lines they're getting paid a six-figure sum to say.'

He laughs and pulls another strand of hair behind his ear. 'That's really cool. Beats working in a bar, anyway.'

'I wouldn't bet on it.'

The food arrives after a rather worryingly quick eight minutes, so I wolf it down as quickly as I can and head back towards my room. As I pass through reception, I notice Jess sat behind the desk, a work colleague filing some papers beside her. I can only presume she keeps her liaisons as discreet as I do, so I throw her a cheeky wink and a smile as I pass by and head up the stairs.

The one good thing about these hotels is the satisfying duet of the *click* and *clunk* as the door to my room closes behind me. It's the sound that tells me I'm back in my nest, safe from the outside world. I think it's the act of locking the door, knowing that there won't be anyone coming in to upset the quiet. No more Mr Duggans. Despite the fact that I've only spent a few nights in this room, its identical similarity to every other hotel room I've stayed in this year makes it feel like home.

I switch on the bedside light and point the remote control at the TV, pressing the big red button at the top. Something catches my eye as I walk back past the TV towards the bathroom. It's the large number 4 in the top corner of the screen. Somehow, the telly seems to have fixed itself. Weird.

Realising that I'll be able to spend the evening watching a couple of channels I didn't particularly have any interest in anyway, I head into the bathroom to brush my teeth and get ready for bed.

I don't usually like seeing myself in the mirror, for fairly obvious reasons. I'm not the best-looking bloke in the world, for starters. As I gaze into the mirror this time, though, the usual face of tiredness and lost hope has something else lurking behind it, shining through. It's that fire I lost a long time ago; something I'm sure has been brought out by Jess. She seems to have a sense of intrigue and yearning for life which leaves me fascinated and motivated in equal measure. The fact that I won't see her again after the next day or two doesn't seem to matter. Sometimes you meet someone – perhaps only fleetingly – who can change your life forever. And that's fine.

I look fresh, invigorated. As if I can take on even the biggest challenges. In that moment, I also realise that I want to try to be a better husband. Sure, I've done bad things. We all have. But if I can do what I want to do and limit, or completely cut out, the amount of time I'm spending staying away from home, that'll kill two birds with one stone. No temptation, no problem.

I spit the toothpaste out of my mouth and take a few slurps from the tap to rinse. I take a towel from the rack and dry my face, and that's when I notice it.

The shower curtain is closed.

That's not particularly odd, I know, but I definitely left it open when I went down for dinner earlier. I always do. These horrible plastic shower curtains look dreadful, so I certainly don't want to be looking at it every time I go to the bathroom.

It starts to make a bit more sense now. Someone's come up to fix the TV and has, for some reason, pulled the shower curtain across as well. I really wish they wouldn't. I take hold of the edge of the curtain and pull it back, the silver rings rattling along the rail as it flies open, revealing the horror behind it.

It's a dead body.

It's my wife.

5

I stare, shock and fear taking over my whole body. I don't know how long I'm standing there, as time seems to stop completely still. Every time I blink, every moment that passes, the panic and horror seems to grow. I don't know if I'm even breathing, if I'm even existing. It's too much for me to take in.

I really have no idea how to react. I veer violently between disbelief, anger, paranoia, sadness and the sense that my whole world has just come crashing down around me. I can feel my lower lip trembling, and I can almost hear my brain trying to kick into gear, searching through the mental files for the one that tells it how to deal with immense trauma. Until the right file is found, I appear to have defaulted to 'freeze and go blank'. There's just nothing there. Absolutely nothing.

I steady myself and try to think straight. It's Lisa. It's definitely Lisa. You aren't married to someone for eight years without knowing what they look like, even in this state. Even when it's obvious there's absolutely no light left in their eyes. They say you can always tell when someone's dead; they no longer look like a person. They become a shell, a husk, the body that once held a soul.

I force myself to look in more detail, to understand what the hell I'm seeing. She's fully dressed, her hair slightly dishevelled, but otherwise looking like the Lisa I know and love. Her mouth hangs open, and I can see her tongue resting gently against the top of her bottom teeth. It looks as though she's been strangled; there's a red mark right around her neck that looks like some sort of rope burn. There's no blood that I can see, which comes as a strange sort of relief. It's an odd word to use, but somehow the lack of blood makes her seem more peaceful.

This is my wife. The woman I married. The woman I vowed to spend my whole life with. And now she's lying dead in front of me. I feel my legs begin to wobble, struggling to hold me upright. I turn and lean against the sink, feeling it creak as my body weight pushes down on it, my chest heaving as I struggle for breath. It's then that I realise I haven't been breathing since I pulled back that shower curtain. My eyes begin to hurt, the blood pulsing at my temples.

But there's one question that comes into my mind before any other thoughts: Why is she here? She's meant to be seventy miles away back home in East Grinstead. She was there when I spoke to her this morning. She just doesn't belong here. It's like seeing an old friend or work colleague in the same resort on holiday. If they're out of context, the brain struggles for a few seconds to deal with it. Now imagine that a thousand times worse.

I blink hard and scratch my face. None of this makes any sense. When I last spoke to her she was enjoying lazing in bed on her day off. She was going to get up and watch some TV, then get on the treadmill for a couple of hours. How did she end up in my hotel room in Herne Bay? Had she come to surprise me? That really doesn't sound like Lisa at all; she's not a spontaneous sort of person. It wouldn't even cross her mind. No, I know from the way she sounded when I spoke to her this morning that she had no intention of coming here. I know my wife, and she couldn't keep a secret if her life depended on it. She even managed to tell me about the surprise birthday party she'd organised for me last year. I pretended it didn't matter and that it was the thought that counted, but secretly I was gutted. She's just completely incapable of keeping her mouth shut.

The mark around her neck is what's freaking me out the most. Knowing that's what killed her. I hover the back of my hand in front of her nose to feel for any sign of breath. There's nothing. My hand shakes with fear, and it brushes the tip of her nose as I draw it towards me. It feels cold. She can't have been dead more than twenty minutes – I left the room barely half an hour ago – but her nose is already cold. It's possible she was killed before she got to the room, but how on earth would someone drag a dead body through a hotel without anyone noticing? To me, it doesn't look like she's been dead long at all, so I can only assume she died here, in this room.

I think back to when I returned to my room. Was the door locked? Yes, I'm sure it was. They lock automatically from the outside anyway, don't they? I don't think it even has an actual lock that you can operate without the key card. There wasn't any sign that anyone had broken in. No broken windows, no damage to the door. So how did she get in here? Who brought her here? Why did she come in the first place?

The realisation suddenly hits me – far later than it should have done – that Lisa died by someone else's hands. It sounds stupid to say it, seeing as it's perfectly clear, but it's something I observed rather than registered and understood. And now it's hit me. Not only that she's dead, but that she isn't coming back. And someone has killed her deliberately. I can feel the tears dropping down my face, the adrenaline pulsing through my limbs. But I know I need to think clearly.

There's no sign of what she was strangled with, so whatever was used has been taken away. By the person who did it. My wife has been murdered. In my hotel room. Seventy miles away from where she's meant to be.

It's like a dream; nothing makes sense and yet I can do nothing but accept that it's all entirely true. There's no other option. It's here, right here in front of me, laid out as if it's the most obvious thing in the world, yet it seems to be completely and utterly random. It feels like there's a huge electrical charge going through my brain as it tries to comprehend what's going on in front of me, trying to find some sort of logic in what's happened. But it really isn't working.

I look at Lisa's body more closely, slumped in the bath like a discarded rag doll. Many times I've watched her sleeping late at night when I've been unable to relax, but she looks completely different now. There's something in her hand. Her mobile phone. I pick it up, gently, trying not to come into contact with her body, and I look at the phone. The screen is on. The screen's never on – it's set to turn off automatically after thirty seconds. I've been here much longer than thirty seconds already, so she must have disabled that setting. Why? She never fiddles with the settings on her phone. She's a complete technophobe, and she'd be terrified of breaking it. She wouldn't even take the protective plastic stickers off the front of it for a good four months after she bought it. That all seems so pedestrian now. Now that she's dead.

The adrenaline is still surging through me and my hands are shaking, trembling as I look at what's on the screen. It's a text message.

Come up to room 112. I have something I need to tell you.

My eyes rise to the top of the screen as I look to see who sent it.

It's from me.

6

I dart into the bedroom and grab my phone from the bedside table. It's exactly where I left it before I went down to dinner. I always leave it up here. I'm not the sort of person to sit playing on my phone in the middle of a restaurant, no matter how bad it is. It takes me a couple of attempts to unlock my phone, my fingers shaking as I jab in the four-digit pin code.

I go into my Messages app and open up the conversation thread with Lisa. We don't really text much, so the only messages there are spread out over the past couple of weeks. The message on Lisa's phone isn't here on mine, though.

I go back into the bathroom and pick Lisa's phone up off the floor, where I dropped it. I tap my name at the top. It was definitely sent from my phone number, from my phone. I look at the time the text was sent. I can't be sure, but I reckon it was only a couple of minutes after I went down for dinner.

The only thing I can be sure of is exactly how this looks. I'm not stupid. My wife's lying dead in my hotel room, seventy miles away from home and anyone she knows, shortly after a text was sent from my phone to tell her to come up to my room. After I'd spent a good deal of the year working away from home as our marriage slowly broke down. Oh, and I'd been screwing the receptionist.

Again, that mix of emotions flips and turns inside me. Anger, fear, paranoia, desperation. Not only has someone murdered my wife, but they've tried to pin it on me.

Everything's a blur. I can't have been back in my room a minute, if that. Two, tops. Yet my brain seems to know exactly what to do. Even though this whole situation is confusing the hell out of my conscious mind, my subconscious is right there, dealing with this quickly and instinctively.

What can I do? Call the police? There's no way I can prove this wasn't me. I was downstairs in the restaurant for twenty minutes, perhaps half an hour at the most. They can't be that specific about a time of death, particularly as she will have died at most fifteen minutes apart from me either leaving the room or re-entering it.

I try to think about whether or not the hotel has CCTV. Even if it does, it'll presumably show Lisa heading to my room, then me doing the same a few minutes later. Around the time she was killed.

The husband is the prime suspect in any murder, I

know that much, and this one is going to look like a pretty open-and-shut case for even the laziest police detective.

My instincts take over. I walk steadily back into the bedroom, collect my things together, shove them into my holdall and leave the room.

I don't know where I'm going. I don't know what I'm going to do. All I know is that running isn't going to make things any worse this time. If I stay, I'm doomed to the same fate that I could possibly, just possibly, get away from. It sounds crazy, but that thought pops into my head again: the desire to up sticks and disappear, embracing my free spirit. In this moment, I know I will never truly be free, but right now the only option I have is to try.

My legs feel like jelly as I descend the stairs. I can hear the blood pulsing in my temples and feel my heart trying to burst through my chest. Everything else appears to be silent. I can't even hear my footsteps on the floor, nor can I feel them. Everything is numb. It's almost as if I'm cocooned, unable to take in any sort of external stimuli. As I push open the door to reception and head for the exit, the sound of Jessica's voice bursts through my bubble and yanks me back into reality.

'Dan? Is everything okay?'

I just look at her, unable to say anything. I can see that she's spotted something in my eyes as they well up, the tears clouding my vision as I blink furiously to hold them back. I manage it.

'Fine,' I say.

'Are you sure? Where are you going with all your stuff?'

'I have to go,' I say. 'I need to check out.'

'You're not due to check out until tomorrow,' she says, almost as if I've somehow got the days muddled up – silly me – but with more than a hint of concern in her voice, too. 'You don't look well, Dan.'

'No, I feel ill,' I say, hoping this somehow explains everything. 'Sorry, I have to go.'

I pick up my bag and head for the exit, my hand fumbling in my pocket for my car key as I walk quickly in the direction of where I parked. My head's pounding and I can't even remember what my car looks like. Did I even drive here?

Before I can answer any of those questions, there's a hand on my shoulder. Jessica.

'Dan, what's wrong? What's happened?' she says, a real look of concern in her eyes now.

'I'm sorry,' I reply. It's all I can think to say. I kiss her on the forehead.

I press the unlock button on my car's key fob and walk over to where I heard the bleep and saw the lights flashing. Jessica's still trying to talk to me as I open the boot and throw my bag in, closing it before I walk round and climb into the driver's seat. Before I get there, Jessica's opened the passenger door and got in.

'What are you doing?' I say.

'I don't know, but I'm not letting you go like this. Something's not right, Dan. Tell me. I'm not taking no for an answer.'

I sit in silence, staring through the windscreen for what

seems like an age. Suddenly, it feels like I've got all the time in the world to work out my reply, almost as if the solitude of the car has provided some sort of barrier. I know I need to tell her. She'll find out in a few hours anyway, but she should at least know that I'm innocent. The police won't believe a word she says, but I hope that at least she will know. Someone needs to know.

'My wife. Lisa. She's here.' All that time sat silently and that's the best I can come up with.

'Here?' she replies. 'Where?'

'In my bathroom.'

'I'm not sure I understand.'

'She's lying in my bathtub. Dead.'

Jessica just sits looking at me. I'm still looking straight ahead, but I can feel her eyes burning into the side of my face.

'Dan, what happened?' she whispers.

'I don't know. I came back up to my room after dinner and she was lying there. I swear.'

'But how? How did she get in there? How did she die?'

'It looks like she was strangled.'

Jessica takes her eyes off me for the first time. 'Jesus, Dan. We need to call the police.'

I sigh. 'We can't. They'll think it was me.'

'Why would they?' she says. 'You were down in the restaurant. If it wasn't you, you can prove it. They have forensics and stuff. If you didn't do it, what's the matter?'

'I can't explain,' I repeat.

'I really can't get my head round this,' she says. 'This is crazy.'

'Tell me about it.'

She puts her hand on my upper leg. 'Dan. Look at me. Look me in the eye and tell me you didn't kill Lisa.'

'I told you, I didn't. I just came back up to my room and—'

'I need you to look me in the eye and tell me, Dan. It's important.'

I do as she says. Her eyes look lost, hopeful and desperate.

'I didn't do it.'

She closes her eyes and nods, then puts on her seatbelt. 'Start the car.'

7

Before I even know where I'm going, I've put the car in gear and I'm driving out of the car park, my tunnel vision focused dead straight ahead of me.

'Head for town,' Jessica says, pointing out over my front-right headlight.

'Why? Where are we going?'

'As far away as possible,' she says, 'but we'll need money. The banks will still be open if we're quick.'

'What about an ATM?' I ask, my head filling with a mixture of a fog of confusion and the screaming of a thousand violins.

She just looks at me. 'How far's three hundred quid going to get us? We need to be able to go into the branch and withdraw as much as we can. What's your bank's limit?'

Right now I don't even know my name. 'I dunno. I've never asked.'

'Which bank are you with?'

'Lloyds.'

'There's one on the High Street,' she says. 'Keep going and I'll show you.'

I try to start to make sense of my thoughts. 'Should we not be getting as far away as possible? I don't feel comfortable staying around here.'

Jessica smiles and chuckles slightly. 'You need to try to keep a level head. No-one's going to know about Lisa until tomorrow mid-morning at the earliest. That's when the maid service will be up to clean the room. We've got, what, eighteen hours? We can be on the other side of the world by then. Let's take our time, think this through and stay calm.'

Now it's my turn to laugh. I can't help myself.

'What? What are you laughing at?' she says.

'You. How can you stay so calm? The wife of a bloke you've known a couple of days is lying murdered in a hotel room and you decide to jump in the car with him and escape to God knows where.'

She's silent for a couple of moments before she speaks, whispering, 'I trust you.'

'I wouldn't trust me.'

'Why not?'

I shake my head. 'It doesn't matter.'

We drive in silence for the next minute or so, weaving slowly through the traffic, towards the High Street, before Jessica speaks again.

'I haven't always worked on a hotel reception. I've known some bad people. I know when I'm looking into the eyes of a killer. If you'd ever looked into the eyes of a killer, you'd know, too.'

I consider this for a moment. This young slip of a girl, barely – actually, I realise I don't even know how old she is, but she can't be any older than twenty-three – how can she have looked into the eyes of a killer? I know from work I've done in the past on documentaries that everyone has a story. There are children who've suffered the most horrendous physical and sexual abuse before they've even reached their second birthday. I've been there and seen it myself. So why not a young adult who's seen murder?

'Do you want to talk about it?' I ask.

'No. I don't,' she replies, firmly enough to let me know that this subject is off limits – but only for now.

When we get to the High Street, Jessica points out the branch of Lloyds and I swing into William Street, parking up on the double yellow lines. An elderly couple sitting on a bench give me a look of reproach, but I don't care. There are at least two other cars doing exactly the same further down the street. I get out and jog across the road and into the bank.

I already know what I'm going to do: I'm going to draw out as much as I possibly can. Yeah, it'll arouse suspicion, but so what? In a few hours' time I'm going to be suspected of murder, so what the hell do a few raised eyebrows in a bank matter?

There's a queue, as there always is in any bank. I guess this is a busy time for them – lots of people have already finished work or are trying to get something done before the bank shuts for the day. I'm torn between panicking over the fact that more people here means more people might see me and the sheer desperation to get as far away from this place as possible.

Slowly, the queue moves forward. The only person left in front of me is a young mother with a screaming baby. That might not be so bad under any other circumstances, but right now my head is pounding and I just don't need the added aggravation. I can see we're going to be here a little while longer, though: the two clerks are each occupied serving their own pensioner, neither of which looks like they're going to be done any time soon.

'Sorry about the noise,' the young mum says. 'She's had a right day of it.'

'Her and me both,' I say, trying to sound as polite as possible.

'Can't tell them to shut up at that age, neither. They don't listen.'

I smile and nod. 'How old is she?'

'Four months.'

The first thing that pops into my head is how mothers always refer to their children's ages in terms of months. *He's eighteen months.* No, he's a year and a half. *This is my son Malcolm. He works as an insurance broker. He's four hundred and twelve months.*

'She's probably teething,' I reply.

'I bloody hope not. Don't much fancy having to deal with that.'

Before I have to fight too hard to bite my tongue, one of

the pensioners has cashed in his five hundred pounds in ten-pence pieces and is shuffling towards the door, leaving the single mother clear to land. Not long after, the other pensioner has finished, too, and I approach the clerk, trying to look as normal and comfortable as possible.

'I'd like to withdraw some money, please,' I say, placing my debit card into the privacy tray.

'You'll need to pop your card in the machine, love,' she says, pointing at the chip-and-pin machine next to the bulletproof glass. 'How much would you like?'

'What's the limit?' I say, sliding my card into the slot at the bottom of the machine. 'I'm buying a car and the guy wants a deposit to secure it.' I'm impressed by my own quick thinking.

She looks at me for a moment. 'There's not a limit as such, but it depends on what cash we have in the branch. It's getting towards the end of the day.'

'Right, I see. How much do I have in my account?' I say.

'One moment,' she replies, tapping a few keys on her computer keyboard before getting up and walking off behind the partition wall that presumably separates the cash desks from the offices behind. A minute or so later, she's back, accompanied by a man in an immaculate suit who looks no older than thirty, but whose well-styled hair is already greying at the temples. I assume he's the manager.

'Can I help, sir?' he says, as if he hasn't already been briefed by the cashier.

'Yeah, I'm looking to take some money out. I'm buying a

car,' I say, trying to make it sound like the most normal thing in the world.

'And how much are you looking to take out exactly?'

I swallow, trying to hold back the panic that's surging inside me. 'Well, it depends what I'm allowed to take out.'

'How much is the car?' he asks, throwing me off balance.

'Does it matter?' My voice wobbles slightly.

'Presumably, yes, if you're looking to buy it,' he replies.

'Well, obviously I need to know how much I've got in my account,' I reply.

The manager pauses for a moment. 'This isn't your usual branch, is it?' he says, knowing damn well it isn't.

'No. I use the East Grinstead branch. I'm in Herne Bay because that's where the car is. I came to view it.' My voice is more confident now. This seems to placate him.

'Do you have any ID?'

'Of course,' I reply, fishing into my inside jacket pocket and pulling out my wallet. I extract my driving licence and put it into the privacy tray. The manager slides the guard across, picks up the licence and looks at it, comparing me against the picture. Fortunately for me, the licence is only a few months old so I still look like the picture.

'Did the seller not tell you how much he wanted for a deposit, then?'

'No, I forgot to ask,' I say, immediately regretting doing so. 'Stupid, I know. I need to get it insured and taxed and everything, so I can't drive it away until tomorrow. I'm staying overnight, but I just wanted to secure the car.'

'I see. We can authorise a withdrawal of one thousand pounds this afternoon. If you have some sort of documentation or sale agreement for the car, we could look at authorising more.'

I can't quite believe what I'm hearing. There's at least ten grand in that account. The red mist descends and I can't help challenging this.

'Wait a second. This is my money we're talking about, right?'

'Yes, sir, but we have to abide by very strict rules to protect ourselves from money-laundering regulations.'

'Money laundering?' I say. 'Are you serious? I've been paying *my* money into *my* account for years, and now you're telling me I can't take it out?'

'We have to abide by the guidance of the Financial Conduct Authority,' the manager says. 'If you can—'

'It isn't your money,' I say, more forcefully this time.

'I appreciate that, sir, but I'm afraid I can't do anything more at the moment. Would you like to withdraw the one thousand pounds?'

I look at him for a moment, and then at the female clerk. I don't want to be drawing too much attention to myself.

'Yes, please.'

Crestfallen, I head back outside with the one thousand pounds in my pocket and climb back into the driver's seat of my car.

'How much did you get?' Jessica asks.

'They'd only give me a grand. Some shit about money-laundering regulations.'

'Fuck. I thought they might try pulling that one. We can't do anything with a grand,' she says.

'Well, there's not much else I can do, is there? This is stupid. We should just go to the police, tell them what happened.'

'Are you mad? Tell them what? "Hello, officer. My wife, who's meant to be seventy miles away, is lying dead in my hotel room. Yeah, I know it looks like I killed her, and I know I did a runner and tried to clear my bank account straight after, but it wasn't me, honest." That'll work a treat, that.'

'Do you have any better ideas?' I say, trying to keep my cool.

'Yeah, I do. Do you use PayPal?'

'For eBay and stuff, yeah,' I reply.

'Right. Is it linked to your Lloyds account?'

'Yeah, I've only got one bank account. Why?'

'Go to the PayPal site on my phone,' she says, handing it to me. 'Then send a PayPal payment to my account and make sure it takes the money from your Lloyds account. Then I can transfer the money to my HSBC account and withdraw it myself. If you do it quickly enough, we can get it out before the banks shut for the day.'

My head's spinning, but I do as she says. 'Won't this implicate you, though?' I say, watching the progress bar fill as the browser loads the website. 'If my money is transferred to you, they'll be looking for you, too. How are you going to explain that one?'

'I don't need to explain anything to anyone,' she says. 'I'm already implicated, aren't I? Besides which, I've got plenty to be getting away from myself. I'm not exactly panicking at the idea of leaving the country.'

It makes me feel slightly sad that a woman of her age feels the need to get away from things. She should be having the time of her life. But then I don't know what her life up until now has been like.

'Will you tell me about it? One day, I mean.'

'One day,' she says. 'One day.'

8

When he's outside, Daniel feels like a free spirit. Most young boys do, the wind in their hair, their imaginations running wild. One minute they're a pirate, then a footballer, then they're a soldier. Right now, the game is much simpler. Daniel doesn't know where the frisbee came from. All he knows is that there's no way the Mother Superior would allow them to play with it. If she knew. It would be ungodly, he's sure of that. Most things are.

He thinks it probably came over the wall from outside. Lots of things come in that way. Usually toys – footballs, bags of marbles, now a frisbee. He's never seen any of it come over, but he knows it happens. The other boys tell him. Besides which, there's no other way it could get in here. There are never any visitors, apart from Mr Duggan. Laurence Nelson reckons the toys come over the wall from people who used to live here. People who know what it's like. Teddy Tomlin calls Laurence Nelson a shit-stirrer.

Around this side of the building, they can play without getting told off. There aren't enough nuns to keep an eye on every boy in every part of the grounds. If they're found – when they're found – they'll be marched back inside and given a dressing-down, but it'll be worth the half an hour of fun and forgetting about everything else. It's a regular routine, and it's one they actually quite enjoy.

One of the boys throws the frisbee too far, and it clatters against a tree before falling to the ground. Daniel chases after it, laughing and grinning as he runs, the oxygen burning his lungs in the happiest way imaginable. When he finally reaches the tree, he bends down and picks up the frisbee, the plastic warming in the late-morning sun. He knows he'll not be able to throw it as far as the others from here, so he closes the distance with a run-up before releasing the frisbee at a perfect angle, the disc continuing to rise upwards on its cushion of air.

He realises it's going to overshoot the rest of the boys at about the same time as he sees it's heading towards the window of the morning prayer room. The first thing that goes through his mind is how stupid a place that is to put a window – not only eight feet up in the air so no-one can actually see out of it but also right in the path of a flying frisbee.

His thoughts are punctuated by the shattering of the glass pane and the deathly silence that follows it. None of the boys say a word, but they all look at each other and then at Daniel. He knows he'll be in trouble, but he doesn't know how much. This is unprecedented.

The silence is broken by the all-too-familiar call of the Mother Superior. It helps that the boys are all stood stock-still, looking guilty as sin, but Daniel will bet she already knew who it was before she even left the building. She seems to have eyes and ears in all places.

She doesn't even look at the other boys; just marches straight up to Daniel and tugs at his arm, pulling him back towards the house – which now looks five times its usual size – and his impending fate.

The Mother Superior's office is a place he's been seeing far more of recently. He's already over the hump and on the home run, and he's beginning to get antsy. Seven years, one month and twenty-two days to go. There's an atmosphere around Pendleton House, too, like something's about to change. Transformation is in the air, and Daniel can tell that the Mother Superior has picked up on it as well, and she isn't all that happy about it.

She sits him down on a cold, hard plastic seat before taking her own rest in her plush leather armchair.

'Do you care to explain yourself?' she says after a few moments of silence, her eyes looking at him in her trademark neutral manner that had all of the emotion and anger hidden far behind, out of sight.

Daniel doesn't know what to say.

'Do you know when you were first brought into this office for disciplinary purposes?' the Mother Superior asks, her warm Irish lilt belying the menace of her intentions.

Daniel shakes his head. He does know, but he knows he's not meant to. 'The twelfth of February this year. And do you know how many times you have been here since?' Again, Daniel shakes his head. This time, he really doesn't know the answer. 'Nine,' the Mother Superior tells him. 'Nine times this year, after a previously unblemished record.'

Daniel says nothing. He just continues looking at a dent on the top of her desk, studying its every angle and line. He wishes it could grow, open up and envelop him. He wants to be anywhere but here.

The Mother Superior leans forward, the desk creaking as it takes her weight through her forearms, her hands clasped together.

'We've had talks about you, Daniel. Myself and the other nuns. We were all of the view that your continued bad behaviour cannot be tolerated. You have no idea – no idea – of the sacrifices we have made and continue to make in order to ensure that you're safe in the eyes of God.' As she speaks, Daniel notices her voice becoming firmer and angrier. She's trying to hold it back, trying to keep a lid on it, but the pressure is building. 'I'm afraid we're going to have to move on to the next stage of punishment,' she says, having taken a moment or two to calm herself down.

She stands and walks around to his side of the desk.

'Stand, Daniel,' she says calmly. 'Undo your trousers, pull them to your knees and lean over the desk.' Daniel does as he's told. The first time he was in this situation he had the nerve to ask why she wanted him to do this. That's not a mistake he's going to repeat again. Behind him, he can hear *the Mother Superior rummaging through a drawer. She finds what she's looking for, exhales and then shuts the drawer. 'It gives me absolutely no pleasure to do this, Daniel,' she says, the pleasure clear and evident in her voice.*

Daniel clamps his eyes shut and clenches his buttocks as he hears the air whistle and feels the sharp pain searing through his flesh.

9

It seems like I'm waiting forever, sat in the car while Jessica goes into the nearby branch of HSBC.

I look at the people walking past the car, milling around as they casually get on with their shopping. It seems like a bizarre antithesis to what's going on in my life right now. Will I ever wander around the high street and do my shopping again? It sounds like an odd thing to say, but I really don't know. I don't even know what's going on now, never mind what's going to happen in weeks, months, years from now.

I must look like shit. I can't be anything but, and an elderly gentleman peers into my car for longer than I'd like him to as he slowly saunters past, his walking stick wobbling as he balances far too much of his weight on it. I want to scream *Fuck off, you daft old bugger!* but I think better of it. If the idea is to remain inconspicuous, that's not likely to do the trick.

There are kids running around and screaming, having a great time. The whole outside world just seems so weird – a mix of people going about their daily business and completely unaware of what's just happened only a few hundred yards from here. There's an ever-increasing feeling that people are watching me, judging me, remembering me. I feel like I'm seven years old again, just waiting to be caught for something else I've done wrong, waiting with my pants round my ankles, ready to feel the searing pain.

I try to tell myself that this is one of the tricks the brain plays on you when you've gone through a trauma. I need to remain calm, keep a level head. But right now that's the hardest thing in the world, because my entire life has just been turned upside down in the space of a few minutes, and I don't know why.

Christ, where is she? It feels like she's been in there for hours. The clock in my car tells me it's barely four minutes, though, before she's back out and walking towards the car with a big smile on her face. She opens the passenger-side door and dumps a white padded envelope on my lap.

'Three grand,' she says. Just like that. As if it's the most normal thing in the world and nothing that went on earlier today has actually happened.

'What? Is that all? Where's the other seven?' I say, at a complete loss for any other words.

'Relax, Dan. It's to do with some sort of fraud prevention thing. They said I can get the rest tomorrow.'

'But we won't be here tomorrow,' I reply.

'So what? We've got four grand. It'll have to do. I

couldn't exactly go kicking up a fuss, could I? I told them a story about selling a car and needing some cash to buy a new one.'

'And they wouldn't let you?' I ask.

'They would, but only if I did it over two days. On the plus side, it backs up your story if the banks decide to speak to each other. They probably do, you know. Money-laundering checks and all that.'

I can't help but laugh. It just seems so stupid and irrelevant right now. 'Oh yeah, that's a great relief. At least when we're being hunted by undercover police for the murder of my wife we'll be safe in the knowledge that at least we won't be getting a stern letter from our banks.'

'How much fuel have you got?' she says, ignoring my sarcasm.

'Practically a full tank. I filled up yesterday.' I look at the instrument panel, which tells me I've got 420 miles to go until my next fill-up. I have no idea where we're going, but I know I want to eat up those 420 miles as quickly as possible and get as far away from here as I can.

'Good. In that case, we'd better get going.' Jessica puts on her seatbelt and settles back in her seat as if this is the most natural thing in the world. It's both scary and oddly reassuring to know that at least one of us is staying calm. I wonder what sort of traumas she's had to endure in the past to retain this level of calm.

'Where?' I ask.

'Folkestone. It's only thirty or forty miles. We'll be there within the hour.'

'Folkestone?' I know exactly what this means.

'Yeah. The Eurotunnel leaves every half an hour. It'll cost us a packet at such short notice, but we can't do much about that. We couldn't exactly book in advance. Come on. We need to get going.'

'And after that?' I say, ignoring her efforts to gee me up.

'I know a place in France. My family had a holiday cottage there.'

I can't quite believe what I'm hearing. 'Isn't that a bit risky? Surely that's the first place they'll look, if they know you have ties there.'

'We're not staying there, doofus,' she says. I'm intrigued by the Americanism. 'I know someone in the area who can help us out. We'll need to dump the car, for starters. They'll be all over the place looking for this one by the morning. Now come on. We need to get out of the country while we still can.'

'Shit. My passport.'

'What? Don't you have it?' she asks, as if I'm mad.

'Well no, I didn't see the need in bringing my passport seventy miles up the road to Herne Bay. I suppose you just carry yours around everywhere with you in case you need to skip the country, do you?' As I say this, she pulls the small burgundy booklet from her inside jacket pocket. 'Yes. Of course you do.'

'Where's yours? At home?'

'Yeah. But I can't risk going back there.'

'Why not? It's not as if Lisa's going to be there, is it?'

She's got a point, but East Grinstead is the last place I

want to be right now. I'm just about clinging on for dear life, managing to keep a rein on my emotions. I don't want those reminders, those flashbacks to the mainly happy times we spent there. I don't want to smell the home-cooked meals and the scent of her shampoo. I have no other option, though.

'Do I need it? I've been to France on the train before and didn't need it.'

'They do spot checks,' she says. 'Be a bit stupid if we get stopped by an overzealous customs officer. Besides, if we get there quickly enough, your name won't be on any watch lists.'

'Watch lists?' I ask.

'Yeah. When they find Lisa's body and can't find you, they'll put you on a watch list at the ports and airports. So you don't leave the country. Which is why we've got to get out before they find her.' She says this like it's the most normal thing in the world.

Without saying anything, I tap the route into my satnav: from here to East Grinstead, then back over to Folkestone. 'Nearly three hours,' I say. 'It's about a hundred and forty-odd miles.'

Jessica just looks at me. 'We'd better get going, then, hadn't we?'

10

I'll have about 280 miles of fuel left by the time we reach Folkestone, according to my calculations. They should be right, too, because I've done them over and over, about twenty times since we left Herne Bay. I know that if I don't keep doing the calculations, my brain is going to try to think of other things, and I can't handle that right now. The thoughts going round and round in my head are making me feel sick, and I'm struggling to cope.

I don't know France that well, but 280 miles has got to get us somewhere over towards the German border, from what I know with my limited geography. We could fill up with more fuel, but there'd be number plate recognition cameras at the petrol stations. Thinking about it, there'd probably be cameras all over the place: on the motorways, at the side of the road, on the edge of buildings. Whichever way you look at it, cameras are going to pick us up. And that's why I know we need to get as far away as possible as quickly as possible, so they've got a much longer trail to have to trace by the time they realise one exists at all.

I don't know where in France this contact of Jessica's lives, and I don't want to ask. I want to know as little as possible. What I don't know can't hurt me. As long as we're able to get there, get some help and put as much space between us and the police – not to mention Lisa's killer – as possible, that's about all we can hope for right now.

The drive over to East Grinstead seems to take an age. They say a drive always seems longer when you're heading home, but East Grinstead already feels alien, like a location from another part of my life. From history.

It's not helped by the fact that we're now in rush hour – the time when everyone's trying to get home from work. Being very much in the commuter belt, that makes a huge difference to the traffic. It's not too bad heading over the Kent Downs, but once we're on the M20 motorway things seem to grind to a walking pace. I can feel the time ticking away as everything in the universe counts down towards the moment that cleaner walks into my hotel room in Herne Bay tomorrow morning and discovers my wife's dead body in the bath. She doesn't know it yet, but tomorrow morning her life will be changed forever, and I don't even know her name.

Even that poor cleaner will have her day, her week, probably her life, turned upside down because someone wanted not only to kill my wife but to frame me for it. That's something that takes some doing to get my head around, and I'm still not quite sure I've come to terms with it. Secretly, deep down, I don't think I want to.

The M20 merges onto the M26, which merges onto the M25. If I thought the M20 was slow, this is something else. I look at the clock for the hundredth time since we got in the car. It's nearly six o'clock. Finally, we get off the M25 and make the relatively short drive down the (congested, naturally) A22 to East Grinstead.

My heart is in my throat as I pull up in my road, a good few houses further down from mine, the hedges and the curve in the road hiding the direct line of sight between the car and my house. I don't particularly want the neighbours seeing Jess sitting in the passenger seat, nor do I want her seeing where I live. I've no idea why; I'll probably never come back here again after tonight, so what does it matter?

Fumbling with my key in the lock, I finally manage to get the door open and make my way up the stairs to the bedroom. I don't turn any lights on, and instead feel my way up the staircase and around the corners of the landing. My passport's tucked away in my underwear drawer, where it always is. I take it, close the drawer and make my way back down the stairs again, stepping carefully in the darkness.

Once I'm back outside, something tells me not to lock the door. It's almost as if I'm looking to lay a false trail of clues. What possible significance could an unlocked front door have when the police inevitably turn up tomorrow morning? I don't know, but I'm pretty sure it's not going to do me any harm. Even better, a burglary would complicate matters further for the police. Whatever I do, I need to give myself a head start.

In my mind, right now, this all makes sense.

I try to keep my feet firmly on the flagstones as I hopscotch my way back up the driveway, trying to avoid the crunching gravel underfoot. As I get to the end of the drive there's a cat sat there, looking at me. Two thoughts cross my mind: firstly, the ridiculous notion that this cat is a witness to the fact I've been back home; secondly, that I'm really pleased right now we don't have any pets or children. That would make this whole situation so much worse. I couldn't just up and leave if I had those sorts of ties. But what ties do I have? A wife who's been murdered and a house that I wouldn't be allowed – or want – to go back into anyway.

Before long, I'm back at the car.

'Got it?' Jessica says, as if I've just popped home to grab something innocuous I forgot. There's a charming innocence about her, as if no situation could ever faze her. To avoid letting that thought play on my mind, I start the car up again and head for the A22.

11

They're queuing for the Eurotunnel much further up the road than I'd imagined. I've only used it once before, and that was very late at night, so I guess I'd had a skewed idea of what was involved. I wonder how many of these people are going home after a day's business in London, how many are going on holiday, visiting friends, attending funerals. Either way, I wish they'd all fuck off. Jessica booked our tickets using her mobile on the way down here, but now I'm worried we'll miss our boarding.

'You have to keep calm,' she says, as if this is a perfectly common situation to be in. It makes me realise how disturbed she must be as a person. I don't mean that in a bad way, though. It actually intrigues me. Quite a lot. There seems to be some sort of deep understanding within her; a sense that she's known all the evil there is to know in the world and knows exactly how to deal with it. Most people would just call her fucked up, but I find it fascinating. I guess we're all a little fucked up.

Being perfectly honest, there's a huge part of me that's getting off on ceding control. I've always been the one to lead by example, do the organising, make the decisions. It's been a case of having to. I've had no other choice throughout much of my life, and until now I'd never realised how much that annoyed me. Having this petite, feisty girl call all the shots is something I'm finding strangely enjoyable. No, not a girl – woman. She's all woman. There's no doubt about that.

There's a knock on my window, and I hear myself audibly gasp as I snap my head round to the side to see who it is. It's a woman in a blue fleece top, with 'BORDER CONTROL' written on it.

'Passports, please?' I hear her say through the window, her voice muffled by the glass. I wind down the window and hand her my passport from my inside jacket pocket. Jess passes me hers and I hand it to the woman. I try to keep calm, appear calm.

She seems to take an age looking through it, glancing at me, then down at the picture, then back at me again. For a moment, I'm certain we've been rumbled. I see it all flash in front of my eyes: Lisa's body being discovered, the forensics experts in their white bodysuits, the glare of the coroner's bulb, the judge's gavel crashing down on the block.

Then she smiles, hands us back our passports and moves on to the car behind us, carrying on with the daily grind.

'The fuck?' Jess says, taking her passport back. 'We don't even need to show our passports to get into France. They're in the Schengen Area. Bloody jobsworths.'

'You said earlier they might. Spot checks, you said.'

'Yeah, spot checks are one thing, but that woman's going to every single damn car. No wonder it's taking so long to board. We'll be here all night at this rate.'

'Maybe they're looking for someone,' I say quietly.

'Clearly not us, then.'

'Wait a sec. Why do you have your passport on you? You just carry it around with you all the time, do you?'

Jess laughs. 'When you look as young as I do, you always have your passport on you. The dicks at the hotel bar even started IDing me a little while back. They think it's hilarious, but I don't. I don't drive, so my passport is the only form of ID I have.'

'Yeah, but you just walk around with it in your pocket?' I ask.

'Much safer than leaving it in my bag or just lying around at work. You get some dodgy sorts staying in hotels, you know,' she replies, giving me a knowing look. I still can't get over how casual and playful she's being. Perhaps it's just her coping mechanism. I've yet to find what mine is.

My thoughts run away with me, and before I know it we're boarding the Eurotunnel. A man in a hi-vis vest waves me forward, further and further, until I'm fairly certain the nose of my car is already in the backseat of the one in front. A few feet further forward and he signals for me to stop.

Some other drivers get out of their cars. A couple of families congregate around one car and start chatting. I presume they're all travelling together in the two cars. The two dads stand laughing and joking. They're looking forward to their booze cruise, I can tell. One of them seems to be about five and a half feet tall at best, with a pot belly and milk-bottle glasses that make his eyes appear to bulge like a frog's. If I couldn't see his children right now, I'd imagine they were the sort of kids who'd be dressed in matching clothes. Thankfully, they're not. A couple of the kids start to tag each other and dart around behind their parents to avoid being tagged back. The others just look completely bored.

At any other time, I'd be really fucked off at the kids running around, worried that they might dent or scratch my car. Kids just don't care about anything. They have no concept of being careful. Right now, though, I've got other things on my mind. I'm not going to lie – there's a big part of me that's trying to suppress a lot of bubbling rage and anger that could quite easily be directed at these little shits, but I'm keeping a lid on it. I've got bigger fish to fry.

It feels utterly bizarre, seeing these two families – complete strangers to me – going on holiday together; everything carrying on as normal, as my wife lies dead in a bathtub in Herne Bay. A huge part of me wants to scream at them about their lack of respect, but then I realise how ridiculous that sounds. It feels like everyone should know. Why don't they?

This feeling, like all of the others, comes and goes

quickly, to be replaced by another equally strong emotion. Every time it does so, it makes me feel sick. I don't handle adrenaline well at the best of times, but this is something else altogether. I know my brain is struggling to cope. Whose brain can possibly be wired up to deal with such a set of circumstances?

Well, Jess's, it seems.

She's sat in the passenger seat, quietly playing a game of solitaire on her phone. I don't know whether to be seriously impressed or scared by her complete lack of emotion. Oddly, I think it's exactly what I need right now. Without her, I think I would have flipped out and started smashing stuff up. I'm still not entirely sure how I'm coping, but then again I'm still not entirely sure what's going on, either. It's all happened so quickly, so unexpectedly. And I have absolutely no idea what's going to happen next. All I know is that we need to keep moving and that Jessica's scary calmness could actually prove to be what keeps my head above water. For the time being, anyway.

'Shit,' I say, suddenly snapping back to reality. 'Why the fuck didn't I grab the phones?'

'What phones?' Jess asks.

'My mobile. From the hotel room. And Lisa's.'

'Why would you want to grab Lisa's?'

I pause for a moment. 'Don't know. No reason.'

'Bullshit,' she says, looking at me. 'What's on the phone?'

I take a deep breath. 'A text sent from my phone asking

Lisa to come up to my room. But I didn't send it,' I add, quickly. 'I promise.'

She nods, but I can't tell if that means she's accepted my explanation or that she doesn't believe me. 'You wouldn't want your own phone, either. They'd use it to track you.'

I nod, silently.

After a few minutes, there's an announcement over the tannoy in the carriage (which I barely hear, my brain tuning it out) and the shuttle starts to pull away. It's at that point I know there's no going back.

12

Thirty-five minutes later, the doors of the carriage open and we're led out into northern France. Our passports aren't checked at this end, and it strikes me that we're now free to go wherever we want. By road, we can reach almost anywhere: Russia, South Africa, China, India. How far can we get before the manhunt begins?

I look at the clock in my car: 9.20 p.m., UK time, 10.20 p.m. here in France. We've got at least twelve hours. I don't know if I could drive for the next twelve hours solid, but I damn well want to try. I want to get as far away from England as possible. I reckon we could be in Austria, the Czech Republic or Poland by then. Or even Italy. A drive through the Swiss Alps, around Lake Como and down into Milan. It sounds like I'm trying to take a luxury holiday off the back of finding my wife murdered and realising I've been framed, but the human brain does strange things in situations like this.

Jessica directs me onto the motorway and in the direction of Dunkirk. That name evokes all sorts of thoughts for British people, and at the moment I'm trying to summon up my own Dunkirk spirit. I know that I need to find out who killed Lisa, why, and what reason they have for trying to frame me for it. Only by proving that I wasn't involved will I be able to clear my name and live peacefully – wherever that might be. I also know that it's going to be an almost impossible task, especially once the manhunt begins tomorrow morning. Saying that, though, I need to get as far away from the UK as I possibly can, and I can only do that while no-one is looking for me.

We've been on the motorways for something approaching two hours when Jessica tells me to come off. We end up on a long country road, vast fields to either side of us. It's pitch black and my headlights do next to nothing, even on the main beam. I've got about 170 miles left in the tank, but Jessica assures me we're nearly there. She made a call once we'd got onto the motorway from Calais, speaking in garbled French to what sounded like a man on the other end. I don't speak French, so couldn't understand a word. I presume this is the person we're going to see. I didn't dare ask. A large part of me didn't want to know.

We pass through the villages of Orsinval, Villereau and, later, Locquignol, then off up a narrow country lane and past a couple of impressive-looking houses before pulling over onto a gravel lay-by next to a farmhouse. It seems as though it's all on one level. Like a bungalow, almost. I suppose the French would call it a *chalet*. It looks a bit big for a chalet, though. A *chateau*? No, too grand. I'll stick with farmhouse.

Next to the gravel road is a small grassy area, with a chicken-wire fence running alongside the road, a low wrought-iron gate at one end and a walled courtyard with low wooden gates at the other. There's a dainty little mailbox just outside the wooden gates and some sort of vine trails across the chicken-wire fence. It looks very French, and my first thought is that it's a shame I'm not getting to see it during the day with the sun shining.

'What's this?' I ask, noticing that Jessica's not moving.

'It's somewhere I never thought I'd come back to,' she says, staring straight out through the windscreen in front of her.

'Bad memories?'

She pauses for a moment. 'Yes and no.'

I don't feel I can ask anything more. Whatever the memories are, they're clearly affecting her or distressing her in some way. For a second, I realise that I've become more concerned about her than I have about the fact that my wife's lying dead in a bathtub in Herne Bay. Never mind the fact that I'm going to become Britain's most wanted man in just a few hours' time. Down here in France, all that seems to have been left a million miles and a hundred years away.

Before I can say anything else, she opens the car door and gets out, walking purposefully across the gravel road and pushing open the wooden gate. I follow her.

We make our way under a wooden archway, again

covered with vines, and I stop as Jessica knocks on the heavy wooden door, which has been painted an odd shade of turquoise. A few seconds later, I hear the latch unlocking on the door and it swings open, revealing a man who I can only describe as very French. His greying hair is swept back, and he has an Albert Einstein moustache. He holds out his arms and embraces Jessica, with a kiss on each cheek. All he's missing is a stripy T-shirt and a string of onions. I can see immediately that there's some sort of untold story between these two. The man steps aside and lets us in.

'Dan, this is Claude.'

Claude just looks at me. Almost as if he expects me to know who he is, or perhaps he's waiting to judge my body language before deciding how to engage with me. He seems cautious but friendly.

'Very nice to meet you, Dan,' he says in heavily accented English. 'Please, come through.'

He leads us into his living room, which has beautiful exposed brickwork and beams. It has an airy, open-plan feel. Yet again, I feel incredibly guilty at just how detached I feel about the whole Lisa situation. I wonder if my brain has shut down my emotions and gone into survival mode. They say traumatic experiences can do that – it's a way of the brain protecting itself. Fleeing so quickly has given me some space, both physically and mentally, to be able to try and process what's happened – and why. I feel safer, as though I'm a long way away from whoever's decided to do this to me. I don't have anyone particular in mind, though people always want revenge for something. But to commit murder in such cold blood and set the scene to look as though I did it?

I can only assume that I'm being set up. If someone just wanted to kill Lisa, why not do it in East Grinstead? Why not cut the brakes on her car or burn the house down? Why lure her seventy miles away to the hotel I'm staying in and make it look as if I killed her? The amount of planning that must have gone into it: getting her there, waiting until I was out of the room, somehow getting her upstairs . . . The only possible conclusion is that someone's looking to ruin my life as well as end Lisa's.

I still can't get my head around that one. Lisa didn't have enemies. She didn't need to be the victim in all this. She was always bubbly, lively, true to herself. I can't understand why someone would want her dead. Nor can I understand why or how that text got onto Lisa's phone from my number.

Claude pours a bottle of red wine into three large glasses and passes one to me and one to Jessica.

'Just water, please,' I say. 'I've got to drive.'

Claude smiles and looks at me. 'You do not need to drive. Tonight, you can stay here. Tomorrow morning, we will see again.'

Jessica senses I'm about to protest. 'You've just driven all the way from England. It's late. And it's been a busy day,' she says, as if I've just had a stressful day at work or had to redecorate the bathroom. I wonder how much she's told Claude. Presumably not much, judging by how comfortable he seems. He heads into the kitchen to put the empty wine bottle away.

'Jess, we need to keep moving.'

'Why?' she says, almost before I've finished my sentence. 'Who's going to be coming here to look for us?'

'I don't know. I don't even know who this guy is,' I reply, lowering my voice but knowing damn well Claude can hear me and understand every word.

'I've told you who he is. And no-one's going to be looking for us until late tomorrow morning at the earliest. And they aren't going to be looking here.' She offers no more information and just takes a large gulp of wine. The fruity tang wafts under my nose from my glass and I raise it, taking a small mouthful myself. It feels so good.

'You want something to eat?' Claude says, returning from the kitchen. I go to say no, but my stomach disagrees and decides to tell me how hungry it is. Fortunately for Claude, he's French and has already returned to the kitchen and started clattering about in cupboards before even waiting for an answer. *Of course they want something to eat; they're guests.*

I look at Jessica and she looks back at me. Neither of us says a word, but, in that moment, so much is spoken.

13

Over the next hour or so, I feel the bizarre mix of adrenaline and tiredness starting to subside and a deep sense of panic begins to set in.

Jessica and Claude have been talking in French for most of the meal, which has got me wondering what they're saying. Claude clearly speaks perfect English, so why would they choose to speak in a language they know I can't understand? I know exactly why: because they don't want me to understand.

Everything's happened so fast. My wife's dead, I've been framed for her murder and I'm sitting in a farmhouse in France eating dinner with essentially two complete strangers. Why am I even here? What possible reason could Jessica have for wanting to help me? She's a runner – I get that. She's probably run away a hundred times before, and she's clearly had issues in her past. But she barely knows me. Why would she trust me so implicitly, especially after what happened to Lisa? I'm not sure I even trust myself. And how does she know Lisa's even dead? She didn't ask for any proof, didn't want to see the body. How do I even know she was dead? At the time I was certain, but could I ever be completely sure? Time will tell, I suppose. I'm comforted by the tiny possibility that Lisa isn't dead at all, Europe's police won't be out looking for me tomorrow morning and I can return home having just had a rather impetuous but nice trip to France.

Except I know that isn't going to happen.

I'm broken out of my reverie by something odd. I've been pretending to pay attention to Claude and Jessica the whole time, my eyes casting over in their direction regularly, watching them and looking as though I was present. But now I'm caught by the look on Claude's face.

I think back to that indescribable but perfectly clear vibe I was getting from Jessica out in the car, that she knew she had to come here – felt it was her duty to do so – but really didn't want to. If this was the place – if Claude was the person who could help us – why would she have such reservations about coming here? Something doesn't quite seem right about that. And that look he's giving her right now as she tucks into the last few spoonfuls of her stew is starting to creep me out. It's almost as if I'm not even here.

A thought occurs to me. She's calm and collected because she's in control. She's always in control. That's who she is. But how long has she been in control? That's the thought that worries me. Has she been able to prepare for this? Was she involved earlier than I thought? Was she somehow responsible for what happened to Lisa? I shake the thought from my head. I've known Jess mere days and she's never met Lisa. It's not as if she's fallen for me and wanted me for herself – she's told me often enough she's not the commitment type. It just doesn't add up.

As Jessica finishes her stew, Claude raises one side of his mouth into a half-smile, leans across to pick up her bowl and takes it out into the kitchen.

'Are you alright?' I ask her.

'Fine.'

I give it a second or two. 'What was that all about?'

'What?'

'The talking in French for the past hour. And those weird looks he was giving you.'

'What weird looks?'

I struggle to tell whether she's as innocent and naive as she makes out, but I somehow doubt it.

'Nothing. I just . . . It seemed a bit odd, that's all.'

Claude comes back in from the kitchen. 'Forgive me,' he says. 'I have to go and see to Baiard.'

Jessica seems to know what this means. I haven't got a clue. She waits until he's walked out through the back door from the kitchen until she explains.

'It's his horse. He's got a stable down at the back of the house.'

'A stable? Jesus.'

'Trust me,' she says. 'That's nothing.'

There's a few seconds of silence before I speak again.

'So how do you know Claude?'

She takes a deep breath. 'He was a friend of the family,' she says through a sigh.

'Was?'

'They had a bit of a falling out,' she replies, her eyes blinking a few times as she says it.

I nod. 'I don't mean to be rude, Jess, and I'm not being funny, but I need to know who this guy is. I'm in the biggest shit I've ever been in in my life, my wife's lying dead in my hotel room back in England and you've dragged me down to a farmhouse in France with Poirot here. I don't know who he is, I don't know who *you* are and I don't know what the fuck's going on.' My voice cracks as I speak, the panic starting to break through the protective buffer my brain had created for me.

'Claude's a good man. He protected me. He cares for me. I feel safe with him. And you don't need to know who I am.'

'I do, Jess. Believe me, I do. I don't even know who I am right now, so I need some sort of security. Some constant.'

'You have security,' she says quietly but confidently. 'You can trust Claude.'

'So you tell me, but how do I know I can trust you?'

'What do you mean?' she replies, looking at me for the first time since dinner, her eyes narrowed.

'I met you only a few days ago, Jess. I know every fucking inch of your body but not a single thing about *you*. I don't know what's happened, I don't know who killed Lisa, but all I know is someone did. Now I'm down here with two people I don't know, who are trying to convince me they're looking after me, but why would they? Why would you? You don't know me, either. You don't know I didn't kill Lisa.'

'I do know,' she says, looking me in the eye. 'Trust me, I know a bad person when I see one, Dan.'

'But you don't know for sure. You can't ever know for sure if you weren't there. This is weird. *Fucking* weird. Don't you see that? Why wasn't your reaction to call the police and tell them you were my alibi? Or to at least come upstairs and see for yourself what had happened?'

She lets out an ironic laugh and whispers forcefully, 'You think I wanted to see your wife's dead body? Seriously?'

'I would've wanted to know what happened, to at least ground myself somehow. I wouldn't have just suggested disappearing off into the night.'

'You did, though, didn't you? You came down those stairs with your bags packed. You said you were going.'

I shake my head. 'I'd just found my wife dead. Someone had set me up to look like I'd killed her. Do you know how you'd react in that situation? No, neither did I. I panicked. I needed space to think and get my head round it.'

'And is it any clearer now?' she asks, knowing full well what the answer is. 'There'll be a way of proving you didn't do this, Dan. We just need the distance, mentally and physically, to be able to work it out.'

I put my head in my hands. 'This was a stupid idea. A really fucking stupid idea. Even if we can prove something, how do we explain running away as soon as we found the body?'

'Why should we need to?' she says. 'Just tell them the truth. Tell them what you just told me. If it was your honest natural reaction and instinct, why should you need to explain it? You'd just been set up for murder, you were in an extreme situation and you reacted instinctively. You didn't commit a crime.'

'I'm pretty sure not reporting a dead body is a crime,' I reply.

'Yeah, because that's the crime they're going to be investigating.' Strangely, Jessica's sarcasm seems to calm me slightly. It adds an odd sense of normality to the situation. No matter how much that puts me at ease, though, I still can't shake off the nagging suspicion about Claude. It's become overpowering.

'You're not the only one with good instincts, you know, Jess.'

'How do you mean,' she asks, more as a statement than a question.

'I mean Claude. I know there's something not right there. There's been something between you two, hasn't there? Something . . . wrong.' She says nothing, so I continue. What I say is more a stream of consciousness than anything. But there's an almost false facade to Jess. As if her controlling, confident manner is just a mask to cover traumatic events in her past. 'I've heard about girls like you. You jump into bed with every guy who wants it because that's what's natural to you, isn't it? You told me after the first time we did it that sex had been devalued for you. I didn't know at the time what that meant, but now I think I do.' I see her jaw clench. 'Jess, were you abused?'

'You don't know anything,' she says, fighting to wipe a tear from her eye.

'Is that why you felt safe here? Is that why, when the pressure was on, you felt you had to come here? I mean, it was pretty obvious you didn't want to be here, but felt you had to be. What do they call it, Stockholm syndrome?' She doesn't say anything. 'Jess, did Claude abuse you?'

'What the actual fuck?' she yells, looking at me with her raging red eyes. 'Are you shitting me? Of course he fucking didn't. I can't even believe you'd say that.'

'Jess, just tell me. I . . . I care for you. I want to know. I want to understand. I want to help.'

'You can't help. I don't need help. And you don't need to understand.' I say nothing, but she speaks anyway. 'Claude did not abuse me. Alright? That's all you need to know.'

What seems like only a couple of seconds, but must've been more, is broken by the sound of Claude's footsteps on the gravel, making their way back towards the kitchen.

14

The winters at Pendleton House have always been cold, but this one has been particularly brutal. The snow has come in droves, coating the grounds with layer upon layer of thick white blanket. It's drifted up the walls and the trees, smoothing the sharp angles and making everything look as though it's melted into a huge mass of white. The boys shiver in their beds, each of them knowing damn well the nuns won't be shivering.

The radiators have been clattering and clunking for weeks, working overtime to try and keep the house warm. So far, they've managed to stop it completely freezing over, but the night-times are still bitter. Some nights, if he breathes out carefully and catches the light of the moon in the right way, he can see his breath misting in front of him.

Daniel knows that in some of the other rooms, the boys huddle together at night for warmth. He can only imagine the Mother Superior in her own bedroom, the radiator no doubt searing hot, her doubled-up duvet keeping her warm and toasty. The boys have only recently been allowed an extra blanket – a heavy, coarse woollen throw that scratches at his arms if he doesn't keep them below the covers. Not that arms outside of blankets is an option in this weather.

Teddy Tomlin isn't the sort of boy who'd want to huddle together for warmth, anyway. He's a lone soldier, a boy who prefers to keep himself to himself. Earlier this evening, Mr Duggan came to visit. A couple of the boys were passing through the lobby when he arrived and they said he stank of whisky. Not long after, the Mother Superior came to take Teddy Tomlin. He'd been in a bad mood all day, Teddy. All week, really. All the boys went through periods of resentment, of hating everything about the place. Daniel was the same. But he'd learnt to keep it under lock and key. Teddy was a little slower to learn. He was reluctant earlier when the Mother Superior came in and asked him to follow her. He already knew that Mr Duggan was here and was well aware what it all meant. For the first time since he'd been there, Daniel saw signs that Teddy Tomlin was starting to rebel. He didn't realise it at first, but that began to stir up feelings of rebellion within him, too. When a troubled yet peaceful and gentle soul like Teddy starts to fight back, you can't help but be stirred.

It's been deathly silent in the room since he went. Daniel hadn't really noticed it before, but the silence he thought he experienced every night was actually far from it. When Teddy is here, his gentle breathing fills the room. The light sound of cotton on skin as he turns over in bed. The faint scratching as he catches an itch. And even when Teddy's not here, there are sounds from outside. A fox scuttling across the lawn. The distant thrum of traffic. The solemn hoot of an owl. In this desolate, desperate winter, though, outside simply does not exist.

The sheer quiet of the silence means that Daniel can hear Teddy's footsteps from further away than he usually would. Daniel can tell a lot from footsteps. That's what sleeping in this sort of place does to you – it gives you an extraordinary skill set that no other child would have. Tonight, Teddy's footsteps sound lonely, forlorn. They sound like the footsteps of a boy who's given up.

A few seconds later, the door opens and Teddy closes it behind him gently. He pulls back the corner of his bed and climbs in, not even bothering to take off his clothes. Anyone else would presume this was because Teddy's cold, but Daniel knows Teddy never sleeps in his clothes. Not even on the coldest of cold nights.

Daniel turns over to look at him, pulling his head back from the shaft of moonlight and allowing it to reflect off the whitewashed walls and cascade down on Teddy. When he sees him, Teddy is looking right back at him, his eyes sad, desperate and wet. Teddy doesn't say a word, but Daniel can see the bruising already beginning to form on Teddy's left cheek, the strong handprints and finger marks already visible in crimson red around his neck.

Daniel swallows. Before he even knows what he's doing, he feels the rage roaring inside him, pushing at his throat to burst free. He's on his feet, he flings the bedroom door open *and he's marching down the corridor, barefoot in only his pyjamas, no longer feeling the cold. The rage and adrenaline is fiery inside him, warming his taut growing muscles with energy.*

He knows Mr Duggan will be in the lounge, where he always is, drinking a glass of whisky from the Mother Superior's secret stash. She doesn't drink herself – the supply is kept purely for Mr Duggan's visits.

When he gets to the end of the corridor, down the stairs, across the hall and into the lounge, Daniel cranks the door handle down and flings the door back against the wall with a clattering sound. Mr Duggan is startled, and he turns around in his seat, beginning to stand but then caught off balance as Daniel throws himself at him.

Daniel hears the whisky glass land with a thud on the carpet, the ice cubes clattering against the inside of the tumbler as his fists pummel into the side of Mr Duggan's head. The old man is gurgling, grunting some words that Daniel can't quite make out. Daniel is crying, the fits and sobs pouring out of him as he unleashes years of fury and rage into Mr Duggan's skull.

Eventually, the adrenaline begins to subside and he feels the searing pain in his knuckles and wrists as he becomes aware of the arms tugging at him from behind, willing him to let go.

He falls to the floor, barely registering the pain from his kneecaps as he collapses into a deep and guttural sob.

15

I look at Jessica, my mind consumed with anger and frustration. Not anger at her, but anger at whoever did whatever they've done to her. I asked her if she'd been abused, and she didn't say no, couldn't say no. All she said was that it wasn't Claude. I'm glad, because if she hadn't told me that, I'd be on top of Claude right now, caving his head in.

Jessica and I don't say a word, but Claude's clearly no idiot. He can see from her bloodshot eyes what's been happening. He's the sort of man who can tell just by looking at a person. Whatever these two have been through, it's enough to build that sort of deep connection.

'Okay, so your car is outside?' he says eventually.

'Yes, right opposite,' I reply.

'Come.' He signals with his finger for us to follow him. We leave by the front of the farmhouse and walk past the car, a hundred yards or so further up the lane and around a hedged bend, where we stop at a large barn. It's an enormous brick-built building, but it looks ancient. It has huge white wooden doors on the front and one smaller plain wooden door near the top of the building. It must've been a grain store or something, I figure.

Claude takes a bunch of keys from the pocket of his waistcoat and fumbles around with them for a second before unlocking the huge doors and swinging one open. The inside is fairly bare – it's beamed, with bales of hay stacked to the left- and right-hand sides. To the rear is another similar set of doors which I assume lead out onto the fields behind. Sat proudly in the middle is a car. It looks like a late-eighties or early-nineties Citroën. It's not aged too badly, but even in this low light I can see some signs of rust and certainly plenty of dust.

'Tonight, you will rest. We will bring your car in here, and tomorrow you take this car. Okay?'

I nod, although I'm still trying to process everything. Is he helping us run away? If so, Jessica must have told him everything. If that's the case, why would he trust me, a complete stranger? Clearly, he wouldn't; he'd trust Jess's judgement. But surely he'd be a little more suspicious of me, I think. That only leaves the possibility that she hasn't told him exactly what happened – just that she has to get away and needs his help. Would that be enough for him to just offer his car? I don't know. All I know is it's happening.

I turn to look at Jessica for some sort of approval or clarification, but she's just standing, staring at the car.

'What's wrong?' I ask.

'Nothing.' Her reply is terse but full of meaning.

'I'll go and fetch the car,' I say, eventually.

My legs feel heavy on the ground, as though they're full of lead, the half-bottle of red wine clouding my brain and somehow making everything seem far more positive as I make my way back down this strange French lane towards my car. It's surreal. Absolutely surreal. None of it quite makes sense, and I can't come to terms with any of my emotions. I haven't cried; I haven't yelled. I'm just numb. It's almost as if my brain and my body don't know how to react. It's not a situation anyone ever expects to be in.

When I get to the car, I open it and climb inside, sitting for a moment and registering the familiarity of the car's interior. It seems so disconnected from this alien world around me and everything back in England, yet it provides a sort of connection to it. I look over at the passenger seat, the seat that Lisa sat in so many times. The door handle she touched. The climate-control knob on her side of the car, always set five degrees lower than mine. In that moment, I realise just how glad I'm going to be when the morning comes and I can leave all this behind. I'll be free of the car, free of any association with home.

It sounds weird saying that, but England no longer feels like home. It's been tainted for me many times over the years, but now my brain has just associated the whole place with what happened earlier, with Lisa. It's not like I'm going to want to go back to the house we shared together, the house she chose, and carry on living a perfectly normal life. Even in this time of utter despair, I have the level of consciousness to know that things have now changed forever.

I start the engine and pull the car onto the lane, trundling slowly up towards the barn as my headlights light the way.

For some reason, we decide to stay in the barn that night. Claude mentioned making up a spare bed for us in the farmhouse, but it didn't seem right somehow. Jessica said we'd burdened him enough and this way we could just get up and go, and he needn't get involved. It seemed strangely right, although I wouldn't have minded a hot shower and a proper bed. I've got a feeling it'll be a while before I have either of those again.

I sit on a bale of hay and try to clear my mind before going to sleep. I'm in that horrible situation where I'm as tired as hell, but I know my brain won't switch off if I try to bed down now. Jess comes back into the barn, having gone to the farmhouse with Claude to fetch some blankets.

'Here you are,' she says, tossing something in my direction. I catch it. It's an iPhone.

'What? Why?' I ask.

'In case we get separated at any time. I've got one, too. They've got each other's numbers programmed in. Don't worry, it's got an unregistered pay-as-you-go SIM – with about five hundred euros on it, so fill your boots.'

It's an older model than the one I had, and certainly older than the one Lisa had – she always had to have the latest model – but the operating system is the same. It's good to have some means of communication, but I can tell I'm going to get about as much use out of this as I have out of any of the mobile phones I've had before: next to none.

'Thanks,' I say, trying to sound appreciative.

Claude covers my car over with a tarpaulin before he leaves, and I wonder why the Citroën wasn't covered with one when we arrived. It clearly never had been, either, judging by the layer of dust over the top of it. I just hope the Citroën's going to run alright and not break down three miles along the road. Once my car is covered, it's out of sight and out of mind.

I look at the floor. The calmness of it seems to soothe my mind for a moment. Jess sits down and presses herself against me, pulling me into her, my head nuzzled in her bosom as she hugs me, kissing me on the top of the head.

'We're going to be alright,' she says, the first time I've ever seen her truly caring. 'We'll sort this.'

We lie down on the hay, embracing, and very quickly fall asleep.

16

It's the first time I've ever been woken up by a crowing cockerel, and as I open my eyes I feel the laser-thin shaft of sunlight searing my face as it sneaks through the gap between the two large doors at the entrance to the barn. It takes me a few moments to realise where I am, even though I've been awake in fits and spurts for most of the night. The events of yesterday weren't exactly conducive to a good night's sleep.

I look beside me and can't see Jessica. There's a surge of adrenaline as I worry about where she's gone. Has she run off? Has she gone to the police? A moment or two later, she appears from the other side of the Citroën, clambering to her feet from her hands and knees.

'Morning, sleepyhead,' she says. 'I thought I might as well get this dust and crap off the car. If we're trying to lie low, we're probably better off not drawing attention to ourselves.'

'Time is it?' I ask, my throat red raw, presumably from snoring.

'Just gone six. Five back in England,' she says, as if realising that my first instinct was going to be to work out how much time we had left. To be fair to her, she's right. Again. 'I reckon we've probably got until midday our time before your room gets cleaned. It'll be longer before the police work out what they think happened and who they're looking for, and longer than that before they check the CCTV footage at the ports and alert Interpol, but we can probably use midday as a decent benchmark.' She speaks so matter-of-factly, it scares me. 'I've had a look at the map. We've got six hours. We've also got options. We could head south and probably just about reach the Swiss border by midday. East, the roads are better and we can be halfway across Germany.'

It's a bizarre choice to have to make. This whole situation is just bizarre. I want to be back home, mourning Lisa, helping the police find out who did this. The cold light of day makes me realise what I've done – what *we've* done. This isn't me, running away from something I didn't do. It was a moment of sheer panic, my inbuilt fight-or-flight response kicking in. And with Jess staying calm, taking control, it was just so easy.

'I need a moment,' I say. Jess just looks at me, as if I've suggested kicking a puppy.

'You're not getting cold feet, are you?'

I rub my eyes. 'I dunno. I just don't think I'm doing

myself any favours going on the run. I haven't done anything wrong. I didn't do this.'

Jess lets out a snort of derision. 'And you think they're going to believe you? I'm not being funny, but your wife lying dead in your hotel bathtub is one thing. Running off to France with the receptionist doesn't exactly back your story up brilliantly, does it? But hey, go back if you want. Go back to your new life on the inside of a jail cell. Is that what you'd prefer? And what if you do manage to convince them you're innocent? It's a big if, but what if? Let's face it. Your wife will still be dead and everyone will still know you're the guy who ran off to France with the receptionist a few minutes later. The police get things wrong. The courts get things wrong. Do you think they're going to believe you didn't do anything? The papers will have you for breakfast.'

She's right. I know she's right. And the problem is that even she doesn't know how right she is.

'Jesus Christ, this is all just so . . .'

I break down before I can finish the sentence. It's all got too much. The thought that I left Lisa lying there, in that bath. Even though she was dead, it was still Lisa. It was still my wife. And I left her. I should've stayed, should've fought. So what if I'd been arrested, or even convicted? It wouldn't have come to that, surely. There'd be DNA evidence, for a start. Like what, though? My DNA in the bathroom? My DNA on her? Well, yeah, she's my wife. What else would they have to go on? The text message? The fact that she was murdered in my room?

All of that aside, there's one enormous elephant in the

room: the fact that the idea of running away, starting afresh and using this awful situation to do just that, is hugely appealing. It's something I couldn't deny if I wanted to. I was happy enough with Lisa, but I've never been the kind of guy to get emotionally attached to people. I learnt the hard way that most people aren't to be trusted. And who can honestly say they've never wanted to just up sticks and leave, start again?

'Where's the nearest airport?' I say, once I've managed to recover myself.

'Dan, we can't just—'

'I'm not going to go home,' I say. 'I mean to get further away. If we get on a plane, think how far away we can be by lunchtime.'

'So you want us to book tickets in our own names and use our passports, too, yeah? Great idea. We're trying to keep away from where people might spot us. As far as anyone is concerned, the last time we were seen anywhere was at Calais.'

'What about CCTV and cameras on the roads?' I ask.

'Not since we left the motorway by Valenciennes. Anyway, even if they manage to get that far and start looking for the car, they'll be looking for yours. Not this one.'

This is fucking with my head. 'So they're going to start searching the area for my car. And eventually they'll come here, and they'll find it.'

'I doubt that,' Jess replies. 'Not if I know Claude. And they're hardly going to manage that by lunchtime, are they?'

I scratch my head. Just when I thought I'd got it all squared with myself, she goes and throws these spanners in the works, getting me even more worried and confused. 'What about a train?' I say.

'Same problem. We need to stay away from cameras. We should be okay on the roads, as they won't be looking for this car. If you're worried, we can stick to the back roads but we won't get as far in the time we've got.' She looks me in the eye, a moment of deep seriousness. 'You need to learn that you can't have it both ways, Dan.'

I swallow, stand and walk over to the Citroën before opening the car door and looking back at her. 'Which way's Switzerland?'

17

We decide to use the main roads, and for the first three hours the car seems to be doing surprisingly well. Considering its age, it's holding out. I drive the car at a steady speed, keeping up with the bulk of traffic, without trying to stand out in any way. Around the cities, most of the cars seem to be much newer and I worry that we're going to stick out like a sore thumb, but Jess tells me I'm worrying too much.

At the end of the day, we're on French roads in a French car, and no-one has any reason to think there's anything suspicious about that. With the probability being that no-one will yet have realised Lisa's been killed, we have the added advantage of being on the run from people who don't yet know they're meant to be chasing us.

As we come within touching distance of Dijon, though, the car starts to become noisy and I convince myself I can smell burning. Jess tells me she can't smell anything, but I pull over at the next service station, sure something's wrong. We were going to need some petrol at some point soon, anyway.

I drive up and let the car sit idling for a while.

'It probably just needs to rest for a bit. It's an old car,' Jess says. 'It's probably not been used for a while. Certainly not on long runs like this.'

'Judging by the layer of dust on it last night, it's not left the barn in the best part of a decade,' I reply.

'I know Claude. He will have made sure it was in good shape. He wouldn't let me down.'

'You put a lot of faith in Claude,' I say, after a few seconds of silence. She doesn't respond. I decide that if we're going to be spending God knows how much time in each other's company, and if we're going to be essentially beholden to this Claude guy, I need to know what the deal is. 'Tell me what happened with him. I need to know.'

'It doesn't matter,' she says. 'Isn't it enough to take my word for it that he's a good guy?'

'I'm not being funny, Jess, but I don't know him and I barely know you. Do you actually realise what you're asking me to do? What you've already had me do?'

'Do I look like I'm an idiot?' she asks, quite curtly.

'Jess, this isn't a fucking game. This is my life. My marriage. My—'

'Your marriage is over. Your wife is dead.'

I look at her coldly. It's because of her that I'm here, in a petrol station in France, filling up a car belonging to some bloke I don't know, with a girl I met only a few days ago, about to become the most wanted man in Europe. I'm angry at Jess for taking advantage of the situation, I'm angry at myself and I'm fucking furious at whoever's done this to me. 'She's not the only one, it seems. Is there any spark of emotion inside you at all?'

'Dan, I didn't leave my wife's dead body in a bathtub, then run away to France with the hotel receptionist I'd been screwing for the past few days. Don't talk to me about morals, alright?'

I can't help but laugh. 'So now you're trying to take the moral high ground here? You think you're completely blameless?'

She shakes her head. 'Believe me, I'm far from blameless.'

There's a good minute of silence before I speak again. 'Tell me.'

She seems to be mulling this over in her mind. Just as I think she's not going to say anything, she decides it's in her best interests to open up.

'I lived here for a while. In France. I was brought up in England but my family had a holiday home here. When I was fourteen, they let me come over on my own for the first time in the summer holidays. I did some work on Claude's farm, helping him out. They lived about half a mile away, but he was still their closest neighbour.' I want to ask her why the hell her parents let a fourteen-year-old girl travel to France on her own, but I don't want to interrupt her. It's taken long enough to get her to open up this much. 'They came out to stay as well. They came to surprise me. It was nearly my birthday.'

There's a couple of seconds of silence before she speaks again. 'They got to their holiday home, and I wasn't there. I was at Claude's. They came to find me, to find out if I was there, but Claude said I was staying with a friend and would be back home the next morning. That night, their holiday home burned down with them inside it.'

'Jesus Christ,' I say, almost involuntarily. 'That's . . . I'm sorry. That's horrible. I can't imagine what that would feel like.' She doesn't respond, so I ask the obvious question. 'Why did he tell your parents you weren't there?'

Jess lets out a deep sigh. 'Because earlier that evening I'd panicked when I heard they were coming to visit. Claude realised something wasn't right and I couldn't bottle it up any longer. I told him everything. About my parents and how they'd abused me.'

'Abused you?'

She nods slowly. 'My dad wasn't my real dad. Mum never knew who my real dad was. This was my stepfather. Ever since I can remember, he used to . . . Look, I don't know why I'm telling you this.' I can see the tears forming in her eyes. The first time I've seen any sense of emotion from her.

'And your mum?' I ask.

'She knew it was going on. I never told her, but she knew. You don't have a mother–daughter relationship and not know everything that's unspoken as well as everything that's spoken. That night, Claude protected me. He promised me that everything was going to be alright. That we'd find a way to make sure they couldn't hurt me again. I looked him in the eyes, and I knew I could trust him.'

'And that night they . . .'

'Yes. The place burned to the ground.'

I don't want to say it, but it's left hanging there in the air, completely unavoidable. 'Claude?'

She swallows, wiping the tear from her eye. 'Can we talk about something else?'

18

Fortunately, the car seemed to sound and drive a lot better for being allowed to cool down a bit. We spent twenty-five minutes sat in the car park of the service station just outside Dijon, and by the time we reached the Swiss border it was already quarter past twelve.

In my mind's eye I could see everything that was going on back in Herne Bay. A middle-aged woman in a cleaner's uniform unlocking the door to my room, worrying about her husband's impending redundancy and her tearaway teenage son's school record. Tutting as she sees the state of the bed and the fact that I've left my bath towels on the floor. She'd run a hoover round, wipe down the surfaces and maybe even make the bed. Then she'd open the bathroom door and there'd be a terrible blood-curdling scream as her life as she knew it ended, and her husband's job and her son's schooling became minor, secondary worries at best.

The oddest thing about the drive here was the silence. Jess never seemed to be particularly keen on conversation, even when I was asking her direct questions. Even about basic things, such as where we were going to stay. We couldn't just check into a hotel, especially not once our faces were all over the news. The good thing is, they wouldn't be looking for us in Switzerland specifically. When I asked Jess about what we were actually going to do, she just told me she had it all in hand.

I find it bizarre that I'm just driving someone else's car through a foreign country, with a girl I barely know, acquiescing to her entirely. Putting my whole life, future and liberty in her hands. It's something very difficult to put into words, but there's a strange reassurance about her. This petite, demure, troubled girl with a dark side, who somehow seems to know exactly what to do. In the strangest and most mind-fucking twenty-four hours of my life, she's been the only constant; the comforting presence and voice of reason.

Would I have done the same if she wasn't working at that hotel? If she hadn't been at reception when I went down? If I'd pushed her away and driven off on my own? I don't know at which point the story would've changed. Would I have even packed my bag and left the room in the first place, or was that my guilt speaking because of my involvement with Jess? Would I have even got as far as the car? Would I have had a moment of clarity and phoned the police? And if so, what then? Jess is right. I'd have been arrested, or questioned at least, and my life would've changed forever. My life has already changed forever, but at least this way I've got a chance of steering it in my own direction. That's the paradox: even though I've completely handed my life over to Jess, right now it's the only thing keeping me in control of my own destiny.

We arrive in a small town called Kerzers. It's big enough that we'll be able to stock up on supplies as well as blend in and not stick out like sore thumbs, but it doesn't strike me as the sort of place to be littered with CCTV. Right now, that's our best bet. I've got a baseball cap in my bag, which I take out and hand to Jess. It was the same when we stopped for fuel – the cap is a far better disguise on her than it is on me. In fact, I'm starting to think a potato sack would look good on Jess. She thumbs through the wad of euros she got from Claude – something else she neglected to tell me until very recently – and a realisation hits me.

'They use Swiss francs here, don't they? Not euros.'

She lets out an endearing yet slightly patronising laugh. 'They'll take anything. Especially euros.'

'Won't we stand out, though?' I say. 'I mean, young woman in a baseball cap paying in a foreign currency?'

'We're in Switzerland, Dan, a few miles over the border from France. It's not Cambodia. Most of the stuff is priced in euros. It's certainly going to be a better option than going to a bank and having to provide ID to change it all into Swiss francs, anyway.'

'Fair point. I'll just wait here, then, shall I?' I say, feeling utterly useless. She doesn't even reply – just opens the car door and goes marching off in the direction of the shop. And here I am, sitting in a stranger's car in Switzerland, waiting for a virtual stranger to spend another virtual stranger's money on supplies that we're going to be living off of, God knows where.

I watch the people walking past on the pavement, going about their daily lives. Some are probably on their lunch break, or out to grab a coffee. I yearn for that normality. But I know that my life will never be normal again. This is normal now – being on the run, trying not to be seen, flying under the radar. And why? I did absolutely nothing wrong. The sheer injustice is what makes me mad and confuses my feelings.

The underlying anger isn't helping me to think straight. Why couldn't I just have stayed and pleaded my case? The simple truth is that I know it would've been futile. I know deep down that whoever killed Lisa, whoever set me up like this, is far cleverer than I am. This had been thought about, pre-planned and executed with precision. That's not something I can match my wits against. Not without the space – both physically and mentally – to come to terms with what's happened.

A few minutes later, Jess leaves the shop. I panic for a moment as she turns out and heads to her right, rather than back in the direction of the car. Then I see her enter the phone box. My body fills with adrenaline. What's she doing? Who's she calling? What if this is all one massive set-up and she's phoning the police, telling them she's caught a murderer? No, that's stupid. Why wouldn't she have phoned from inside the shop? If that was the case, she wouldn't be out here doing it in full sight of me. That's madness. Before I can even process my thoughts properly, she's left the phone box and is heading back towards the car. I watch as she opens the door, plonks the carrier bag in the footwell and sits down.

'What was that all about?' I ask.

'Hmm?'

'The phone box,' I say, as if she's already forgotten.

'Oh, that. I didn't want to make a traceable call on my mobile and I needed to wait until I had local currency. The shop would only give change in francs, so I thought I'd do it then. Handy, really.'

'What? Who were you calling?' I ask, now starting to get a little irate.

'Claude,' she replies. 'He asked me to call him when we were well away.'

'Are you serious?' I say. 'What did you tell him?'

'Nothing. Honestly, don't fret. I trust him.'

I shake my head in disbelief. 'You might, but I don't even know him. Did you tell him where we were?'

She places a hand on my upper thigh. 'Dan, relax. The only way we're going to get through this is with a level head, alright? Now, we need to head out past Zurich. We're looking for a place called Uster. There's a campsite near there that we're looking for.'

'Campsite?' I ask.

'Not just camping. They have caravans and lodges as well. And they take cash without a passport.'

'How the hell do you know this?'

'Claude,' she says, as if that explains everything.

'Jesus Christ,' I reply, feeling myself getting deeper and deeper into this confusing spiral of the unknown. 'How far is it?'

'A little under two hours away,' she says. 'Less if you actually start the car up and get going.'

19

We're not long past Bern, and the open road behind us is starting to enable me to think a little more clearly. I'm still nowhere near as lucid as I want to be, the shock having warped my mind, but I'm starting to get there.

The main problem with my mind clearing is that the paranoia is starting to set in. I've not even realised it, but ever since we left the hotel in Herne Bay I've been looking in the rear-view mirror at every car that approaches, expecting to see a police car that'll pull us over and arrest us. I know it's daft, because they'd have no reason to. Now, though, I'm fairly sure Lisa's body will have been discovered and the hunt will be on.

How long will it take them to know we've left the country? Presumably they'll find my mobile in the hotel room, see my bag is gone, find out that Jess disappeared around the same time and put two and two together. They're not stupid, after all. What's it going to look like? Unhappy husband murders his wife and runs off with his new girl-friend. Open-and-shut case, as far as they'll be concerned. Beers are on you, Detective Inspector.

Next they'll probably check CCTV, see us driving off in the same car and check CCTV and number plate recognition cameras on the major motorway networks. They'll see us getting on at Folkestone and coming off at Calais, after a short bit of diplomacy with the French border police to get hold of their footage. Or do the British control the French entrance side of the tunnel? I think I remember reading that somewhere. Makes sense, I suppose. And how long would that all take them? In the digital age, probably not long. An hour or two at the most? Maybe longer if they've got facial recognition or something like that. That means there's a very good chance they already know we've been to France. From there, they'll have worked out the furthest we could have driven: likely only to Germany or Switzerland, and the police in those countries will be on red alert. The French police within a few hours' drive of Calais will have their eyes peeled, too. They'll all want a piece of being the ones who manage to nab the fleeing murderers.

What if it's worse than that? What if someone in a neighbouring room reported a smell from my room? Would a dead body start to smell that quickly? What about the blood? Would that have come through the ceiling? *No, of course not,* I tell myself. Her body was in the bath. It'd just go down the plughole. But what if a plumber was working on the drains at the time? Wait a minute. Was there any blood? Thinking back, I don't think there was. So why is there an image burned onto my retinas, branded onto my mind, of Lisa lying in a pool of blood?

What if Lisa was seen entering the hotel and not exiting? What if someone else on reception noticed Jess had gone and they searched all the rooms? My mind's running away with so many ideas and possibilities, and I'm trying my level best to keep it calm and rational. It's all I can do right now.

The roads are actually pretty clear, and I can see why so many people have said they like driving in Switzerland. There's an almost serene beauty in the gentle curvature of the road as it delicately body-swerves natural obstacles.

But that calmness and rationality soon disappears when I take the umpteen-thousandth glance in my rear-view mirror just outside Bern and see the livery of the Swiss police car. The two male officers sat up front appear to be staring straight into my eyes as I look back at them, and I quickly realise I have been making eye contact for too long. What if they can see the fear? They can probably smell it. They're trained to.

I swallow and tighten my hands on the wheel.

'Jess, don't look now, but there's a police car behind us.'

'So?' she says, as worryingly calm as ever.

'What do you mean, so? I'm five miles an hour under the speed limit and they're just sitting behind us while everyone else overtakes.'

'Speed up, then. You're going to look suspicious if you drive that slowly.'

'Won't that look even more suspicious, though? Seeing a police car and totally changing the way I drive?'

'Dan, you need to calm the fuck down,' she says, both slowly and sternly at the same time. 'Right now, you could be fast asleep and still look suspicious.'

Before I can say another word, and before I can alter my speed, the police car pulls out to the left and starts to coast past, barely walking pace above what we're doing. I try to keep my eyes focused straight in front of me, but I can feel the eyes of the non-driving officer boring into my skull.

I quickly assume that the game's up. They've found Lisa, they've circulated a photo of me and Jess and we've been rumbled. Game over. Where they'd find a recent picture of me, though, I don't know. They couldn't exactly ask Lisa to provide one. Facebook? No. I never put pictures of myself on there.

In the space of a split second, I register that the police car's presence next to me has blocked the blinding sunlight from streaming in through that window. Because of the light, I'd pulled the sun visor out and turned it across the side window about fifteen minutes earlier. That same sun visor that'd now be obscuring the top half of my head quite nicely.

With newfound confidence, I tilt my head slightly and smile and nod at the police officer. It's kill or cure.

The officer smiles, then points to our car, gives me a thumbs up and laughs.

It's weird, but my first thought is to be slightly offended. Yeah, the other cars on the roads in Switzerland are all new Mercedes and BMWs, but I'm still a little affronted at him taking the piss.

Then it dawns on me.

We're clear.

20

When you're a child, you have a hierarchy of dependence. Your first port of call is your parents, closely followed by the rest of your family. In Daniel's case, calling on his parents wasn't possible and his family was right here in Pendleton House. This was the only family he'd ever really known. People who weren't flesh and blood but who he ate with, lived with and grew up with. The nuns were the closest thing he'd had to parents in a long time – perhaps ever. But the looks in the eyes of the junior nuns in the early hours of that morning told him everything he needed to know.

He didn't know who'd called the police, nor from which phone. He could tell from the Mother Superior's face that it wasn't her, but he didn't know any other rooms in the building which had a telephone apart from her office. Judging by some of the questions the police officers were asking him, he assumed it must have been one of the boys.

The police hadn't let the Mother Superior sit in the same

room when they spoke to him, instead having told her they'd speak to her separately afterwards. The officers were both dressed in plain clothes – something that even Daniel's young brain knew meant something was serious.

'Do you know who made the phone call to the police, Daniel?' one of the officers asks. Daniel says no, he doesn't. He hopes the officer can see that he's telling the truth. The police have to know these things. It's their job.

The other officer speaks. 'The person who called the control room made some very serious allegations. About Mr Duggan. Do you want to tell us what that was all about?'

The officers sound curt and accusatory.

'No,' Daniel says. 'Because I don't know what they said.' This time, he hopes they can't see the truth behind his eyes.

'Are you sure?' the same officer replies.

'Yes.'

A moment of silence. 'Well, in that case we can only presume that it isn't true, can't we?'

The first officer speaks again. 'We know it can't be easy for you having to live here, but it doesn't excuse boys from making things up about other people. Especially about people who put a lot into the community and who keep a roof over your head. Do you know what it's like out there on the streets? Cold and alone, without anywhere to live?'

Daniel shakes his head.

'That's what they had to do in Victorian times. Then after that there were workhouses. Life isn't perfect, but you should think yourself very lucky that you live in a society that looks after you when you get in trouble.'

The way the police officer says these things makes even Daniel start to question his own attitude.

'If you were outside this house, on the streets, and behaved in the way that you did earlier tonight, what do you think would happen?'

Daniel shrugs, his knuckles starting to throb now that the adrenaline has well and truly subsided.

'I can tell you what would happen. You'd be going down to the police station. You'd be arrested and put in jail. Would you prefer that?'

Daniel swallows and shakes his head. He's pretty sure they wouldn't do that at his age, but he still isn't particularly keen to find out.

'Good. Now you'll be pleased to know you've got a second chance. A last chance. Mr Duggan has told us he doesn't want to press charges. Do you know what that means?'

Daniel shakes his head again.

'It means he doesn't want to take it any further. He doesn't want you to be arrested and put in jail. Do you think that's a good thing?'

Daniel thinks for a moment, then nods. 'I suppose.'

'You're lucky Mr Duggan is a gracious man,' the officer says. 'He didn't have to do that for you. But he did. Because he's a good man. Do you understand that?'

Daniel nods, and begins to pick at the seam of the armchair he's sitting in. He knows what this means. Even at his age, he understands the concept of them doing him a favour as long as he promises not to say any more about Mr

Duggan. He's not happy with it, but he doesn't particularly want to go to jail, either.

Part of him wonders if Mr Duggan might change his ways after tonight. After seeing how close he came to being found out. After Daniel fractured his eye socket, broke four of his teeth and burst his eardrum. Even though he's the one sat here being spoken to by the police, he knows who came off worse tonight. And he knows one thing for sure: he doesn't have to worry about being the boy to be called out of his room on Mr Duggan's next visit.

21

We finally arrive at the campsite. On any other occasion I would describe it as 'lovely', but that hardly seems like the right sort of word to be using now. A place to bed down and gather our thoughts is what it is. Here, we can lie low and keep away from motorways and police cars, at least until the initial buzz has died down and we can work out how to prove I had nothing at all to do with any of this.

That's what I keep telling myself, anyway, because deep down I just want to keep running. I don't feel safe anywhere – not here, for sure. Interpol will soon know we've been through France. My car went through the tunnel and was seen leaving at Calais. Jess went into the shop in Kerzers, too, and she's not exactly the sort of woman a shopkeeper's going to forget seeing – particularly not if he's male. And what about the police officers who saw us on the motorway just a few miles back? No, this isn't good. As far as I'm concerned, we need to be a lot further away, and it's only really Jess's insistence and apparent total control over the situation that's actually keeping me here.

I need to have my escape route planned. The only problem is, I don't really know where we are or how to get anywhere. We've been doing everything based on an old map we found in Claude's glovebox and Jess's intuition and sense of direction. She wasn't keen to activate the GPS feature on her iPhone for fear of being tracked, and I wasn't going to argue with that.

After Jess has paid (in cash, naturally) for the caravan, she makes her way back to the car, the baseball cap pulled down as far over her head as it'll go with her hair tucked up inside it, and looks back over her shoulder before leaning through the window to talk to me.

'Come on. It's this one over here. Try and keep out of people's sight until we're inside, though.'

Once I've parked the car up next to the caravan and made sure I can't be seen, I grab my bag out of the car and step inside. My first impression is that it's actually not a bad place to stay. Sure, it's just a caravan, but it's clearly laid out for people who want to have a half-decent holiday.

Jess puts the carrier bag from the shop in Kerzers down on the table and rummages through it, taking out a few items.

'Right, here's some razors and some scissors. We're going to have to use accents while we're here, too. I told the woman on the reception we were Norwegian.'

'Jesus Christ, Jess! Norwegian? At least pick an accent I can actually do.'

'What, like French? Yeah, because they won't see right through that one,' she replies.

'Seriously, though. Who the hell knows what a Norwegian accent even sounds like?'

'Exactly. It's foolproof. Now, get that beard off. When you're done, I'm going to cut your hair.'

I stare at her. 'Cut my hair?'

'Well, yes. I'll need to cut it before I shave it off or it's going to hurt like hell.'

I open my eyes wider. 'Shave it off? No way. We didn't say anything about this.'

She picks up the scissors and the packet of disposable razors. 'It's not negotiable, Dan. Pretty soon now the police are going to be looking for an English bloke with hair over his ears and a scruffy beard, not a Norwegian bloke with a shaved head.'

She's got a point.

'I hope I'm not going to be the only one doing this. What's your plan for yourself, O mistress of disguises?'

'I'm going to cut my hair shorter. Not as short as yours, mind. Or, more accurately, you're going to cut it for me.'

'Me?' I yelp. 'What the hell do I know about cutting hair?'

'Oh yeah, cool, I'll just call the mobile hairdresser out, then, shall I? Or maybe pop into the salon in town and ask for a Fugitive Special?'

'There's no need to be like that,' I say, completely refusing to acknowledge the fact that she's right and I know it. To be fair to her, she looks pretty damn good with the short hair and baseball cap combination. She'd look good in anything, though.

'What about supplies?' I ask. 'Food and stuff like that.'

'There's a little shop on-site. Does everything you need, apparently. Not much point going there while we still look like this, though.'

It's been a while since I've had a haircut, and I've never gone as short as having my head shaved, but I can see Jess's reasoning. To be quite honest, I don't give two hoots about my hair or my beard – they're both pretty low maintenance aside from the occasional beard trim, and it saves regular trips to the barber's or constant shaving, which I hate. I've always been lucky that my hair grows pretty slowly and always tends to look neat, plus I had the advantage that fashion actually seemed to catch up with me for a change in terms of my facial hair. Deep down, I know that my reluctance to do this isn't because of me personally; it's because I know how much Lisa likes – liked – my hair and my beard. It feels as though it's the last thing keeping the memory alive, as daft as that sounds after she's only been dead a matter of hours. However, out here in a strange country in a strange car with – let's face it – a strange woman, it's one of the only constants I've had.

'It'll grow back soon enough,' Jess says, as if she's been reading my mind.

I swallow and nod, then pick up the razors and head for the bathroom.

22

After my haircut and shave I feel as though I'm starting to think more clearly. It's as if the hair was somehow clouding my brain.

I can't help but keep touching it. It feels odd.

'Right, we need to sit down and go through everything,' I say as Jess tries to neaten up her new fringe in the mirror. Thankfully she can't see the back, because I'm fairly sure I've butchered it. 'We need to try and make sense of all this.'

'I think you need to tell me something first,' she says.

I swallow. 'Like what?'

'That text message. Are you sure you didn't send it?'

'No! Yes. Yes, I'm sure. Why would I? She was seventy miles away. That's just the thing: I didn't even know she was in Herne Bay, never mind at the hotel, so why would I tell her to come up to my room?' I sigh loudly. 'Jess, she didn't even know which hotel I was staying at. I don't even know for sure that I specifically told her it was Herne Bay. I might've just told her it was Kent. I go away on work that often, it's not even a talking point in our house any more.'

'So why was she there? And how did she get there?' Jess asks.

'I don't know. That's what's really freaking me out.'

'Was her car in the car park?'

I think for a moment. I hadn't even thought about that until now. 'No. I don't know. I mean, I didn't see it, but then I wasn't exactly looking out for it. It's a silver Fiesta, so it's not exactly an uncommon car.'

'And she didn't tell you she was coming?' As she speaks, Jess starts rifling through the cupboards.

'No, of course not. I think I'd remember that.'

'Score. Minibar,' she says, pulling a bottle of red wine out of the cupboard. 'Right. Glasses . . .'

I can't help but shake my head. 'Are you actually taking this seriously? My wife's dead, I've been framed for her murder, we're . . . fuck knows how many miles away from home in fuck knows what country, and you're more worried about wine glasses?'

'Switzerland,' she says, opening another cupboard and pulling two wine glasses out.

'What?'

'The country. It's still Switzerland. We're not far from Germany or Liechtenstein, though.'

'Jesus Christ!' I yell at the top of my voice, all of my

emotions finally bubbling to the surface. I stand and slam my hands down on the table before marching over to Jess, towering over her as she stands in front of me, her face neutral and a wine glass held in each of her hands. 'What is wrong with you? Are you some sort of mental case or something? This is serious shit, Jess! Why can't you grasp just how serious this is? This is my whole life, fucked up by one act that wasn't even my fault! I've lost my wife, I've lost my freedom and I'm about to become the most wanted man in Europe!'

'Probably the world, to be fair,' she says.

I grab her by the shoulders and start shaking her. 'I'm serious! Will you stop being such a fucking idiot and grow up for a minute so we can get our heads round this?'

'Grow up?' she says, her voice calm. 'You want to talk about growing up?' As she speaks, I hear the anger starting to come through in her voice, bit by bit until she's roaring at a full crescendo. 'You're away on work, having a great time and you decide to bed the young receptionist while your good little wife waits at home for you, completely unaware of what you're doing? Is that what you call grown-up?'

'Oh, so that's what this is all about, is it? You can hardly talk, Jess. It takes two to tango.'

Before I can realise what I'm doing, I've done the stereotypical soap opera turn-away-towards-a-window move.

'What do you want me to do, exactly?' she says. 'I got you out of there. I got you safe. I got you the time and space to think, but I can't think for you, Dan. I don't know who would've wanted to kill your wife and frame you, do I? I barely fucking know you.'

She says those last few words in a way which has them laced with hidden meaning.

'And what do you mean by that?' I ask, turning back to her.

'Exactly what it sounds like. You need to get your brain into gear and work out what's gone on here, because I can't help you with that. I mean, yes, I'm a pretty good judge of character after the stuff I've been through over the years, but what's to say it wasn't you who killed Lisa?'

'It wasn't,' I say quietly, almost whispering.

'Of course you'll tell me that. Look at it from my point of view, though. A guy I don't even know – in terms of his life and background anyway – seduces me and then convinces me that the dead body in his hotel room has nothing to do with him. Dan, I don't even know that there was a dead body. I've only got your word for that.'

'This is stupid,' I say.

'I almost hope there wasn't. Lies, I can deal with. I've dealt with plenty. But assuming there *was* a dead body in your bathtub and assuming it *was* your wife, I've only got your word and my judgement that it wasn't you. And my judgement's been wrong before.'

'Jess, I don't know how else I can—'

'I mean, no-one even knows we're here. We don't have contact numbers for anyone. What if I were to die? What if you were to do the same to me? No-one would ever know.'

'I didn't do it, Jess.'

She nods slowly. 'I know. I believe that. For now.'

'For now?'

'What more do you want?' she replies, turning to unpack her bag. 'I'm just a child, remember.'

23

There's paper everywhere. This was meant to help me organise my thoughts and try to work out what had gone on, but it's just making things worse. It's clutter, and I can't deal with clutter.

Jess is furiously scribbling away on another piece of paper, which she then puts on the table, moving two other pieces slightly further away from each other to make room for the new one.

I've been trying to tell her everything I can – everything I want to, at least. It feels utterly bizarre giving my life story and intimate details to someone I barely know – and someone who less than an hour ago accused me of murdering my wife and wanting to kill her. But if I'm not able to get my head around what's happened, I need to give the facts to someone who could.

As far as I'm concerned, Jess has now become the police detective who *should've* been helping me, were it not for the fact that I'd be arrested on the spot and likely charged with my wife's murder.

'I still don't get the whole thing with the phone,' Jess says, as we reach that point.

'Me neither. The weird thing is, the message wasn't appearing on my phone as being sent from it. I guess the police would just say I deleted it, though.'

'Does anyone know the passcode for your phone?'

'No,' I say, having not even considered that up until now. My phone needs a four-digit code to unlock it before use – and that's if I don't use my fingerprint to unlock it.

'What I really don't get, though, is why that'd prove to the police that you did it. Surely the phone could've been hacked or something? They can prove these things.'

'I dunno,' I say. I've already told her more than enough. She wanted to know all about my relationship with Lisa, for starters. I told her it was a marriage like any other – we'd had our ups and downs, occasionally argued but nothing serious. Before I knew it, she'd had me opening up about my own feelings on the marriage. The problem is I've always been a lone wolf. I've never been the sort of person who's felt comfortable being tied down to one particular person or place. I think that's part of why escaping to Switzerland has allowed me to start to gather my thoughts again.

I made the mistake of telling Jess I've never really believed in love. She gave me an odd look that I couldn't quite decipher, and I had to try and explain to her that it didn't mean I never *loved* Lisa, but that I have a different concept of what love is. I know my own personal concept of love is there for a reason: it allows me to get away with whatever I want to get away with. After all, it's my life, isn't it? I've never hurt Lisa.

Jess wanted to know about affairs. I couldn't help but laugh. I've not been the best-behaved bloke in the world, but who has? As for Lisa, I truthfully don't know. I'd always worked off the assumption that she'd been faithful, and whether she had or not I failed to see what bearing that would've had on someone wanting to murder her. Would a psychotic ex-lover or his wife do this? It seems doubtful. If Lisa didn't know I was staying at this hotel, how is some mythical lover meant to know? The only thing I could think of was that if she'd been having an affair it would be yet another sign that pointed to me being her murderer.

We go through everything. I tell her about people I've fallen out with at work, neighbours we don't particularly like and long-forgotten family feuds. I know why she's doing it, but I really don't see the point. How many people murder a bloke's wife because he forgot to put sugar in their tea, or because he cuts his privet hedge a bit too short? True, there are some seriously unhinged and deranged people out there, but I think I'd know if I'd come across one of them. Sure enough, I have, but I've always kept a wide-enough berth not to get involved.

The harder I try to think, the more clouded and confused my brain becomes and the more I have to try and calm myself down. Thankfully for me, Jess is a pretty calming presence in herself.

I tell her I can't think straight; my head is buzzing.

'I didn't want this to be the first resort, but this is serious now. We really have to get your head straight,' she says, rummaging in the inside of her jacket pocket and pulling out two sizeable roll-ups. I've never taken illegal drugs, but I recognise this straight away.

'The fuck?' I squeak, unable to come up with anything wittier.

'To clear your mind. It'll loosen you up and let you think better.'

I can't even think of a response. 'You tried to cross two national borders with a coat full of weed?' I say, trying to get my head around the way this girl's brain works.

'Tried and succeeded, I think you'll find,' she says, lighting one roll-up and handing the other to me, with the lighter, at least giving me the choice of whether to spark up or not. She waits a few seconds before speaking again. 'Go on. It'll help.'

'From what I've heard, it'll make me paranoid, too, and that's something I can do without right now. I've got plenty of paranoia to keep me going for about a decade.'

'Suit yourself,' she says, taking a huge drag and leaning back on the chair. The sweet smell of the smoke is familiar, and takes me back to my college days. I never indulged myself, but I knew plenty of people who did.

Jess is the dictionary definition of contradiction. To look at, she's a slim, petite and incredibly attractive young woman. She's got a face like butter wouldn't melt, and seems like the perfect church-going daughter. Close your eyes, though, and you've got the devil incarnate. A temptress. A sex goddess. A girl who thinks nothing of smuggling a coatful of drugs across two national borders whilst escaping a murder scene with the prime suspect. A girl who knows people, who can summon up a getaway car and a bagful of euros at a moment's notice.

This is a girl in control.

And all I can do is sit and watch.

24

That night, the first news reports start to roll in. We've had BBC News 24 on the TV screen for a good few hours now, but it's taken a while for what happened in Herne Bay to hit the public consciousness.

The news story on the ticket at the bottom of the screen changes to BREAKING: HERNE BAY HOTEL DEATH and I reach for the remote control to turn up the volume as the newsreader begins to speak.

'Kent Police have appealed for witnesses in the Herne Bay area to come forward after the body of a woman was found in a bath in a local hotel. The woman's body was found in the TruMotel on Thanet Way. The woman, in her thirties, was not believed to have been a guest at the hotel. The room's occupier has since been declared missing, along with a member of staff from the hotel. Peter O'Dell's at the scene. Peter, what more can you tell us?'

The camera cuts to the news reporter, who's stood in a

very familiar-looking hotel car park, the hotel behind him surrounded with police cars and vans, with officers in hi-vis jackets standing around the police tape billowing in the wind.

'Duncan, Kent Police have naturally been quite cagey with the details so far, but we do know a number of things.' The man glances occasionally at his notepad as he speaks to the camera. 'Shortly after eleven thirty this morning, a call was made to the emergency services reporting that a woman's body had been found in a bathtub in one of the rooms at this hotel. We believe she was found by one of the cleaners at the hotel. We don't have any details on how the woman died, but the police have told us that she had been dead for some hours, and that they are treating her death as suspicious. They've told us they want to speak to two people: one, a man who was staying at the hotel, a Daniel Cooper, of East Grinstead, Sussex, and another, a woman, Jessica Walsh, who was employed at the hotel.'

Walsh. I didn't even know her surname until now.

'Neither Mr Cooper nor Miss Walsh have been seen since yesterday afternoon, and police are keen to speak to them. They've released a picture of Miss Walsh, and ask that members of the public should call the police immediately if they see either Mr Cooper or Miss Walsh.'

As the reporter speaks, a picture of Jess pops up on the screen. It's her staff picture from the hotel – the one that was on her name badge.

'Peter, have the police said what connection these two

people have with each other or the victim, and whether or not they are suspects?' the newsreader asks from the studio.

'No, the details are still a bit sketchy, but the police have told us they're concerned at the fact that neither Mr Cooper nor Miss Walsh has been seen since yesterday afternoon, and that Miss Walsh was employed on duty at the time of her disappearance. I did ask the senior investigating officer, though, where they believed Mr Cooper and Miss Walsh might be, and he seemed to indicate that there was a possibility they could have already left the country. That's something we'll get more on as the facts start to become clear, I'm sure.'

Almost before it's even begun, the news report is over and the presenter is back onto a story on the latest deaths from a conflict in the Middle East.

Neither of us can say anything for a good few minutes. Jess's face is emotionless, as it so often is. I think that's what scares me the most about her: that I never quite know what she's thinking or feeling.

It's a bizarre feeling, hearing your name mentioned on TV, especially considering the circumstances. Even though there was no photo of me on the screen, and although the foreign news channels are unlikely to have picked up the report yet, I feel all eyes are on me. I instinctively slide down a little on my seat, trying to take myself out of the eyeline of the windows of the caravan.

Without saying anything, Jess gets up and walks over to the kitchen area. She opens cupboards and looks through them before starting to rummage through drawers.

'Christ, there's all sorts of shit in here,' she says as she opens one drawer. 'Looks like a man drawer to me.'

'Man drawer?' I ask, still unable to take my eyes off the TV screen, which is now focused on a story about a Premier League footballer's latest sex scandal.

'Yeah, all men have a man drawer, don't they? A drawer filled with old keys, drawing pins, radiator keys, curtain hooks . . . And tennis balls, apparently.'

She pulls the tube out of the drawer, the plastic screeching against the laminate edge as she does so, before popping the red cap off the end and taking a tennis ball out, which she throws towards me.

'Catch.'

I make a cursory effort at flapping my hand in the general direction of the ball, but I miss and it bounces off the formica-topped table. Before I've even seen it, another ball hits me on the shoulder.

'Hey, pack it in,' I yell.

'Alright, chill,' comes Jess's reply.

'Don't tell me to chill. How can you be so calm? The biggest news network in the country has just named us as prime suspects in a murder case.'

'Not the biggest news network in *this* country.'

'What?'

'Well, it's not. Besides, no-one watches those things. Unless it's on BuzzFeed, no-one'll take a blind bit of notice. And what are you worried about? There wasn't a photo of you. As long as you don't walk around introducing yourself as "Daniel Cooper of East Grinstead, Sussex, wife murderer extraordinaire", you'll be fine.'

'There wasn't a photo of me *yet*, you mean. That's a matter of time.'

'Yes, time by which the whole of Europe'll be looking for a scruffy bastard with floppy hair and a beard. Meanwhile, you'll be strutting your shaven head around a Swiss campsite saying "Good morning" to everyone in Norwegian.'

No response I can think of will drag this conversation back into the realms of sanity, so I just shake my head and continue to watch the newsreader mouthing silently to me.

25

It all happened very quickly. A good week or so went by after the incident with Mr Duggan and the police before Daniel was called in to see the Mother Superior.

'Sit down, Daniel,' she says, gesturing with one of her tree-trunk arms. Her voice is calm, maternal. But there is still something in the air that tells Daniel this is not simply a friendly chat. 'Pendleton House always does its best to try and make its boys happy and healthy, especially when they haven't had the best start in life.' The Mother Superior crosses her arms and leans forward on the desk. 'Many of the boys who have grown up here over the years have flourished and become responsible, successful young men. But it would be remiss of me to assume that the same approach will work for every boy.'

Daniel isn't entirely sure what all these words mean, but he's learnt to pick up a lot through tone of voice and he can see where this is heading. He swallows and shifts his weight in the chair.

'Sometimes, Daniel, boys don't flourish here. That's no fault of theirs, or of ours, but it's the way God intended. Daniel, do you know what foster parents are?'

Daniel shakes his head. He does know what they are – not long after he first arrived, one of the older boys was sent to live with foster parents – but he wants to hear it straight from the horse's mouth.

'There are a lot of families, a lot of people who have the kind hearts and souls that make them want to do God's work and take young boys in as part of their family. To give them a regular family home and give them a second chance. Would you prefer to live in a regular family home than here at Pendleton House?'

Daniel thinks for a moment. He wants to make sure this isn't a trick question. He looks up and meets the eye of the Mother Superior, looking for any indication of what the right answer might be. All he sees is genuine benevolence – something he's never seen in her eyes until now. He nods his head slowly.

'There's a family, Daniel. Mr and Mrs Cooper. God has not been able to bless them with children of their own, so they would like to give the gift of family to a boy who doesn't have one. They're a fine, upstanding couple. Mr Cooper is a doctor, and Mrs Cooper is a legal secretary. Would you like to meet them?'

Daniel nods slowly again. All that's going through his mind is that he might finally be able to get out of this hell-hole. He has plenty of apprehension, though, after the way he's already been shoved from pillar to post in his young life.

The Mother Superior smiles.

Mr and Mrs Cooper's house is quite a drive from Pendleton House. As far as Daniel is concerned, that's a good thing. He'd rather forget all about the place and try to become a normal boy, whatever one of those was.

After a few minutes, Daniel stops looking at the glass in the rear-view mirror. Every time he does, he sees the eyes of Mr or Mrs Cooper in the front seats glancing back at him. The drive to their house is quiet, the tyres humming on the road as Daniel rests his head on the cold glass window and looks out at the rolling fields.

The front driveway to their house is gravelled, bordered with conifers. The Jaguar makes a satisfying crunching sound as it rolls over the gravel, gliding to a stop in front of a large bay window. Inside, he can see a light-brown dog jumping up, his tongue lolling from his mouth as his head appears, then disappears; appears, then disappears.

Daniel stays in the car, looking up at the house in front of him. It isn't anywhere near as big as Pendleton House, but he knows that he will be the only boy here, with his own room and his own freedom.

The door opens beside him. 'Are you coming in, Daniel?' the woman asks, her voice friendly and as fresh as summer daisies.

Daniel unclips his seatbelt and follows her to the front door, the man fetching his bags out of the boot of the car.

Inside, the house is immaculate. He hasn't felt carpet under his toes in years. Not carpet like this, anyway. It is soft and luxurious, the fibres tickling the undersides of his feet like clouds. There's a scratching sound from behind the living room door. Daniel looks at the door, amused.

'Do you want to meet Skip, Daniel?' the woman asks.

'Honey, he might not like dogs. One step at a time, yeah?' the man replies.

'Do you like dogs, Daniel?' she asks him.

Daniel nods. The woman smiles and opens the door. Skip comes bounding in and circles Daniel twice, sniffing his legs and investigating the new addition to the family.

'I think he likes you,' the woman says.

'I like him,' Daniel replies, bending down and stroking Skip's head. The dog pants and grins.

Later that night, Mrs Cooper makes sausages and mash. Daniel likes sausages and mash. He wolfs it down inside a few minutes, Mr and Mrs Cooper watching him with barely concealed amusement. He noticed earlier that Mr and Mrs Cooper have a large television in their front room. Daniel would kill to watch some television, but he daren't ask them. He doesn't want to offend Mr and Mrs Cooper.

Afterwards, they go for a walk around the local neighbourhood, Daniel filling his lungs with the freshest of fresh air. Although he was allowed outside into the grounds at Pendleton House, the air never felt fresh there. It was always tainted with a heavy fog, a sense that this air was only borrowed. Now, though, Daniel knows this was the air of home. The air of freedom.

The scuttling of browning leaves skipping across the pavement seems louder and crisper than usual, as though they are singing their way across the path. It seems like another world.

When they return home, Daniel is tired. He takes a bath and then gets ready for bed. Mr Cooper comes in to see him. He tells Daniel he's really very glad he's come to live with them and that they're going to do everything they can to make life happy for him. They want to give him the best life they possibly can, he says. Daniel smiles.

Mr Cooper strides over to the bookshelf and takes a moment to select a book, his fingers rasping through his beard as he contemplates which one to choose. Finally, he picks a book and takes it over towards Daniel, sitting on the bed. Daniel can see it's a book for children, much younger children than him, but he doesn't say anything. He can see Mr Cooper is trying hard, and he doesn't want to hurt his feelings. The story is fun, though, and Daniel realises for the first time in a long time that he's happy.

When Mr Cooper reaches the end of the book, he smiles and places it on Daniel's bedside table.

'I think that's enough for one day,' he says, switching out the light. 'Goodnight, Daniel.'

Daniel pushes his head further into the soft, plump pillow, smelling its freshness.

'Goodnight, Dad.'

26

For some reason, it feels weird sleeping next to Jess, so I decide to bed down on the padded seats in the dining area and let her take the bedroom. I feel safer, actually, in full view of the front door and knowing that I'm near the kitchen – and its knives. It's strangely comfortable; probably more comfortable than the bed itself, and it gives me the space and solitude I need to be able to get my head around everything.

I feel for Jess. Just knowing a little more about her past has allowed me to connect with her on an emotional level I'd never expected or intended. I've been there myself – without a proper home, without a proper identity. I'm not quite sure which of us is looking out for the other. Until now it's been her guiding me and keeping us out of harm's way, but I feel the need to step up to the plate myself. I'm just not sure how.

We didn't stay up long after the news report, as we

were both so tired. Knowing that we'd reached the next step of our journey was more of a ticked box than an actual event. We'd both known it was going to happen, although that did little to dull the shock on my part. I've started to feel prepared, though, which is always a good thing from my point of view. Perhaps going through the possibilities and permutations earlier this evening helped more than I realised.

I hadn't expected to get so tired so quickly, or to want to actually sleep so quickly after finding out we were the most wanted people in Britain. My brain had already turned to mush after trying to piece together what had happened and going over and over my life story with Jess. I feel really uncomfortable with her knowing so much, but I don't see what difference it makes now.

For the first time since it happened, I can feel my brain starting to clear properly. Just lying here, in the darkness, with the pale-blue moonlight pushing around the edge of the curtains, I feel as though I've got a little breathing space. Even though I'm lying inside a tin box in the middle of a field, I feel like I'm cocooned in an underground shelter, safe from the goings-on around me. As a child, this used to be my way of getting to sleep. Whenever anxieties took me, I would pull the covers over my head and pretend I was anywhere else – a tent and a lorry cab were two regular favourites – and for some reason I felt much safer and more relaxed. It's bizarre, now I think about it: neither of those two places could be considered safe, and particularly not when compared to my childhood bedroom, but the key was that they were *somewhere else*.

I think that's what's helping me now. I think that's why I so readily fled the hotel after finding Lisa's body. I've never been good at staying put and facing up to my problems. I've never been someone to actually deal with things. I'd far rather run, get some distance between me and the problem. I think disappearing from Herne Bay so quickly was far more of a subconscious decision than a conscious one. And yet again my subconscious mind has been proven right over my conscious mind. Maybe I just need to stop thinking so much. The problem is, I've always been a thinker. That's often been my downfall.

I can't remember the last time it happened, but I soon realise that I'm actually thinking of nothing. Absolutely nothing. I'm almost completely relaxed. For the first time in a long time, I'm starting to feel peaceful. It feels wrong, like I shouldn't be allowed to, but I'm going to enjoy it while I can. I'm aware of, but barely notice, the sound of a wild dog crying somewhere outside. It doesn't bother me in the slightest, though, as I'm allowing myself to enjoy this – no doubt brief – moment of calm.

Just as I feel my eyelids are starting to get heavier and my brain begins to conjure up safe, fictional worlds, I'm jolted back into the moment by the noise of the bedroom door clattering open and Jess marching out towards me. The look on her face is neutral, as it so often is, but I detect a deep undercurrent of anger. She has this wonderful way of conveying anger without showing it. It's then that I notice her jawbone jutting out, her jaw clenched tight as she heads into the living area. Before I can ask her what's up, she's opened a kitchen drawer, taken out a rolling pin, flung back the latch on the front door to the caravan and has jumped down the three steps to the grass below.

I sit bolt upright and look towards the door, confused in my half-asleep, half-awake state. Right now, none of this seems to make any sense. I'm not entirely sure what's going on. I hear her footsteps marching across the grass. Then silence. It's then that I hear the unmistakable sound of the dog yelping and howling in conjunction with the violent thwacking of the rolling pin bouncing off various parts of its body. One after another, after another. In only a few seconds, the howling has been reduced to a mere whimper, and I hear Jess's footsteps on the ground outside as she makes her way back up the steps to the caravan. I don't dare look at the rolling pin as she lobs it into the sink with a clatter, locks the door behind her and heads back for the bedroom.

I blink a few times, trying to come to terms with what's just happened. I sit, blinking in the darkness, unsure of what to do next. I get up and go to the bedroom. I don't know what I'm going to say, but I can't leave it like this.

'Jess, what the fuck?' I say, my mind unable to come up with anything more intelligent, my eyes clouded with tears.

'It was keeping me awake,' she says, her voice emotionless. 'I don't like being kept awake.'

And with that, she rolls over and closes her eyes.

27

The next morning, it's almost as if it never happened.

I'm woken by the sound of Jess rummaging through the cutlery drawer. She pulls out two spoons and drops each one into a china mug. It's then that I register the sound of the kettle boiling.

She looks over at me, sees that I've woken up, but doesn't say a word. Instead, she takes a carton of milk out of the fridge and pours a small amount into each mug.

I rub my eyes, vague memories of last night starting to come back to me, and I notice a selection of newspapers on the table in front of me.

'Where did they come from?' I ask, going to run my fingers through my hair and instead being met by the rasp of stubble.

'The shop,' she replies. 'Sugar?'

I don't usually take it, but I think today I'm going to need the extra glucose.

'Yeah, please. You've been out?'

'Yes. You were snoring away, so I didn't want to disturb you.'

I nod, not quite sure what to say. I sit up, my spine creaking, and take a look at some of the papers on the table. There are copies of *Le Monde*, *Blick* and *La Repubblica*. I don't understand a word that's written on any of them.

'Maybe you'll be able to make a bit more sense of this one,' she says, slapping a copy of *The Sun* down in front of me. It's the photo of Lisa that I see first. She looks so happy, carefree. I recognise it immediately as the photo she used as her Facebook profile picture. Next to it is a photo of me, taken on last year's weekend away in the Cotswolds. Although it's been cropped, I identify it as the one where I'm standing next to a sign for Cooper's Hill. We'd found it funny at the time.

Then I see the headline. BLUDGEONED IN THE BATH: HOTEL HORROR AS POLICE SEEK HUSBAND. The usual tasteful, intelligent headline from *The Sun*.

To the right is a boxed-off section which is titled CLOSE FRIENDS REVEAL HUSBAND'S SHADY PAST. Underneath, there are a few words:

Close friends of murdered woman Lisa Cooper revealed yesterday that her husband Dan was 'dangerous' and 'could not be trusted'. Full Story – Pages Four and Five.

I don't even need to turn to pages four and five, nor do I want to.

'Care to explain?' Jess says, holding out a steaming mug of tea.

I take the mug.

'Do I need to? No doubt you've already read it.'

'Is it true?'

'How do I know? I don't even know what they've said. It's the British media. It'll either be spot on or completely made up. In which case there's either no point lying to you, or no point trying to convince you it's lies.'

'The company. Russ Alman. The bankruptcy,' she says, surely knowing by the look on my face that she doesn't need to say any more. I look away. It was something I'd tried to block from my memory since it happened, but I could tell Jess wasn't going to make that so easy.

Russ and I set up a company a few years back, based around a concept Russ had for a free-standing lighting rig that could be set up and taken down in a couple of minutes at most. He was convinced it was going to make millions. We both were. I'd managed to build up a good network of contacts who were all really interested in the product, but we couldn't get it to the point where it was ready for production. The whole process of testing and development killed us, not to mention having to go through applying for patents and trademarks. Sure, perhaps I put a little too much pressure on Russ. But all I had to offer was the pure, hard facts: that so many people were interested in our product, we'd be multimillionaires if we could just get it to market. Russ took that at face value and put everything he had into it – his life savings, his house, everything. By the time the last penny was rattling around in the tin, we still weren't any closer to launching the product.

'It was a long time ago, Jess. And it's got nothing to do with Lisa's death.'

'How can you be so sure?' she says, sitting down opposite me. 'Dan, you screwed that guy over for two hundred grand. He was your business partner. Wouldn't you be a little fucked off about that?'

'He was fine. Well, not fine, but we sorted it out. We'd been on speaking terms. And I didn't "screw him over", either. We both lost out. Heavily.'

'You didn't go bankrupt, though.'

'No. I wasn't quite as naive as he was. Look, it was business. It happens. We both knew the risks when we set up the company.'

Jess takes a sip of her tea. 'The paper said you were arrested and cleared of fraud.'

I shake my head vehemently. 'No. There was a tax investigation after the company was liquidated and I was found to have done nothing wrong. The police weren't involved at any point.'

She says nothing for a few moments.

'He lost his home, Dan.'

'I know.'

It hurts to think that the papers have uncovered that episode in my life. It was a difficult enough time for me as it was, almost losing my home and everything I knew, but to think that they are actively using it as some sort of proof of my guilt over my wife's death is an entirely new level of shitty. But could Russ really be behind all this? Personally, I can't see it. He's always been the quiet, inventive one. The Nutty Professor, we used to call him. He'd be in his workshop at all hours, playing around with new ideas and testing different types of rig. He certainly never struck me as the crazed-killer type.

'I just can't believe they're bringing that up now. It's got nothing to do with Lisa. It's just the tabloid bastards trying to dig up dirt and make out I'm some sort of monster. Trial by fucking newspaper, yet again.' I can feel the veins in my head throbbing.

'Dan, you need to calm down,' Jess says, placing a hand on my shoulder. 'We knew this was going to happen. The media attention, I mean. And anyway, in a few days' time everyone will have forgotten your name and my name and they'll be on to the next new scandal. Sod them.'

'I dunno,' I say, rubbing my forehead with the palm of my hand. 'I don't think I can handle this. What other stuff are they going to dig up?'

'What is there *for* them to dig up?'

I shake my head. 'Nothing like that. That's not what I mean. I just . . . I just know what these people are like. They'll find anything they can and twist it in any way that suits them. They're parasites.'

'Yep, they are. And parasites move on to a new host when they realise they're not getting anything out of the old one. Don't give them the satisfaction. Let it wash over you.'

I'm not really even listening to a word she's saying.

'I mean, fuck's sake. *"Dangerous"? "Can't be trusted"?*

What the fuck's that all about? Seriously, those people are going to ruin my fucking life.' I'm yelling now, feeling the anger and resentment flowing out of me like lava from a volcano.

Jess pulls me towards her.

'This isn't doing you any good at all. We're going to get through this, alright? This is the tough bit now, but if we sit it out we can get through this.'

I look up into her eyes, feeling like a lost puppy.

'Who's doing this to me, Jess? Why?'

'I don't know,' she says, kissing me on the head. 'I don't know. But we're going to sort it out, okay? I think the best thing for you to do is to keep yourself busy. You need to give your head some space. Thinking about things over and over isn't going to help at all. Why don't you go into town and get some bits? We could do with some proper milk, rather than that revolting stuff in the fridge.'

I think for a moment before realising she's right. I nod, stand up and go to fetch my shoes.

28

It's about a mile and a half's walk into the town from the campsite, which is just enough to start to get my head clear. The only problem is, every car that goes past is a potential threat, as far as I'm concerned. My photo's out there now. Jess is right – it's unlikely anyone's going to recognise me from those old photos, particularly with my head shaved and my beard gone – but that doesn't stop me feeling paranoid.

I'm wearing a pair of reading glasses we found in one of the cupboards in the caravan, presumably left by a previous guest. It goes some way towards being a disguise, I guess, especially seeing as I've never worn glasses in my life. They don't look too obvious as a disguise, either. I didn't particularly fancy walking around in a massive top hat and a false nose.

As I reach the town, I find a small supermarket. I check my pocket to make sure I've still got the money. I don't know how much stuff costs, or how much a Swiss franc is even worth, but Jess said she thought a hundred francs would get us some food and stuff. Not that I can carry much home with me with that walk, and I wasn't going to risk taking the car out – especially as we'll no doubt have been seen driving it at some point. I'm desperate for Jess to get rid of the car somewhere, but she thinks that'd be too risky. We're better off leaving it at the campsite, she reckons, as it's hidden well out of the way as it is. I'm not so sure.

Once I'm inside the supermarket, I grab the milk as well as some ham, bread and a large carton of orange juice. I find what looks like a packet of roasted nuts, so I grab those, too. The weight's going to add up quite a bit, so I decide this'll probably do for now.

When I get to the checkout, there's a British family in front of me who seem to be taking their time paying for their stuff. What's really worrying me, though, is their young daughter, who's turned around and is staring up at me blankly.

'Nick, will you hurry up, please? I wouldn't mind getting these ice creams back to the car before they melt,' the wife says. She seems like a bit of a cow, from what I can see.

'Give over, Tash,' the man replies, insisting on counting out every last coin from his large handful of change, rather than just handing over a banknote like most people. 'She's pregnant. It's the hormones,' he says to the cashier whilst receiving an icy glare from his wife.

Their bloody daughter's still looking at me. Just staring. As if she knows me. As if she knows everything that's gone on. Children are meant to be perceptive. Her family's British, so there's a good chance they've read the newspaper and she's recognised my face from the front page. I try my best not to smile, not to look like I do in the photo. Before I can worry too much, the man's finally paid for his shopping – to the last centime – and they're trying to coax their daughter from the shop.

'Ellie, come on,' the mother says, grabbing her hand and pulling her along behind her.

I'm not going to lie; I'm panicking. But I try to keep that panic off my face as I step up to the counter to pay for my shopping. My brain's already conjured up the little girl's voice as she tells her parents *That's the man from the news-paper!* Little brat. Fortunately for me, neither of the parents so much as glanced at me, so there's no chance of them being able to take her seriously. One of the benefits of those sorts of parents being so self-absorbed, I guess.

Once I've paid for my shopping, trying to avoid making eye contact with the shopkeeper the whole time, I saunter over towards the exit. There's a stand selling magazines just inside the door, so I pretend I'm browsing through those, whilst actually looking through the glass door and watching the British family disappear off towards their car. I can't risk them looking back and seeing me. Eventually, I see them all climb into a hired Skoda Octavia and drive off towards the north. That's particularly handy, because I'm headed south.

Walking back towards the campsite, I start to feel more

positive. It's almost as if the shopping bags have provided the ultimate disguise. I look just like any other holiday-maker or local walking through the streets. The most normal bloke in the world.

It's allowing me to think more clearly, too. Emotion has started to subside a little, and I can feel myself thinking logi-cally and sensibly. I'm starting to be able to put my anger behind me somewhat and focus on the facts.

Firstly, Lisa came to the hotel in Herne Bay for a reason. It can't have been off her own steam, either, as she didn't know where I was staying. Sure, if she'd hacked into my laptop and found the email confirmation it might have been possible, but my passwords are pretty strong and Lisa didn't know a laptop from a rucksack. Someone else must have lured her there. The killer.

That person needed a good reason to get Lisa to come all the way over to Herne Bay from East Grinstead. A really good reason, too. They also needed to be able to get into my room and send text messages from my phone. It's that last bit that I can't quite fathom. How would someone manage to get into my mobile phone when they would've needed to know my passcode? It's not even something someone could guess, either. It's 7297 – I chose it because it makes a triangle shape when you type it in.

Getting into the hotel room without breaking in sounds difficult, but there were a fair few people staying in that hotel and I'm pretty sure each key card must open more than one door. Anyway, aren't they all just magnetic sensors or RFID chips or something? I'm fairly certain someone could've used some sort of gadget, battery or device to fool the doors into opening. That's one of the downsides of computer technology – it's never as safe as a big brass bolt.

Or, of course, there's always the chance that the killer could've got a spare key card from the reception desk.

The reception desk where Jess worked.

The people who worked on reception would've had access to my room.

Jess would've had access.

29

Daniel's life had changed irrevocably over the past few years. It had initially been difficult for him to come to terms with the feeling of belonging. He'd always felt like he had an identity at Pendleton House, but he'd quickly come to realise that the identity he had there was the same as all the other boys'. His identity had been that he had no identity. Now, though, he was a son. He had parents.

Mrs Cooper was a strange sort, always fussing around and seemingly desperate to make sure Daniel was happy at all times. She was constantly asking him if he was okay, asking him if he wanted to go somewhere for the day, giving him sweets and cakes. Mr Cooper, on the other hand, would just sit and look at him while Daniel watched TV in the evenings. Daniel could see him out of the corner of his eye, just looking at him and smiling. He could tell Mr Cooper was happy, though, so he didn't ever let on that he could see him watching him.

He knew Mr and Mrs Cooper weren't his real parents, but that didn't matter. They were the only people in his entire life who had actually wanted him. His birth parents had rejected him from the start, and he'd always felt like he was an imposition on the nuns, as though they were resentful of having to look after him.

Those days at Pendleton House seemed like an age ago, as if they were happening to someone else and Daniel was watching the memories like a film. Small things like being at school occasionally reminded him – the formal, stilted nature of a class of children obediently listening to every word the adult said. Sometimes it ran shivers down his spine. But school had its own perks, too. School had Roseanne. But today, things were changing yet again.

He should have realised something was wrong when Roseanne refused to meet his eye when he said hello to her that morning. She'd tried to slink through the school gates unnoticed, but Daniel always noticed her. It was as if she carried a permanent glow, an aura which made her stand out a mile off and made everything else seem insignificant.

She'd seemed genuinely impressed with the roses the day before. A dozen bright-red flowers picked specifically by him, for her, for Valentine's Day. It was the first time he'd ever done something like that – the first big romantic gesture of his fourteen years. He'd fancied many girls over the past few years, more and more as time went on, but Roseanne Barker was the first one he really wanted. The one he could see a future with. The one that was worth going the extra mile for.

Her friends had giggled and tittered as he said hello at

the gates that morning. He presumed she was just shy, that she didn't know how to approach the situation. That was understandable. It was a big thing.

That morning, he had double chemistry. It was a subject he usually quite enjoyed, as it had that wonderful mix of set rules and logic as well as a smattering of pure magic, watching substances change their states and come together to form something with completely different properties to its constituent parts. Daniel thought he might like to be a chemist one day, but he knew that he lacked the academic ability to do it. Besides which, he knew he'd get bored of it eventually. He got bored of everything eventually.

Today, though, the chemistry lesson dragged on interminably, the clock seeming to slow down with every minute, every second. The whole of time seemed to slow. All he wanted was to reach morning break and see Roseanne again, to speak to her and make her feel comfortable. She didn't need to feel embarrassed in front of him. He'd make her feel happy.

After what seemed like an age, at eleven o'clock the morning break bell rang and Daniel gathered his things and made his way out to the courtyard. Roseanne and her friends were already waiting near the languages block, and Daniel caught her eye as he left the science building. Within a split second, he saw the look of shock on her face before she looked away, diverting her gaze down towards the floor.

'Oh look, it's Casanova!' one of her friends called, Daniel not noticing which one as he was still trying to catch the eye of Roseanne. She clearly had no intention of looking at him, *though. 'What you got in your bag today, Daniel? An Italian violinist?'*

'Make a speech! Get down on one knee!' another one of the girls called. Daniel could see Roseanne's face going bright red at around the same time he felt the blood rushing to his own features, pulsing in his ears.

She'd told them. She'd told her friends. And it hadn't been in a good way, either.

'Roseanne?' he called, trying to catch her attention as he walked closer to her. At the sound of her name, she looked up, gazing at him like a policeman on one of those television programmes who'd come to deliver bad news.

'I'm sorry, Daniel.'

He didn't go to any of his lessons that afternoon. He sat on the bench at the edge of the sports pitches, his toes turning numb in the cold, the blood pulsing through his veins keeping everything else warm. The adrenaline hadn't left him since morning break, and he could feel himself getting angrier and more humiliated by the minute. The more he thought about what had happened, the worse it got.

The bells continued to ring between lessons, but they all blurred into one in Daniel's mind. Between morning break and lunch, a couple of teachers had come up to him to check that he was alright. He'd nodded, and they'd gone on their way. The teachers at the school all knew Daniel's history, that he had been adopted, even if it had been hidden from the other children at the school. Right now, though, he felt like he wanted to tell all of them – let every kid in the school know that his parents weren't his real parents. He was sure that the shame and humiliation he'd feel from that could never be as bad as what he felt now.

'Daniel?' called the voice from his right-hand side, getting closer to him. He turned his head. It was Mr MacArthur, his head of year. 'Daniel, the bell's gone for the end of the day. Are you okay getting home or would you like me to call your parents to collect you?'

Daniel shook his head and stood up, his knees creaking as his cold legs struggled to fight back to life.

He walked slowly towards the school gate, skulking behind groups of older lads, hoping to blend in and make his way home without further humiliation. He was doing well, too, until he came to walk through the recreation ground that provided his route home from school. Sat on the wall next to the cricket pavilion was Craig Power, a year-eleven boy who had a reputation as one of the toughest kids in the school. Unlike many of his less fortunate compadres, Daniel had managed to avoid Craig Power's sights since he'd been at Stanbrook Upper School. Had Craig known about Daniel's parentage, no doubt that would have changed very quickly.

But it wasn't the sight of Craig Power that left Daniel's heart lurching and his legs carrying him as quickly as possible in the opposite direction. It was the girl in his arms.

30

I walk quicker now, heading back towards the campsite whilst trying to process the thoughts in my mind. To think you know everything, to feel like you understand someone, and then to have that all ripped away from you in one horrible moment of realisation – that's the worst feeling in the world. It's not the first time I've been led or destroyed by a vindictive woman, but I sure as hell know it's going to be the last.

I can't quite get my head around what it means. But the problem is it all makes sense. Jess would've been able to get into my room with very little difficulty. After all, she worked at the hotel and could've easily got a spare key or used a staff key to get access to all sorts of areas. Could she have sent the text message? I suppose so. It wouldn't surprise me if she was some sort of secret computer hacker. Nothing would surprise me about her.

But killing someone? I suppose she'd need to have taken Lisa by surprise. Then it'd be possible. I can't imagine Lisa taking any prisoners if she was being attacked, but then again I reckon Jess could put up a pretty good fight for such a slim, petite girl.

It would also explain why she didn't need to see the body when I told her what had happened. She would have already known damn well that Lisa was dead. Because she killed her.

It explains, too, why she was so keen to go on the run with me and to know I was innocent. She knew I was innocent because she'd done it. And who would want to go on the run more than the actual killer?

Plus, she would've known how to either avoid the CCTV cameras or disable them for a few minutes. She'd know the way everything worked at that place. She was in complete control of the whole situation and she's played it to perfection. And what now? Does she intend to kill me as well? If so, why hasn't she done so before now?

I don't know the answers to these questions, but I suddenly start to realise how everything falls into place. Yes. It's all starting to make perfect sense now. The only thing I don't understand is *why*. Jess has never met Lisa. Not as far as I know, anyway. How would a hotel receptionist from Herne Bay possibly know my wife? I've never been to Herne Bay before, and neither has Lisa. So why would she want to kill her? So she could have me? No. Not a chance. She told me enough times herself that she wasn't a relationship sort of person. She was happy to have the fun while it was there, but that was it. She doesn't get emotionally attached. And I could tell from the look in her eyes that she was telling the truth. She's purely a have-fun-and-fuck-off kind of woman. So that's that theory blown out of the water.

But it still doesn't explain *why*.

Right now, I don't need to know why. I can find out from her. I need answers, and I'm going to demand that those answers come from her. I know I need to tread carefully here, though. If she can kill a grown woman, she'd have a good old go at me, too. Particularly if she's been planning this for a while. She might be lying in wait for me, ready to bash me round the head with a cricket bat when I walk through the door. I doubt it, but I know I need to be careful now. Too careful, though, and I could arouse suspicion. I can't go pussyfooting around and making it obvious that I know she's a cold-blooded killer. Jess might be many things, but she's not stupid.

I think it's a suspicion that has been in the back of my mind for a while, now I think about it. Something's been not quite right about her from the start. And what surprises me the most is that I seem to have this instinctive knowledge of how to handle the situation. Maybe it's the male instinct to fight for your life and protect what you love and cherish. Or perhaps I've just been watching too many films.

I feel my heart start to beat in my chest as I get closer to the campsite. My legs feel like jelly as I walk through the main gate, and I have to tell myself to stop being so silly. I need to stay calm. Stay vigilant but don't let her suspect a thing. Thinking about it logically, I'm fairly sure she doesn't want to kill me. She would've done so by now, otherwise. She's had plenty of opportunities. *She killed the dog, though,* I tell myself. That should've been a sign in itself.

As I get closer to the caravan, I notice the door is ajar. Not by much – it's closed, but not shut. I swallow heavily and step carefully towards it, pulling it open with my finger as I peer inside, half expecting to see that cricket bat swinging towards my head.

'Jess?' I call out, pleasantly surprised at how confident my voice sounds.

I make my way up the three steps into the caravan and look to my right, towards the bedroom. The door's closed, but it's then that I notice the broken plate on the floor. It looks like it's been swiped from the work surface and landed here.

I look into the dining area and see Jess lying on the floor, her face and arms covered in cuts and bruises, the blood having trickled down her face and onto the floor. She's not moving.

My first instinct is to check whether or not she's still alive. She doesn't look it to me. I throw myself to my knees amongst the broken glass and crockery and start to shake her.

'Jess? Jess, answer me!'

I put the side of my face to her nostrils.

I can't feel her breathing. There's nothing at all.

I take her arm in my hand and feel for the pulse on her

wrist. She's still warm. I count two seconds. Three. Five. Ten.

It's no use. There's nothing. Not even the faintest flutter of a pulse.

She's dead.

31

In an instant, I realise what this means. Jess wasn't the killer. Not only that, but the real killer has caught up with us and killed her. He knows where we are. He knows where I am. He could be watching right now.

I head over to the bedroom door and listen carefully. I can't hear anything, but I can't take the risk. I go back to the kitchen area and grab the largest knife I can find. I notice another knife on the counter, blood congealing on its blade as it pools on the surface of the worktop. Jesus Christ. He's stabbed her, too.

I try not to look too closely, don't want to have to look at Jess's lifeless body. All I feel is guilt. Guilt that I ever suspected her. Guilt that I left her, gave the killer the opportunity. I should've known that when push came to shove Jess wouldn't be able to handle this on her own. She needed me as much as I needed her, and I failed her.

I think back to that night at Pendleton House, the night the switch flipped and I tried to protect Teddy Tomlin the only way I knew how. But then I knew what I was fighting against. Mr Duggan was there, a visible, physical presence. Now, my nemesis is far more elusive.

I go back to the bedroom door, listen again for a moment, then step back and kick the sole of my foot into it as hard as I can. The door flies open and slaps against the wall, and then there's silence. I step inside, knife poised and ready, but there's no-one there.

Thank God.

I delve into the holdall and take out the cash I withdrew in Herne Bay. Then I find Jess's coat and take out the Swiss francs. This is all the money we have, but I'm not going to sit around and count it. Whoever killed Lisa and Jess knows exactly where I am.

I stuff all of the cash into the holdall, grab a few clothes and pieces I find lying around, zip up the holdall and walk down the steps out of the caravan. I check no-one is stood waiting for me, close the door behind me and head for the car.

I don't have a clue where I am, so I can't risk trying to get around on public transport. I know I'll need to ditch the car as quickly as I can because they'll be looking for it, but I reckon I can make good ground to a nearby city before trying the trains. Either way, I just have to keep moving.

There's still plenty of fuel left in the car. This thing seems to go on forever, and we filled up not long before arriving here. I know home is north-west, so I need to head south and east. The car starts perfectly first time and I drive as calmly as I can towards the exit from the campsite. I know we turned in from the right when we arrived, so I indicate left and turn out.

None of this road looks familiar, which is perfect. I'm confident I'm heading in the right direction. When I see the signs for the main motorway, I allow myself a small feeling of relief.

In just over an hour I'm crossing the border into Liechtenstein. I only know how long it's been because I distinctly remember the time I left the campsite – 13.44 – and the clock in the car now says 14.53. That time seems to have passed like the blink of an eye. I think my brain is starting to shut down completely, almost as some sort of defence mechanism. I can barely remember anything of the drive.

What I can't quite comprehend is the fact that I'm now completely alone. With Lisa dead, and the prospect of the combined police forces of Europe out to track me down, the only person I was able to confide in or have trust in was this beautiful, intriguing stranger. Even if I'd known her for twenty years she'd still be a stranger. That's the kind of person she was.

Was.

I can't get over how much that word hurts. And what's worse is the guilt I feel at ever having suspected her, even fleetingly.

What's fair to say, though, is that, amongst this utter

confusion, I now know one thing for certain. There's only one constant to connect Lisa and Jess's murders. The killer didn't want to get rid of Lisa because of anything she'd done. He's after me.

32

I drive for another two hours before I start to get low on fuel. I spot a petrol station just outside Innsbruck and I pull in, already knowing what my plan will be. The traffic has started to get denser and I can see the city from here. As I step out of the car, a huge jumbo jet comes in overhead, ready to land barely a few hundred yards away. I'm right on the edge of the city.

I fill the car with twenty-one euros and fifteen cents' worth of fuel. It's enough to blend in and not be noticed or remembered, but it's also not going to waste what remaining money I've got left. And a waste is exactly what it would be, because I don't intend for that car to ever leave this forecourt.

The pump itself doesn't seem to take payment. Not that I'd be risking using my credit cards, of course, but the option to feed cash into the machine and not have to come face to face with other people would've helped massively. Defeated, I walk into the building and look around furtively. I grab a few bits – a bottle of screenwash, a first-aid kit and some bags of sweets. I make a point of looking as though I'm struggling to carry it all in my arms as I dump it on the counter.

There's no-one else there, so it's a bit of a giveaway which car is mine, but I point over to it as I rummage through my pockets to pull out some money.

The man says something to me in German, which I presume to be the total. I glance over at the till and see the price: thirty-two euros and ten cents. I hand him thirty-five and he says something else in German. I look up, confused, and he repeats himself while holding up a large carrier bag. I raise my eyebrows and nod. He hands me the bag and my change and I smile and leave. *No. Shouldn't have done the smile. You were smiling on the front page of the paper. That's what everyone'll be looking out for.* I tell myself I'm just being paranoid, and I walk back to my car, stopping deliberately when I get there to look back at something I've already seen. I need to make it look like I've just spotted it, though. I look at my car, as if appraising its cleanliness, then back at the car wash area, before sitting inside the car, starting it up and moving it over towards the jet wash machines.

The jet wash is to the side of the petrol station's build-ing, with a huge great brick wall between me and the cashier. I have a cursory glance around – nothing too obvious – to watch for CCTV cameras. I can't be certain, but I'm fairly sure there aren't any pointing this way. There are plenty on the roof of the forecourt pointing at the pumps, but nothing here from what I can see. Even so, I know I need to be careful. Anything that raises suspicions right now won't be good. This is my one chance to fall off the radar, if only for a short while.

I open the back door of the car and take the vacuum nozzle from its holder. I put two euros into the coin slot and press the button to start the machine. Hidden by the car door and the noise of the vacuum cleaner, I quickly pull my shirt off over my head, grab a jumper from my bag and put it on. While I'm doing that, I push my shoes off. I change my trousers, too – from a pair of light chinos to navy jeans. I slip on a pair of lighter shoes, too, as well as a beanie hat, before shoving my old clothes back in the holdall with those damned reading glasses and zip it up.

Next, I tip the contents of the large carrier bag onto the backseat and I put the holdall inside it. It just about fits.

Leaving the car door open, I shove the nozzle around in the footwell a few times to keep the noise changing, then I hop over the short wall and onto the grass bank behind it. I check to make sure there are no rear windows to the petrol station – I'd checked from inside, too, but I couldn't be sure there wasn't office space at the back – and I brace my legs widely, getting down the surface of the grass bank as quickly and efficiently as I can.

To my left, the main dual carriageway into Innsbruck

continues to rumble by, with a long succession of cars making their way into the city on the flyover. And before I know it, I'm on the footpath below, walking alongside a fast-flowing river and making my way towards the city.

33

My German is pretty limited, but even I can spot signs for a train station when I need to. The signs are infrequent, but at least they let me know I'm going in the right direction. I keep the river to my left, walking along the pretty pleasant footpath, watching the planes landing and taking off from the airport on the other side of the river.

The worst thing about all this – and the thing that I'm trying to keep tucked away right at the very back of my mind – is that I don't know where the threat's coming from. I have absolutely no idea who killed Lisa and Jess and who's trying to get to me. It could be anyone – that bloke over there – someone watching from an office block. I've no way of knowing. Whoever it is, they've managed to track me down to a campsite out in the middle of Switzerland without too much trouble, so I doubt they'll struggle to find me here. That's why I've got to keep moving.

The police are after me, too, of course. I've been

keeping well away from newspapers and TVs, but I'm not stupid or naive. They won't give up. They don't give up. They'll make it look as if they're scaling back the investigation at some point sooner or later, but that's only really done in the hope that you'll have to put your head up for oxygen at some point. And that's when they pounce. I'm not going to let that happen.

Anyone around me could be an undercover police officer. I wouldn't know. That's the whole point, I suppose. But I also know that thinking these thoughts over and over is not going to help me in the slightest. All I can do is focus on keeping moving and getting myself somewhere safer. Somewhere I can try to figure out in my mind what's happened.

That's the bit I'm not looking forward to. How can I ever do this on my own? With Jess, I at least had half a chance. It was as if she was almost superhuman. I felt like she'd have the answers. And now she's gone.

The fact of the matter is that as hard as I try I really can't think of anyone who'd want me dead. And not only that, but to want to kill two innocent people on the way to it. Or do they want me dead? If so, why didn't they kill me? Why kill only those around me? The killer could've easily waited until I came back up to my hotel room in Herne Bay minutes after they killed Lisa and killed me, too. The same goes for the caravan on the campsite. Why?

The answer is almost more disturbing than the thought that someone wants to kill me: someone wants to terrorise me and make my life a living hell.

That's what I can't come to terms with. Never in my

whole life have I fucked someone off to the extent that they'd want to ruin my life. Not even Russ Alman. It sounds bizarre to say it, considering the fact that he lost his house and his livelihood when the business collapsed, but I knew him well. And I'd know if he'd harboured those sorts of feelings. Above all else, I need to trust my own instincts. It's all I've got right now.

I try to push the paranoia to the back of my mind and simply take in the scenery around me. I feel dreadful at pushing the memories of Lisa and Jess to one side, but it's the only way I'll be able to cope and get through this. I have to go into survival mode. I don't have anything else.

It's a good hour or so before I'm in the centre of Innsbruck. It's a busy place, and I blend in nicely, I think. I feel much more comfortable since changing my clothes and I'm making good progress.

I know no-one's followed me from the forecourt, and although someone working there will no doubt have found my car empty pretty quickly, there's not much they could do. If they looked down to the footpath they'd see what appeared to be a completely different bloke just passing by. If they traced the car, then what? Presumably it'd go back to Claude. I can't be sure, though. For all I know, the car wasn't even registered to him. If it was, then they'd probably find the link with Jess pretty quickly. And then the search would be on in Innsbruck – big time. Otherwise, it might take them a bit longer. They might do some DNA swabs. Is my DNA even on record? I doubt it. My parents are dead and I don't have any siblings or children. Or would they have got it from my toothbrush back at home in East Grinstead? That's the sort of thing you always see on these TV crime dramas.

Either way, they'll track me down to Innsbruck before too long. All I need to do is keep my head down and well away from any cameras. My main advantage is that they'll be looking for someone in a shirt and light chinos carrying a holdall, not a guy in a jumper, jeans and beanie hat with a big carrier bag. That should buy me some time.

I follow the signs for the station, or *Hbf* as they're written here. It's a stunning scene – the snow-capped mountains tower over the station. It's certainly one of the prettiest train stations I've been in. Much better than East Grinstead, anyway. It's just a shame I won't be staying.

I step inside the station and look up at the large departures board. I'm looking for somewhere further east that's still in the Schengen Area. That way, I won't need to show my passport. I know I can't go much further east. There's Hungary and Slovenia, but any further than that and I'll be . . .

That's when I spot it. The name almost jumps out at me, beckoning me. It seems right.

I spin around on the spot and walk over to the ticket machine. I tap the flag to indicate that I want the instructions in English, and then I scroll through the list of destinations. I take a deep breath and swallow as I tap *Bratislava*.

34

Dan hasn't felt anger like this since that night in Pendleton House. Another downside to the once laser-focused local press widening out and becoming more regional is that his own local newspaper has started to include news from the other side of the county. It's not an area he particularly wants to be reminded of, and those reminders are now stronger than ever as he recognises the face beaming out at him from the front page.

It's a picture of Mr Duggan – Frank, according to the article, which describes him as a local businessman and philanthropist – who has recently died at the age of eighty-nine. The article makes no mention of his involvement with Pendleton House – good or bad – and describes him as a stalwart of the local community.

Dan had often wondered what had happened to Mr Duggan. He hoped it was one of two things: either he'd seen the error of his ways and changed his behaviour, or he'd been found out and locked away for a very long time. Mostly, though, he tried to forget completely about what went on all those years ago.

The rage burns inside him. A pure fury at realising not that Mr Duggan is dead but that he lived a long and healthy life, dying peacefully in his sleep. He realises that Mr Duggan will never face justice. Ever since that night, that had been what had kept him going. Now, even if the truth about Mr Duggan comes out – which it inevitably will – Dan knows deep down that it will change nothing. He will never have had to truly face up to what he did.

He tears the front page off the newspaper and scrunches it up into a ball, throwing it and the rest of the newspaper into the recycling bin. A few minutes later he's feeling sick at its presence in his house, so he takes the contents of the recycling bin outside and puts them in the main wheelie bin.

'Everything okay?' Lisa calls to him when he gets back inside the house.

'Fine,' he replies, heading through into the kitchen to make himself a strong cup of tea.

'Are you sure?' Lisa asks.

'Didn't you hear what I said?' he barks, trying to keep a lid on his frustration but failing miserably. 'I just said I was fine. What's wrong with you?'

'Me?' Lisa says, herself trying to remain calm. 'Hang on a second, you're the one responding like this. I only asked if everything was okay. Clearly not, judging by your reaction.'

'What are you getting at me for?' Dan replies, feeling his

eyes misting over with anger. He can almost see the red fog.
'I'm fine, alright?'

'Oh, whatever,' *she replies, turning to leave the kitchen.*

Dan grits his teeth. 'Don't you fucking dare speak to me like that.'

'Like what?'

'Like that. With your fucking sarcasm and attitude problem.'

'Attitude problem? Seriously, Dan? Are you even going to go there right now?'

Whatever he says, and whatever Lisa replies with, it inflames the situation further and infuriates Dan. 'What are you trying to say, Lisa? Hmm? Go on, tell me. What are you trying to say?' *His face is pressed almost right up against hers. He can see fear in her eyes, but he can also see that she knows he won't do anything stupid. She knows he's not that kind of person.*

'Dan, I can't cope with these mood swings of yours. You can't just decide to—'

'Mood swings?' *Dan yells, wheeling away from her before turning back and raising his fist before he even realises what he's doing. He does realise, though, and he freezes on the spot, his eyes burning into his wife's as she shoots him a look of disgust and pity.*

After a few seconds, she begins to nod slowly. 'Great response, Dan. Brilliant.'

He can see the hurt and disappointment in her eyes before she turns and leaves the kitchen. He chooses not to follow her but instead leans back against the kitchen cupboards and slides down, collapsing onto his backside and pulling his knees tight to his chest, the sobs and the memories taking over as he battles with a smorgasbord of emotions. Anger, hurt, resentment. But also relief and happiness that he's no longer in that place. That place, though, will always be with him, tainting his thoughts and his words and his actions.

Dan hadn't raised a fist to anyone, or even contemplated it, since that night at Pendleton House. Had tonight's argument with Lisa happened on any other night, he knows it wouldn't have ended that way. The only reason it did is because the incident with Mr Duggan was fresh in his mind, polluting his thoughts and turning him momentarily back into that little boy, Daniel. The little boy who saw everything but did nothing until it was too late. The little boy who just wanted to be happy.

35

Why Bratislava? I don't know. I really don't. It's a city I've wanted to go to for a long time, but never got round to. Fortunately, I know Slovakia is in the Schengen Area, and I know it's a long way east. It's the farthest I can go without a longer-term plan, but it's also far enough away that I feel as though I'll have the space to actually come up with that plan. It's also of the old Eastern bloc, and I'm fairly sure it would be easier for a man to live outside the law there than in Austria or Switzerland.

I know how terrible that sounds, but I've got to face facts. If I'm going to be able to put enough space between me and the police – not to mention me and Lisa and Jess's killer – I'm going to have to bend the rules a bit. I'm going to need help, and that sort of help is going to be much more readily available in Eastern Europe than it is in a Swiss ski resort.

The ticket costs me eighty-six euros, which I think is

actually pretty reasonable considering it's a five-and-a-half-hour overnight journey. The train will get in at around two o'clock in the morning, with a change at Vienna on the way. I'm going to try and get some sleep on the train, if I can, as I don't much fancy having to try and find somewhere to sleep in the middle of Slovakia at two in the morning.

My train doesn't leave until 8.22 p.m., which gives me about two hours to kill. Having bought my tickets, I find a cafe and a newsagent. The first thing that strikes me is how busy the station is at this time. I suppose a lot of people will be on their way back from work. This both comforts me and worries me. On one hand, a busy station allows me to blend in more easily. On the other, it makes it far more difficult for me to spot an undercover police officer. Or a killer.

On top of that, there are the weird feelings I get from watching these people going about their everyday lives. Men in suits and with briefcases waiting to board their trains back home at the end of a long day. Families with suitcases and backpacks waiting to go on holiday. Couples parting after time spent together. Groups of girls heading off for a night out. It's society in a nutshell, a mix of ordinary people going about their ordinary lives.

But my life is anything but ordinary right now. That's the problem. Yet again, I'm one huge walking contradiction. I feel somewhat calmed by the presence of normality, by people unknowingly showing me that the world hasn't actually stopped turning, but at the same time I'm convinced that it has. Why aren't these people being more respectful? Don't they realise that my wife and my – well, what was

Jess? – have been murdered? That I've been framed for at least one of them, and no doubt will be heavily suspected of the other? Can't they see the injustice?

No, of course they can't, because they don't know me. Is that a good thing? Probably. They don't know me and they wouldn't want to anyway.

I see a sign for the toilets and decide to head that way. It'll give me a bit of breathing space, at least.

When I get there, I do what I need to do and then go to wash my hands in the sink. I look up at myself in the mirror and am both shocked and pleasantly surprised. I don't look good. I look a fucking mess, in fact, but the main thing is that I look completely different from the photo that was on the front page of the newspapers. By now, more photos will have been circulated, but I'm sure none of them are going to look anything like I look now.

For years I've had fairly unruly hair and some form of beard. I can't remember the last time I was without either. Now, though, I have neither. The whole shape of my face looks completely different. I can see the tiredness, too. My eyes are sunken, and I'm sure there are wrinkles which weren't there before. I look like a man defeated, but deep down I know that I'm not.

I barely recognise myself, so I'm pretty certain that no-one else is going to pick me out in the middle of an Austrian train station. The only way they'd manage that is if they already knew I was here. And unless they'd followed me from the campsite and from the petrol station, that just wouldn't be possible. I've been careful; I know I have.

Either way, the possibility is always there and I doubt that fear's going to leave me until this whole episode is over.

What I'm not worried about, though, is the passing policeman or observant member of the public spotting and recognising me. I'm hidden in plain sight, and I'm happy with that right now.

Things could get a bit sticky if there are passport checks at any point. Technically, there shouldn't be. Getting from Austria to Slovakia means staying within the Schengen Area, which means EU nationals can cross borders without passport checks or visas. I know there's the possibility of spot checks on the train, though. All I can do is hope, because it's a long walk to Bratislava.

I exit the toilet and make my way back towards the cafe and the newsagent. In the newsagent, I buy myself a copy of *Kronen Zeitung*, a newspaper I presume to be Austrian. Probably the best way to blend in, I think. I grab a coffee from the self-service machine and take both to the till to pay.

As I thumb through my money, I do my now well-established trick of looking at the price on the till as the cashier speaks to me, but nothing shows. I keep my calm and hand over a twenty-euro note. That should be plenty. The girl looks at me disapprovingly and counts out my change. With a quick *'Danke schön'*, I'm off and back on the main concourse, ready to bed down and try to look normal for the next couple of hours.

36

By the time my train finally flashes up on the board, I feel as though I should be fluent in German. I've read almost the entire paper back to back, and I didn't understand a word.

I make my way to the platform and board the train. I feel a bit of a wally walking on with a carrier bag when everyone else has suitcases or rucksacks, but my holdall is far too recognisable now to risk it being visible. I'll buy a new one in Bratislava.

The train is far smarter and more comfortable than the ones I'm used to back in England. I've found that whenever I've been abroad, though, which is quite bizarre seeing as our railways are mostly owned by foreign European governments anyway. Everywhere else I go, the level of comfort and style always seems to be much higher, except for the metro system in Brussels, which seems to be made entirely of orange plastic.

Despite the fact it's an overnight journey, this isn't a

sleeper train. That means it's going to be a long five and a half hours trying to get to sleep in a chair while we bounce through Austria as I try not to get too paranoid about the people around me in the carriage. I'm not worried about passing strangers recognising me, but what if someone's sat opposite me for a good few hours with a copy of the newspaper right in front of them?

Fortunately, there's nobody sat anywhere near me until we stop almost two hours later at Salzburg, at which point an elderly lady plonks herself down across the aisle from me, facing in my direction. She beams a big, friendly smile at me. I think for a moment, then return an upturned corner of my mouth – so different from my usual smile that'd be in all the pictures that I'm actually pretty impressed with myself.

That's the last time she even looks in my direction, as a couple of minutes later she seems to be fast asleep. At least, I hope she's asleep. If she's not, I'm convinced I'm some sort of walking death magnet.

The effect of the train swaying gently on the tracks as it trundles through Austria is deeply relaxing, but it's not enabling me to sleep. I can't. Not while I'm out here in an open carriage, potentially exposed to all sorts of threats. Even the windows worry me. Despite the fact that we're hurtling along at God knows what speed, there's always a worry in my mind about the blackness outside. There's nothing to be seen save for a few distant lights, and a part of my brain tries to convince me of all sorts of things that can see in, even though I can't see out.

It's paranoia trying to creep in again.

I won't let it.

Shortly before twelve thirty, we arrive at Vienna Central Station. I know it's going to be tight to make the connecting train to Bratislava: it's meant to leave at 00.50, and I don't know which platform it's from. As it's an international train, it might be from a different building altogether.

I make sure I'm first off the train, then I jog along the platform until I see the information boards showing the trains due to leave and arrive. I see 00.50 *BRATISLAVA* on the board. It's platform 9, the adjacent platform, and my ticket tells me I need to be boarding at the carriages A–C end.

The train's already there, so I head for carriage C and show the ticket inspector my ticket. He waves me aboard and, thankfully, doesn't ask me for my passport. All I've got is another hour and a half until I'm clear. If my luck continues to hold out like this, I'll be alright. I'm certainly due a run of luck right about now, that's for sure.

As I wait for the train to depart, I allow my brain to start mulling over the possibilities. How could someone have tracked us to a campsite in Switzerland? We drove all the way to Claude's and changed cars, and there's no way in hell anyone followed us there, as he lives in the middle of nowhere. There's no way they'd be able to get anywhere near us without us seeing. Then we headed to Switzerland in an unknown car. If someone had followed us on that whole journey, we would have noticed. We were so careful.

So what was it? A tip-off? If so, from who? And how would they have been able to tip off the killer? If someone spotted us, recognised us and reported us, they'd call the police. And the police wouldn't turn up and murder Jess; they'd arrest us.

All I can assume is that somehow someone is following me. Not one person, I'm sure of it. More. It's the only way they'd be able to do it without being seen. It still doesn't explain how they twigged about the switch at Claude's place, but I'm sure I'll figure that out, too. Unless . . . unless Claude was in on it. It makes no sense, though, especially as Jess trusted him so much. She might have been a perfect enigma, but she was a good judge of character. I knew that much. She spoke about Claude with such passion, almost like a mother protecting a child. If I trust Jess's judgement, I have to trust that Claude couldn't have been involved. That leaves me with some more thinking to do, then.

It also leaves me with the enormous worry as to why a whole group of organised criminals would be out to get me. Willing to kill Lisa. Willing to kill Jess. Willing to chase me halfway across Europe to see me terrorised and possibly even dead.

As the train starts to pull away from the station, I know that's a question I must answer, and answer soon.

37

The train stops every few minutes. Far from being a direct service, I don't think we've gone more than five minutes without a stop. It's agonising, knowing we must be so close to Bratislava yet unable to get there any quicker. It's even more irritating that no-one seems to get on or off the train at any of these stations. There are nineteen people in this carriage – I've counted them – but not one of them has got on or off since Vienna.

As the train pulls away from Gattendorf station (the fourteenth one we've stopped at in the past fifty minutes – I've been counting), I decide I need a change of scenery to stop me going insane. I pick up my bag and head for the toilet.

I don't need to go – I just want to be able to sit somewhere, quietly, without stressing myself out. Some solitude, perhaps. The frequency of the stops isn't helping my paranoia at all; I'm convincing myself that the next time the

train stops, those doors are going to open and a police officer's going to step on. Not that hiding in the toilet will make
much difference, but at least I'll *feel* safer, calmer.

My heart rate starts to drop from the second I slide the
lock across on the inside of the toilet door. It has an instant
calming effect, and I'm thankful for small mercies. I run the
cold tap and pool some water in my hands before splashing
it onto my face. I do this a few times, enjoying the feel of
the ice-cold water on my skin. The tap's noisy, though, and
I realise there's no way I'll be able to hear the station
announcements from here with it running, so I turn it back
off and sit with my head bowed over the sink, cold water
dripping into the basin from my nose and chin.

I'm aware of the swooshing sound of the intercarriage
doors opening at the far end of the carriage, and the voice of
a man calling out. He says a few words, in a variety of
foreign languages. French, German and something else I
don't recognise. But there are four words I definitely do
recognise, because they're English.

'Tickets and passports, please!'

It takes me a couple of seconds to realise I'm doing it,
but I'm holding my breath. I can hear his voice getting
closer and closer every time he calls out. Something that
sounds like German. Then the language I don't recognise
but presume to be Slovak. Then French. Then those unmistakable words yet again.

'Tickets and passports, please!'

He's now right up near my end of the carriage. Probably
only a few seat rows away from the toilet. I can hear his

appreciative murmuring as my fellow passengers show him their tickets. I wonder if any of them will point out the fact that there's a guy in the toilet? I really hope not.

In England, ticket inspectors are pretty wise to the usual tricks: getting up and going to the toilet when the ticket inspector comes into your carriage, walking down the carriage and jumping off at the next stop before getting back on further up the train. They know all the methods. Right now, I'm just thankful that I got up and went to the toilet before he could even be seen.

All I can do now is hope and pray that he walks straight past the toilet. I certainly can't risk having to show this guy my passport. The game will be up. Here. On a train somewhere between Austria and Slovakia.

My brain runs through a million thoughts in just a couple of seconds. Do we have an extradition treaty with Austria? What about Slovakia? Of course we do – we're in the EU. Would I be put into a local jail or sent straight back to the UK? How would I get a lawyer? How on earth can I explain running away from the scenes of two murders? Will all this circumstantial evidence be enough to convict me? Who the hell's doing this? Why? Why?

They're all thoughts I've had over and over since finding Lisa's body, but now they're all coming at once, firing themselves into my consciousness, screaming and rattling around inside my skull. I can hear the blood pulsing in my ears, my heart trying to jump out of my mouth. My legs and arms trembling, filled with adrenaline.

What will I do if he knocks on the door? Do I ignore it?

No. He'll know I'm there. There's a tiny window, but it's got a grille over it and there's no way I'd be able to squeeze out anyway.

I could open the door and jump him. Kick his head in. Get off at the next station and run. Judging by the current pattern, we can't be more than about thirty seconds from the next stop.

No, I should just sit and wait it out. If I jump him, that'll be game over. They'll be out looking for me, and they'll know exactly where I am. As things stand, no-one can be certain where I am. Even I'm not entirely sure.

I think about the recent migrant crisis in this part of Europe. Surely they'll be even more vigilant with checking passports now? Hiding out in the toilets has to be a pretty common way for people to try smuggling themselves over borders. So many of the borders have already closed thanks to political pressure, and the ones that are open are far more hawk-eyed when it comes to checking passports and identities. I manage to comfort myself by remembering that the migrants are heading west through Europe, *into* Austria and Switzerland – not the other way. Might that make this guy less worried about checking everyone if he's got to be super vigilant when the train's going in the other direction? I hope so.

Only a few seconds have passed, and I can hear his voice right outside the toilet now. He's on the back row of seats, not far from where I was sitting.

'Tickets and passports, please!'

It sounds almost as if he's calling it through the door to

me. I look wide-eyed at the door lock, expecting to see it wiggle but willing it not to move. My heart is in my mouth and I realise I'm holding my breath again. My eyes start to mist up.

And then I hear the anti-climactic whooshing of the doors into the next carriage and the familiar but fading voice of the inspector.

'Tickets and passports, please!'

38

The train pulls into Bratislava at almost exactly two o'clock in the morning. The station's quite impressive, an odd mixture of old Eastern bloc and modern glass. My first thoughts on leaving the building are that I'm actually pretty disappointed. It looks just like any other town or city: bus stops, zebra crossings and what looks to be a shopping centre on the other side of the road, almost completely made from glass. I don't recognise any of the brands, but I presume one of them to be a gym. Tatra Banka, presumably, is a bank. Other than that I haven't a clue.

I turn left and walk a little further down the road, crossing over onto the shopping centre side of the road. At the end of the building is a familiar sign that leaves me chuckling: Tesco Express. My light chuckle becomes a chortle, then a belly laugh as I sit down on the brown brick steps outside the Tesco Express and let it all out.

I feel like a lunatic. It's two in the morning, there's no-one around, and I'm sitting outside a Tesco Express in Slovakia, laughing and crying at the same time. The pure bizarreness of the situation makes me laugh even more. I don't know how long I'm sat there, but by the time the feeling has subsided my stomach hurts like hell, as does my face and the two muscles that run from the base of my skull down the back of my neck.

I look down at my bag and then up at my surroundings. And suddenly I realise this is all I've got in the world. This is now my home. I stand up, pick up my bag and start walking.

The overriding thought in my mind is that I need to find somewhere to sleep. I had tried to get some rest on the train, but it was just impossible. My worries about someone jumping on at the next stop or suddenly recognising me were starting to take over. There was just no way I'd have been able to keep my eyes closed for more than about five seconds. I feel even more tired from the travelling and the almost constant adrenaline rushes, not to mention the amount of walking I've done over the past few days.

That walking's not something that's going to stop any time soon, though, and I find myself criss-crossing the streets of Bratislava, trying to determine where I might be able to find a place to sleep. Thankfully, Slovakia's in the eurozone so I can spend the currency I've already got on me. If I can find somewhere. In this part of Bratislava, it seems, absolutely everything is shut down for the night. Even the Tesco Express had '6–22h' on a big sign outside it.

I spot signs for the Danube and what I think refers to

the city centre, and I follow them. It's nearly an hour before I've worked my way through the streets and crossed the river onto the other side of Bratislava, which is definitely very much still alive. I can hear music from nightclubs and bars, even past three in the morning, and I remember a friend of mine telling me that was the European way: many people don't even go out before midnight. Right now, though, I'm ready to sleep almost absolutely anywhere.

It's only a few more minutes before I spot a sign outside a building. It's called Hostel Maria. It doesn't look like the smartest place in the world, but right now I really don't care. I just want somewhere to lay my head for the night. The tatty poster in the window advertises board at twenty euros a night. That seems pretty cheap to me, even for a place like this, and I wonder how long that poster's been in the window. I just don't care, though. They could charge me two hundred euros and I'd pay it. I wouldn't have a whole lot left, but I'd pay it.

That's when I start to think of something else I've been repressing for a long time: I'm going to have to get some money from somewhere. I'll deal with that in the morning, though. For now, I need to sleep.

I walk up the steps and push open the door of Hostel Maria. The first thing I hear is women laughing. There's a guy with a receding hairline, a large moustache and an even larger beer belly sitting behind a grotty desk, smoking a cigarette. He eyes me with suspicion.

'Room?' he barks. My first worry is that he can work out so quickly that I'm English.

'Please,' I reply, my voice hoarse. I realise it's the first time I've spoken to anyone in hours.

'Twenty euro,' he says, holding out his hand. I put my hand in my pocket and take out a few notes. I hand him a twenty-euro one.

'Private room, forty euro,' he adds, not taking his eyes off of the rest of the cash in my hand.

I think for a moment, then nod and hand him an extra twenty euros. He spins around on his chair, takes a key from a hook and hands it to me. 'Room twelve. Up stairs, then right. At end.'

I nod and pick up my bag before heading up the stairs and along the corridor.

This place is revolting. The wallpaper's peeling off the walls, there are stains of grease, dirt and God knows what else on the floors and ceilings and the whole place smells like smoke and something else I can't quite put my finger on. It's not a place I'd ever want to be in my life, but right now I'm pretty desperate.

The open dormitory is at the other end of the corridor, to the left as I get to the top of the stairs, but I can still hear the laughter and noise coming from it. As I see room 12 in front of me, I wish it was just laughter I could hear. In a room somewhere on this corridor – I don't know which, but it's very close – a couple are having sex. Very noisy sex. I put the key in the lock and make a point of trying to make as much noise getting in the room as possible, but it's no use. There's no way in hell they're going to be able to hear me. They sound like they're having far too much fun.

I slam the door behind me. I know it's not going to stop them, but I feel like I need to make a point.

I go to put my bag down on the floor and decide against it. The carpet is filthy and sticky. Instead, I opt to put it on the table next to the bed. At least that's just dusty. I take off my clothes and put them on top of the bag, then climb into bed. The light's off, but it doesn't make any difference as there's a huge great streetlight outside my window, the light streaming into the room. The curtain's half the size of the window, too, so that doesn't help. All I can be thankful for is that the net curtains behind it are so covered in dirt and grime that it's probably keeping at least some of the light out.

The noise of the couple having sex is still going on. I go to put the pillow over my head, but before I do I notice a horribly suspicious-looking stain on it. I pick up the pillow and throw it at the door, before turning onto my side and clamping my hands over my ears. Home sweet home.

39

When I wake up, everything is deathly silent, aside from the faint murmur of road noise from outside. I roll over and look at the small alarm clock beside me, my neck and shoulders stiff and painful. The clock tells me it's 9.41 a.m. I presume that's right, but I wouldn't know. If the quality of the clock is the same as the quality of anything else in this place, it could be three in the afternoon for all I know.

My first thought is that I'm amazed I managed to sleep so long. I'm not usually one for waking up late as it is, and in my current situation I'm not exactly finding it easy to relax. It's clear to see, though, that something has allowed my brain to subconsciously loosen up and de-stress slightly. It's probably the realisation that I'm fairly unlikely to be found here, because even *I* don't know where I am.

I'll have been caught on CCTV probably hundreds of times between Innsbruck and Bratislava. That doesn't bother me too much, though, as I don't look like *me*. Or, rather, I don't look like the me that people will be looking for. They'll be looking for a guy with scruffy hair over his ears and a beard. Claude's car will be on CCTV, too, but I don't know that they're necessarily looking for that. Not the police, anyway. I know the killer knows, because he tracked us down to the campsite and killed Jess, but I'm very confident he didn't follow me to Innsbruck.

I try to get it straight in my head: the killer knows the car I was using, but doesn't know I took it to Innsbruck. The police will find the car in Innsbruck but won't know it was the one I was using. Presumably they'll track down Claude as the owner, and he'll tell them it must have been stolen from his barn. Then I just have to hope there's no sort of paper trail linking him to Jess, or the chase will well and truly be on.

In short, I don't see a way that I could be traced here, to Bratislava. That doesn't mean I can put my head up above the parapet, though. I'm going to have to be incredibly careful until this whole thing is sorted.

And that's where I get the huge bolt of adrenaline in my chest and the lump in my throat. Because that's what it all comes back to: I have to get this thing sorted.

That's the most difficult part of all. How the hell am I meant to try and work out who killed Lisa and Jess – and why – when I'm too busy worrying about being caught or killed myself? I need help. I know that much. But there's no-one to help me. I can't make contact with anyone back home – that'd be far too risky. Not that I've got anyone I can really trust and rely on. It's not until this whole thing happened that I realised how alone I've been all along. I only ever really had Lisa. Not that I ever treated her particularly well. And then there was Jess. God, yes, I relied on her. I just trusted every word she said, everything she did, even though I barely knew her. And, to be honest, she's probably saved my life. Now I need to make this work for her, and for Lisa, who died needlessly in the room where I betrayed her.

I look across at the large carrier bag I've been carrying halfway across Europe, with my holdall tucked inside it. Another anchor in the past. I know that I need to get myself a new bag. One that no-one will be looking out for. One that I can call my own. One that's untainted.

I don't even bother to try to find the bathroom in this place. Even if I did, I'm pretty sure the mouldy soap and brown water would make me even dirtier than I am now. As I get towards the door, I glance back at the bag on the side. Should I take it with me? No, that might be too risky. Leaving it here isn't without its risks, either, but there's nothing incriminating in the bag. I've got my wallet and most of the money on me. There's only really clothes, some toiletries and general knick-knacks in the bag. Nothing that can identify me, anyway.

I decide it's best to leave the bag here for now, to allow me to blend in better on the streets if nothing else, and I unlock the door.

The corridor outside my room is an eerie sort of quiet, not a peaceful one. The kind of quiet nobody likes. Then again, I doubt that this place could ever seem peaceful. I think 'eerie' is probably as good as it gets. I should imagine that the people staying here will be fast asleep by now. If they've been out clubbing into the early hours their heads will probably be a bit sore. Judging by the sounds coming from the neighbouring room when I got here last night, that's not the only thing that'll be sore.

It would be fair to say that this place looks even worse in the daylight – what daylight there is in this dark, oppressive corridor – and I'll be glad when I can find somewhere to stay more long-term. The problem there, though, is money. The money I've got is quickly running out and I've no way of being able to get more right now. I can't just go sticking my card into an ATM, as that'll link me straight to Bratislava. No, I need cash. Cold, hard cash. And I need to find it in a country I don't know, using a language I don't speak.

A rather depressing and sobering thought occurs to me: Jess would know what to do.

40

The streets of Bratislava look quite pleasant in the morning sun. I spend about half an hour walking in what I believe to be the general direction of the city centre. I'm careful to walk in a straight line where possible, though, and I've memorised the name of the street the hostel is on in case I get lost: Palisády, near the junction with Zochova and Bradlianska. I've devised a little song to help me remember it, as well as the image of the hostel being my safe place, a fort with iron fencing – or a *palisade* – around it. Just to keep things extra safe, I visualise Bradley Walsh, the British quiz show host, standing guard out front. *Palisády. Bradlianska.* It's crude, but it'll do. At least I'll be able to get back home.

Jesus. Home. You know things have gone downhill when you start to call that shithole home. Without any form of income, though, it's the way it's going to have to be. At forty euros a night, even keeping that grotty roof above my head won't last long.

I try to think of what I could do to earn some money. The problem is, I know nothing except the industry I've spent my life in. I don't speak a word of Slovak, either, so I fail to see how I could get any sort of job. Is English widely spoken in Bratislava? I don't know. Getting a job working in a bar in Amsterdam, for example, would be fine if you don't speak Dutch. No-one in Amsterdam speaks Dutch anyway. But this is Slovakia.

Before long, I find a sports shop near the hospital. I go in and buy myself a new bag – one that won't look out of place and doesn't tie me into my past. It's psychological as much as anything. The rucksack sets me back a whopping sixty euros. A bargain compared to being caught at this stage, but still a big chunk out of my quickly depleting stock of cash.

A few feet away from the sports shop, I feel myself starting to break down. The whole thing's become too much for me. I feel my breathing start to increase and get shallower, my heart rate builds and my head fills with an electric buzzing.

No. I can't let this happen. I can't let it get on top of me. I have to keep fighting, keep moving, keep on top of things. If I start thinking, start realising, that'll be the beginning of the end. I need to distract myself. I need some normality.

I spot a bar across the road, the door open and inviting – even at this time of the morning. I can't see inside – it looks dark compared to the bright sunshine out here, but I head inside and shut myself off from the world outside.

It doesn't take me long to decide whether I want alcohol or not. It's not like it really matters any more. I can't go getting blotto and letting my defences down, but I think it's pretty fair to say I need a drink right now. I order a beer, by pointing at it, shying away from the temptation of whisky or whatever the local moonshine might be. The bartender surprises me by speaking to me in English.

'One euro, please.'

The only thing that surprises me more than him somehow knowing I'm English (how do we Brits always manage to give off that unspeakable air of Britishness?) is the price of the beer.

'One? Blimey,' I say, handing over a one-euro coin. 'I could get used to this.'

'Cheaper than back home, no?' the bartender replies.

'Yeah, definitely.'

'Let me guess,' he says, popping a paper napkin under my beer glass. 'Australian.'

I stop myself before I answer, changing my mind. 'Yeah,' I say. 'Australian.'

He smiles broadly. 'Can always tell. Are you here for long?'

I allow myself a small chuckle. 'I don't know. I really don't know. I'm doing a bit of travelling, but I'm happy to stay put if I like the place and it feels good.' Not so far from the truth, that.

We chat for a little longer, mostly idle pleasantries. He

can tell I'm a stranger in a strange land, and he seems keen to ensure that I feel at home here. It's something you get in a lot of places – locals determined to want you to love their city.

'You have accommodation?' he says, pointing to my rucksack. He must presume I've got all my gear in here – it's actually packed out with polystyrene and plastic wrapping to make it look good on display in the shop, but he doesn't need to know that.

'No,' I say. 'I mean, I stayed in a hostel last night but I don't have anything permanent. And I don't have enough money for anything permanent.'

The bartender holds eye contact with me and nods, expressionless. 'You looking for work?'

I raise my eyebrows and drop them again. 'Possibly,' I say, taking a sip of my beer. It's ice cold and feels fantastic. 'Although it's going to be difficult.'

'You can be in Europe ninety days in six months without visa,' he says. 'My brother, he has a building company. An Australian guy worked for him for a few weeks.'

'Oh right.'

'From . . . Melbourne,' he says, suddenly remembering the name. 'You know it?'

'A bit,' I reply. 'Not far from me.'

He smiles. 'Where you come from before Slovakia?'

'Italy,' I say. 'That's where I flew into. Then I went to Slovenia and Hungary before here.' I thank my lucky stars that my European geography is pretty sound. He seems convinced.

'All in Schengen Area. So nobody knows you are in Slovakia, no?'

I swallow heavily. 'No.'

'Okay, so rule is ninety days in six months in Schengen, yes? So you can be ninety days in EU, then ninety days in Romania. Same rule, but not Schengen. Many people do this.'

'Oh right,' I say, not wanting to tell him that it's completely irrelevant as I'm an EU citizen and can stay here as long as I like. 'That's handy.'

'But if you have job, you can stay for long, long time.'

'I couldn't even stay for ninety days without a job,' I tell him.

'How much you pay for hostel?'

I see no harm in telling him. 'Forty euros a night.'

'Two hundred eighty euros a week,' he says, doing the maths immediately. 'Very expensive.'

'Yeah.'

'I have room here,' he says, still not taking his eyes off of me. 'One hundred eighty euros a week. Also, I can help with job.'

'Oh,' I say. 'That's very kind. I might take you up on the room, but I've never worked behind a bar before so I'm not sure if—'

The man laughs. It's a deep, guttural belly laugh. 'No, is not bar work. Bar is not busy enough for extra work. My brother, he have some work. Is good pay.'

'I'm afraid I don't have any experience in building, either. I don't think I'd be much help to him.'

'It is a different work,' he says, taking my beer and topping it up for me. 'Delivery.'

'Delivery?' I ask. 'For a builder?'

He smiles. 'My brother, Andrej, he has many businesses. He is very well known here in Bratislava. With many customers, he need many deliveries. You can ride motor scooter?'

It's not a question I've been asked before. 'Uh, I guess.' I mean, how hard can it be?

'Okay. Room here is cheaper anyway, yes? I must tidy, but you come here after lunch and you can have room. Save lots of money.'

I smile at him, thankful for his generosity. I'd always been led to believe that people in Eastern Europe were far more generous and kind than we are in the West, but I hadn't realised quite how true that was until now.

'I will. Thank you.'

The man holds out his hand. 'I am Marek.'

I take his hand in mine and shake it. 'Bradley,' I say. 'Pleased to meet you.'

41

One of the benefits of wrap parties was the free bar. Not only did it mean the hard work of filming had finished and it was time to hand over to the editors in their warm, cosy studios and suites, but it was an excuse to let their hair down and celebrate the fact that they'd done a bloody good job.

For Dan, the free bar was something he looked forward to through the closing days of filming, knowing that it'd be a perfect opportunity to get hammered without having to worry about the additional next-day headache of checking his credit card bill. What he liked most was that everyone was invited and everyone seemed to be on a level playing field, from the camera operators and the actors, to the costume department and the researchers, such as the particularly glamorous one he was talking to at the bar.

She wasn't what Dan would call a classic beauty – she was curvier than his usual type, but certainly not fat. Her fiery red hair was what first enticed him to talk to her, combined with the charisma and air of sexuality that she seemed to exude. Many people in the TV world had that sort of way about them – particularly the ones who were keen to get out from behind the camera and one day end up in front of it.

'He seemed to understand that, though,' she said, having come to the end of her really not very interesting story about how she'd managed to apply for her job in the first place.

'So what sort of stuff do you enjoy doing?' Dan asked, trying to change the subject away from talking shop. Although lots of people were impressed by the perceived glamour of TV, to him it was just another job. A job that meant he got to see a lot of the country – and further afield – and which paid fairly well, but it was a job all the same.

'Funnily enough, I'm in a field hockey team,' she said, even though it wasn't particularly funny in the slightest.

'Are you? That's really cool,' Dan replied, not wanting to ask the difference between field hockey and normal hockey. 'What position?'

'Fullback, but just recently I've been playing as a sweeper because our regular one's been injured.'

Dan nodded, trying to look interested, but instead only thinking that perhaps her curves weren't curves, but the muscular build of a hockey – or field hockey – player. He'd never been with a muscular woman before. He wasn't sure if he'd like it or not.

He could feel his mobile phone buzzing in his pocket. He didn't know why he even bothered bringing it out with him – no-one ever called him unless it was the most incon-

venient moment possible. Like now. He looked at the screen. It was Lisa. He put the phone back in his trouser pocket.

'Sorry about that. Don't know why I even carry the bloody thing.'

'Don't you find it handy?' the girl asked.

'No, I find it a pain in the arse. So. Field hockey.'

Luckily for him, the redhead didn't want to stay the night. He was never keen on waking up next to a woman – almost as if that made it worse. To Dan, having them leave that same night and then sleeping alone in his hotel room meant that he stayed just the right side of the moral line. It was a moral line that he often blurred, but it was still one he recognised.

He'd just been starting to nod off, the digital clock on the bedside table having ticked over to a few minutes past two in the morning, when he heard the incessant vibration of the mobile phone coming from the pocket of his trousers.

He jabbed the light on, blinked in the brightness and scrabbled on the floor to grab the phone from his pocket. It was Lisa again. He groaned, looking at the time on the bedside clock. Although it was far too late to be taking phone calls, he knew Lisa wouldn't be calling at this time unless it was urgent.

As soon as the call connected, he could hear her desperate sobs, even before he'd managed to say hello.

'Lisa? Lisa, what is it, sweetheart?' he said, trying to keep *his voice low so as not to wake up anybody in the adjoining rooms.*

He heard Lisa fighting for the words, trying to find a way to say what she had to say.

'Oh, Dan. I don't know how to put this,' she said, before breaking off and crying.

'Say what? What's wrong? What's happened?'

Lisa sobbed again, a huge release of emotion. 'I've had a miscarriage.'

42

I feel guilty for lying to Marek. For pretending to be someone I'm not. But then again that's what I've spent my whole life doing. Why change now?

I manage to find my way back to the hostel, thankful that I'd walked pretty much in a straight line from here to town earlier today. At least staying above the bar will mean I'm more central and will be able to find my way back more easily. It seemed to be right in the thick of things.

When I get back to my room, everything's still silent. I'd be willing to bet that none of the occupants of any of these rooms have even moved since I left earlier, never mind got up.

As I open the door, I stop and stare at the carrier bag I left on the side, with the holdall full of my belongings inside it. I can't remember for the life of me how it looked when I left it earlier this morning, but I still can't shake the overriding, all-engulfing feeling that it's moved. It's a feeling I can't explain, but it's strong.

I step cautiously over to the bag, poke my head around to the opening and look inside. It's just a holdall. Just my holdall. Not that I really expected anything else, but something still doesn't feel right here. It feels like the walls have eyes.

I gather I have nothing to lose, so I grab the carrier bag and head back out into the corridor. Instead of turning left towards the stairs, I head right. I remember seeing a fire door at the far end of the corridor not far from my room. I have a decent idea where this will lead.

When I get to the door, I check it for electrical contacts. It doesn't seem to be alarmed, so I push on the bar and shove the door open. There's a brown metal staircase leading upwards against the wall, and a bucket with sand in it, a dozen or so cigarette butts sticking out of it. It seems a bit pointless in this place, seeing as everyone appears to just smoke inside anyway. I take the bucket and prop it up inside the door frame to stop the door from slamming behind me, and I make my way up the staircase, the carrier bag and my old holdall in one hand, the new rucksack in the other.

When I get to the top of the steps, I find myself on the roof of the hostel. It looks like any other roof around here – a few air-conditioning units and water-storage tanks. It's hard to tell where the roof of the hostel ends and the building next door starts, but that's irrelevant right now. I'm up here for a reason, and I don't intend to be long.

I step towards the edge of the roof and look over across Bratislava. The view is pretty impressive, especially on a bright and sunny day like this. It seems a world away from Herne Bay and East Grinstead, from Claude's farmhouse and the constant shoulder checks.

The physical distance allows me to keep some emotional distance, too. I've never been the most emotional guy in the world, but even I'm struggling to cope with what's happened recently. However, coping is exactly what the human body and mind is built to do. It's a ready-built coping machine. I'm well aware that I'm probably in denial, but I really don't care. All that matters is that I can avoid being caught by the police until I've worked out what's going on. Or worse, being found by Lisa and Jess's killer.

That last possibility is one that only occasionally occurs to me. That someone wants to terrorise me.

If that's the case, how do I get out of this? Will I ever get out of it? Somehow I don't think so. I'll never be truly free, but I'm a lot freer here than I would be back home right now.

Home.

What is home, anyway? Surely it's the place you feel safest, the place you want to be. England is neither of those things to me any more. I feel safer here than I have anywhere since Lisa was killed, save perhaps for the arms of Jess. But she's not coming back. And neither is my desire to head back towards England. I know that now, but I've known it deep down for longer. And that's why I came up onto the roof.

I bend down and take the old holdall out of the carrier bag, unzipping it and taking out the contents. I then unzip the new rucksack, shove the carrier bag and the polystyrene foam inside the old one, and put my belongings into the new one.

I keep one thing unpacked, though.

I take the old rucksack over to a more open part of the roof and place it on the floor. Then I bend down on one knee, roll the side of my thumb quickly down the wheel of the lighter and wait for the large flame to settle. It's barely visible in the bright light of the Bratislava skyline, but the air above it shimmers in a hot haze.

Carefully, I lean further over and put the flame to the material of the rucksack. It takes a few seconds to catch, but when it does it's beautiful. I stand up, take a few steps back and watch for a couple of moments. Once I'm satisfied, I pick up my new rucksack and walk back down the metal staircase, never looking back.

43

When I get back down to the reception area, there's no-one around. That doesn't particularly surprise me, but it does mean I don't need to bother about explaining myself. I leave the key on the reception desk and step out onto the street.

It already feels brighter and sunnier out here. It was pretty bright and sunny earlier, but now it feels as if a veil has lifted from in front of my face. I feel lighter, freer. This is the space I need to be in to be able to come to terms with what's happened and to find out who killed Lisa and Jess – and why.

As I make my way back to Marek's bar, a realisation strikes me. It's something I think I realised a while back, but perhaps not consciously. Ever since I left Herne Bay I've been telling myself that being on the run is a way to give myself the time and space to think and to work out what's gone on. The fact of the matter is I don't think I'll ever be able to work out what's gone on. Who could? I'm kidding myself if I think I'm going to do a better job of this than the police. But then that's not the point, is it? Deep down, I know why I ran. And I know why I've continued to run. And I know why I've not made any serious, concerted effort to try and get to the bottom of what's happened. It's because I'm enjoying the adventure.

It sounds bizarre, considering the circumstances. Of course I didn't enjoy Lisa's or Jess's deaths. But that instinct to up and leave and start again is a very male thing. It's all about the adventure. I feel safer here – I don't really feel as though the police are on my tail. Nor the killer. But I also know I have to assume that they are or I'll never be truly safe. I can't get complacent.

Telling Marek that my name was Bradley felt good. Really good. It was like inventing a whole persona. In that flash of two syllables, I could see my whole life story behind me. The childhood growing up in Australia, having barbecues on the beach, surfing with my friends. All a lie, but one I am more than happy to live. After all, I've lived plenty of lies that I've been less than happy to live.

I've already pretended to be the faithful husband, the hard-working provider. I've been living the life of adventure the whole time, but never living it with truth. It's always been hidden behind this false facade of a normal life. Now, though, this *is* my life, and I'd be untrue to myself if I were to pretend I wasn't enjoying it.

It's a case of taking every day as it comes. Sooner or later, the police will have to realise that I wasn't responsible for Lisa's death. Nor Jess's. I don't know how they're going to prove that, but they're going to have a better chance than I am. Sure, they're not going to be trying to prove it because my disappearance is going to make me their prime suspect anyway, but I have to cling on to that hope. It's all I've got.

The text message sent to Lisa's phone is the big problem. The police would surely be able to tell that it wasn't sent by my phone, but I can't guarantee it wasn't. After all, the phone was in my hotel room the whole time. If the killer was, too, then it's entirely possible they sent the message from my phone. How, I don't know. Would they be able to tie in the exact time the text was sent with CCTV images from the restaurant downstairs? If they could, they'd be able to see that I couldn't possibly have sent the text. CCTV would perhaps show Lisa going up to my room and me arriving a few minutes later, but it wouldn't confirm that she was dead before I got there. Whatever happened in that room will remain a mystery in that sense.

Either way, the biggest problem I have is that this whole thing seems to have been very carefully planned. I know from watching enough crime dramas and reading books that the easiest killers to catch are the impulsive ones, the ones who react in the heat of the moment and try to cover their tracks afterwards. The ones who are never caught are the ones who plan well in advance and are always a number of steps ahead.

There are estimates as to how many undiscovered murders happen every year. The number of people who are 'off the grid' is huge. Murders that never go reported. Bodies that are never found. People who won't be missed if they disappear. I wonder if Jess will be one of those. Apart from Claude, who does she have? And I don't know for sure that there's any paper trail linking him to her, so he might never find out about her death. He needs to know. I owe him that much. I tell myself that when this has all blown over and it's safe to do so, I'll tell him. He deserves that. Jess deserves that. She doesn't deserve to be another nameless murder victim, one of the forgotten.

It's amazing how a bit of distance and a change of scenery can change your perceptions. This has always been about justice. Ever since Lisa died. Until Bratislava, it was justice for me – vindication for what happened, clearing my name. Now this is about justice for Lisa and for Jess. For the two who died needlessly. For the two who died because of me.

44

Marek greets me with a warm smile and a bear hug when I get back to the bar, as if I'm a wanderer returning from a long voyage.

'You came back!' he says, beaming. 'Welcome to your new home.'

'Thanks,' I reply, pulling the rucksack off my shoulders. 'Can I put my stuff upstairs?'

Marek smiles even wider and steps aside, ushering me behind the bar and up the stairs to my room.

When we get there, I'm pleasantly surprised. I was expecting something similar to the dreadful room at the hostel, but it's actually pretty good. It's less of a room and more of a luxury flat. It's tastefully decorated, seems to have mostly new appliances and furniture and has a great view out across the streets of Bratislava.

'This is lovely, Marek,' I say, looking around. 'Really nice.'

'I'm glad you like. Now, my brother has job for you. Delivery. You earn some money, yes?'

I'm amazed at just how trusting and welcoming this guy is. 'Uh, sure. But I don't know Bratislava very well. It might take me a while before I can get started.'

Marek waves his arms in front of his face as if he's wading through a swarm of mosquitoes. 'Is easy, is easy. I have map. Listen, is good money. For delivery of parcel, Andrej will pay thirty euro.'

'Thirty euros? What, a day?' It can't be thirty euros a week, surely, I think.

'No, no. Thirty euro every parcel.'

I feel my jaw drop. 'Thirty euros per parcel? And how many parcels are there?'

Marek shrugs. 'This depends. It changes. Sometimes many, sometimes not many. Depends if busy.'

I guess Bratislava is like any capital city around the world. Getting parcels from A to B is actually pretty difficult in a city centre. I know for a fact that a same-day motorcycle courier delivery in the centre of London can easily cost twenty quid for a small parcel. If we're talking valuable items and a city that's even harder to get around in a car or van, the motorcycle courier business could be pretty lucrative. Thirty euros isn't much over twenty pounds.

'That's good pay,' I say, but I can't help myself from asking the obvious question. 'Why does he need a same-day courier, though, if he's a builder? What do builders need to send by courier?'

Marek looks at me blankly for a split second before

smiling and half laughing. 'Andrej has many businesses. He is also in jewellery trade and import of luxury goods. This part of business, I am manager. This bar, we own together.'

'Ah, I see.'

So Andrej is Bratislava's serial entrepreneur. Not a bad person to get involved with, perhaps. At the very least, it should keep me under the radar and it'll earn me some much-needed money while I'm at it. Bratislava feels safe for now, but I'm well aware that I need to be able to up sticks and go at any time I need to. I have to accept that this is my life as of that moment I left the hotel in Herne Bay.

I'm tempted, sorely tempted, to go out and buy an English newspaper or try to find some coverage of Lisa's murder on TV or the internet, but I manage to convince myself that this would be a very bad idea. I know for a fact that the police use the press to try and flush out killers, as the vast majority of them will keep a keen eye on the press to see what the police have managed to work out. I'm not a killer, though, and I need to try and distance myself emotionally from what's happened. I couldn't bear to see Lisa's face in the newspaper, nor Jess's if they've managed to identify her, and it would do me no good whatsoever to pay attention to any of the coverage.

I like the way I'm starting to think. Deep down, I'm well aware that this is a coping mechanism. It's exactly what I noticed in Jess right back when we first left the hotel in Herne Bay. While I spent a while in a state of utter confusion and desolation, Jess jumped straight to this stage – the coping strategy. She must have been through some shit in her short life to have had her brain switch straight to coping mode, almost instantaneously and seamlessly. She was clearly someone who lived with a lot of emotional pain and scarring. I guess I'm somewhat thankful that she no longer has to live with that, but it was obvious that she was a fighter. She was a coper. And now I owe it to her to fight and to cope.

Marek gestures towards my rucksack. 'You take out your things. Be at home. After, you come down to bar and have drink, yes?'

He seems to flit between having a very good grasp of the English language and then speaking in the oddest broken grammar. I nod and smile.

Marek goes back down to the bar and I unpack my bag. I'm going to need some new clothes – that much is obvious. I don't have much with me anyway, and I feel uncomfortable wearing my clothes from back in England. I count out my money and try to work out how long it's going to last me. I figure if Marek can wait until the end of the week for his rent money, I could get some new clothes over the next couple of days. I could eat and drink downstairs in the bar to save some money – I'm sure Marek wouldn't charge me full price – and the money I'll get from delivering parcels for his brother's business should more than cover the shortfall. One delivery a day will cover my rent easily if I work weekends, and if he's one of the biggest entrepreneurs in Bratislava I'm pretty sure there'll be more work than that.

I take a fresh T-shirt and a pair of jeans out of my rucksack and change my clothes for only the second time since leaving Claude's farmhouse. That might actually be quite normal. I don't know. I'm losing track of the days. But then again it doesn't matter to me whether it's a Tuesday, Sunday or a Friday. The days all blend into one now. I'm a free spirit.

45

I decide not to hit any more alcohol just yet. Marek mentioned something about a delivery, and I've already had one beer. I don't know what the drink-drive limit is in Slovakia, but I should imagine it's lower than in the UK. Most places are stricter than in the UK, and back home a pint and a bit will put you over the limit. I stick to orange juice.

Within about five minutes of being back down at the bar, the conversation returns to the job.

'So, you interested in delivery work?' Marek finally says, having skirted around all sorts of topics until then: the weather, Australian culture, the women of Bratislava.

'Yeah, I reckon so. If you can put up with me not knowing where I'm going for a while. Oh, and I don't know how the driving licence rules work. I don't have an EU licence,' I say. I do, of course, but Marek's still under the impression that I'm Australian.

'No problem,' he says, waving his hand in front of his face. 'No problem. Is only small scooter.' I'm not entirely sure what this means – does he mean I don't need a licence for a small scooter or is he saying I shouldn't bother getting one? I'm not sure whether he's asking me to break the law or telling me I don't need to worry about it. 'Local delivery. No problem,' he adds. I'm still none the wiser.

The problem is, I need the money. I don't have another option. Bar work is no good as I don't speak Slovak and it'll open me up to far too many people. The likelihood of being spotted eventually is far too high. Besides which, the money wouldn't be enough. I need to earn enough that I can up sticks and leave whenever I have to. A cash-in-hand parcel delivery job would be ideal.

Before I realise what I'm doing, I'm nodding.

'Yeah, alright then. Let's give it a go.'

Marek raises an index finger, pulls his mobile phone out of his pocket and dials a number. After a few seconds, I hear the indecipherable voice of a man at the other end of the phone. Marek starts speaking in Slovak. As he does so, he jots something down on a small notepad that he's grabbed from behind the bar. The conversation over, he hangs up the phone, puts it back in his pocket and smiles at me.

'Okay, your first job.'

'That was quick,' I say.

'Is always work for you,' Marek replies. 'Andrej is busy man. Okay, so here is where you collect, yes?' he says, jabbing his finger at an address on the notepad. It means absolutely nothing to me, but I nod and make murmurs of agreement. 'And here is where you take to. Is not far.'

'Right. And where do I pick up the scooter from?' I ask.

'He bring here. Five minutes.' He says this as if it's the most normal thing in the world. Maybe that's how things are done here. I don't know.

Marek pours me another orange juice, and we sit in silence until there's a knock at the double fire doors at the back of the pub. Marek walks casually over to them, pushes the bar and opens the right-hand door. He turns and waves me over.

The man at the door is huge. Got to be well over six and a half feet tall. I chuckle as I imagine him riding the moped over here, all hunched over like a circus clown on one of those tiny motorbikes. He hands a helmet to me, his eyes never leaving mine as he does so. There's a white scar running from his forehead, right down across his eye and onto his cheek. It doesn't look recent, but it looks like it's done some damage. If I had to describe his appearance in two stereotypical words, it'd be 'Eastern European'.

I take the helmet and he extends his other hand to give me a set of keys. He turns and speaks to Marek in Slovak. I don't understand a word of it. Marek replies and slaps the man on the back in a friendly, jovial way. The man nods at me and leaves.

'Seems like a nice bloke,' I say, hoping Marek won't understand the subtle English sarcasm.

'He say the gas is full. Every day, return the scooter here in passage behind bar. He will collect.'

'Every day?' I ask, not sure what this means. Does this mean I'll be delivering parcels all day every day? Or that the scooter can't be parked out here overnight?

'Every day,' Marek replies. I decide not to question it.

Marek lifts the seat of the scooter up to reveal a storage compartment no bigger than my rucksack. Inside is a map of Bratislava. He takes a few moments to mark out where we are, and where I need to go. It seems pretty simple to me. At the end of the passageway I need to turn left, and then right onto the main road. The street I want is about a mile down on the left-hand side.

'What do I say when I get there?' I ask.

'Say? Say nothing. They are expecting you,' he replies.

'Right. Fair enough. And what about clothing? I can't just ride this thing in jeans and a T-shirt.'

He laughs. That deep, guttural belly laugh again. 'You have helmet! This is fine. Scooter go maybe forty, forty-five kilometres per hour. You will hurt more if you fall when you walk!' He seems to find his joke far more hilarious than I do. I've not ridden anything with two wheels since I was about eighteen years old. I look more closely at the scooter, trying to work out where the accelerator and brake are, and how to indicate. I hear a door closing behind me, and I turn to find out Marek's closed the fire door and gone back into the bar.

Cautiously, I climb onto the scooter, put the key into the ignition and turn it. The engine purrs and comes to life.

It feels good.

46

When they say you never forget how to ride a bike, it seems that extends to mopeds. It helps that the roads aren't too busy and the scooter's really easy to handle. I feel a little unsafe with only a T-shirt and jeans – despite the helmet – but it's far too hot for full leathers, and I'd feel a bit of a tit wearing them on a moped that can barely hit thirty miles an hour.

The address I was given appears to be a cafe. There's no number on the building, but counting down from a couple of doors up it seems to be the right place. I pull over to the side of the road, cut the engine and take off my helmet. I have a quick look at the map to see where I've got to go from here and I memorise the route.

Inside the cafe, it seems to be a popular place for locals to grab a bite to eat. There's what I can only assume is a Slovakian soap opera on the TV, the sound louder than you'd expect. I'm not sure whether it's so loud to accommodate the fact that the general clientele in here are probably hard of hearing, or whether it's to ward off anyone who isn't a local. It could be either; I certainly don't feel particularly comfortable in here.

There's a man of about forty stood behind the counter, preparing a cup of coffee. He turns to look at me as I approach him.

'Courier?' I say, holding up my helmet as if that will explain everything in international sign language. He nods and curls his finger to beckon me to follow him.

He takes me through a door into a back room, which looks to be some sort of storage area for food. There are cardboard boxes everywhere. The man moves one box aside and fishes a large padded envelope from behind it. He hands it to me. It weighs a good couple of kilos and has nothing written on the front of it at all. It's a good job I checked the delivery location before I left. 'For Mario,' he says, just standing there.

I take that as my cue to leave, and go to move towards the door back into the cafe before I feel a hand on my shoulder, stopping me. I turn to face him and he gestures with his head to the fire door behind him. 'This door,' he says.

I nod and do as he says.

The door takes me out into an alleyway that runs down the side of the cafe. I look around, but the only people about are simply going about their daily business. I head back towards the street, open the under-seat storage compartment on the moped and tuck the padded envelope inside, before putting on my helmet and pulling away as quickly as I can. I'm not sure what that was all about, but I know I didn't particularly like it.

I'm worried now about what's in the padded envelope. It weighs a fair bit, but it could be anything. Drugs? A gun? Worse? I'm not sure what could possibly be worse than either of those, but I don't want to think about it, either. I tell myself I'll drop it off at its destination, go back to the bar, thank Marek very much for thinking of me and politely decline any future work.

The journey to the delivery point seems to take an age. I'm desperately willing the moped to go above jogging pace, but it's not having any of it. I just want to get it done and over with, before I get any deeper into whatever the fuck this is all about. I'm in enough shit as it is without getting involved in drug dealing or gun running.

When I finally arrive at my destination, it looks as if it's a barber's shop. Either these businesses are just fronts for whatever's in these packages, or there's a very hungry Slovakian barber ordering lots of secret bacon sandwiches from the local cafe. I know what my money's on.

Every part of me – every fibre of my being – wants to flee. I want to run, get as far away from here as possible. If I don't deliver the package, I can't be held liable. I could just leave the moped here with the keys in, and hope someone takes it. And then what? Go back to Marek and tell him I lost it? No. I have no choice but to go through with this now.

I walk up to the door of the barber's shop and am pleased to see that there are two customers sat in chairs.

That doesn't mean the shop's not a front, but it does mean I feel a little safer with members of the public around.

One of the barbers seems to know exactly what I'm there for, and he beckons me over to a desk at the back of the shop. He takes the parcel from me and places it inside a drawer, before patting me on the back and indicating that I should go. As if it's the most normal thing in the world. To them, perhaps it is, but this world is completely alien to me.

I leave the shop – by the front door this time – and don't even stop to look over my shoulder. Then I'm back on the moped and heading back for Marek's bar as fast as I can, which isn't very fast at all.

47

When I get back to the bar, I park the moped in the alleyway and go inside to find Marek. He's sat at the bar, as he usually is, waiting for some customers who probably don't exist.

'Ah, Bradley! How was first job?' he says, giving me that big beaming smile once again.

'Well, I did it,' I say, taking off my helmet and putting it down on the bar. 'But I want to know what this is all about. Picking up a parcel from a cafe and delivering it to a barber's shop?'

Marek waves a hand at me. 'Is just business. Do not worry.'

'I do worry, though,' I say. 'Because if this is to do with drugs or weapons, I'm not interested, alright? Thank you very much for thinking of me and giving me the opportunity, but I really don't want to get involved.' The last thing I want to do is get mixed up in any sort of criminal activity. I'm here to try and clear my name, not muddy it.

Marek looks down at the floor and walks over to me, stopping when he gets to me and putting his hands on my shoulders. 'Bradley, this is good work. Good money.' He dips his hand into his back pocket and pulls out a wad of cash – far more than thirty euros. 'This is for you. Payment.'

'What for?' I ask, knowing exactly what it's for.

'For hard work and loyalty.'

'Loyalty?' I say, trying not to break out into a laugh. 'We only met this morning. I've done one delivery.'

'One very valuable delivery,' he replies, staring into my eyes. 'One big test.'

I'm at a loss for what to say. 'A test? Sorry, I really don't know what this is all about. I think it's probably just best if I go, alright?'

Marek says nothing. I head upstairs, taking the stairs two at a time, and shove everything into my rucksack. I just want to get out of here as quickly as possible.

When I'm done, I head back down the stairs and find Marek stood at the bar with another man who I've not seen before.

'Ah, Bradley. This is my brother, Andrej.'

I certainly wasn't expecting that. I'd always been under the assumption that I'd be dealing directly with Marek, and now this mythical business don of Bratislava is standing right in front of me. Andrej cocks his head slightly to one side and smiles at me. I can only presume he can see the look of shock that I can feel on my face.

'Andrej is telling me how happy he is at your hard work,' Marek says.

'Very happy,' Andrej adds, his voice much deeper and more resonant than Marek's.

'I'm glad,' I say, trying to be as pleasant as possible but still making it perfectly clear that I want nothing to do with this. 'But I'm afraid I can't do any more deliveries. I'm only in the area for a little while. Thank you, but I have to go. Here's the money for the room,' I say, handing the wad of notes back to Marek, who looks at Andrej and says nothing.

'Go?' Andrej says. 'But you have only just arrived. You have a job. We have given you work, money and generosity.'

'Yeah, and I really appreciate it, but I need to go. You can have the money back.'

'Back? No. There is no going back, Daniel.' I freeze. Andrej's eyes suddenly look very different. I can't think of a word to say, but fortunately I don't need to, because Andrej speaks again. 'You left your bag in your room. Your passport was inside.'

I can feel my jaw hanging open, my heart hammering in my chest.

'You went in my room? In my bag?'

'It is important that we know who we work with,' Andrej says, as if this is the most normal situation in the world. 'We cannot work with liars and frauds.'

Oh, well at least you've got some form of morality to your business is what I want to say, but I end up saying: 'In that case, you don't have to. I'm leaving.'

I keep my eyes fixed to the ground and walk towards

the door, stopping dead when I hear Andrej's voice behind me.

'The police in England are offering a very big reward for finding you.'

How the fuck have they got into my room, got my passport, identified me and found out about that in the space of half an hour? And why the fuck did I leave my passport there in the first place? I should've burned it along with the old rucksack. Scrap that – I should have left it in France somewhere. Not long after we'd left Claude's place, that passport was completely worthless. I'd have been better off being caught without a passport at all than with that one. If I'd just ditched it earlier, I wouldn't be in this situation now.

'Drug dealing *and* blackmail?' I say, without turning round.

'At least we have not murdered you,' Andrej replies. I'm not sure whether that's a threat aimed at my life or a reference to him being able to take the moral high ground over the Lisa situation.

I turn and address Marek. 'What's this all about, Marek? Why are you doing this to me?'

Marek says nothing.

'We are very generous to you,' Andrej says. 'You have a room. A safe place. Also, you have a job. And with very good money.' Andrej's English is far better than Marek's, and he has that intimidating air of someone far more educated and refined.

'I did not kill Lisa,' I say, looking Andrej in the eye in the hope that he'll be able to see the truth. 'Someone has set me up and made it look like it was me.' I choose not to mention Jess. 'I'm not a bad person, alright? I don't break the law. I'm not a murderer, and I'm certainly not a drug runner.'

'So why are you here?' Andrej asks. 'Why did you run from England and come to Slovakia?'

I look away and shake my head. 'I don't know.' The truth is far too complicated to go into right now. I wouldn't even know where to start. 'It's a long story.'

'Who killed your wife?' Andrej asks.

'I don't know. I really don't. I wish I did.' I look him in the eye again as I speak. He says nothing for a good twenty seconds but continues to look at me. I hold eye contact.

When he eventually speaks, they're not the words I was expecting to hear.

'We can help you.'

48

My legs ache, the lactic acid in my muscles making them feel like they're on fire.

I had to get out of there. I had no other option. The whole room suddenly felt stuffy and claustrophobic, like it was closing in on me. I barely even heard the last few words they said, as it all became far too much for me.

Now I'm walking randomly but purposefully around the streets of Bratislava. I don't know where I'm going and I don't know why. All I know is that I need to get some air, get some space, get some distance. I've barely been here a few hours and already Andrej and Marek have discovered who I am. What hope do I have against the combined police forces of Europe? Not much, by my reckoning.

Even though I disappeared pretty sharpish, I know exactly what's going to happen from here. And I know Andrej and Marek do, too, which is why they didn't try to stop me leaving. Those words. *We can help you.* All I want, all I need and desperately desire, is for someone to help me. To have someone on my side, someone who can find out who's doing this and why, whilst keeping the police well away from me. I don't even trust the British police after my experience of their corruption back at Pendleton House, so I've got very low hopes for the Slovakian police force.

The only problem is, by working for Andrej and Marek I'm undoubtedly far more likely to open myself up to the police. I still don't know what is in these deliveries – and I don't want to know – but I'm fairly sure it's not icing sugar. At the same time, though, I get the sense that these sorts of people are above the law, smarter than the police, able to actually help me. These aren't small-time petty criminals. You can tell when somebody really means business.

I'm far from being a goody two shoes, but I've got to be honest and admit that these people scare me. Sure, I've done bad things in my life. I've broken laws; I've upset people. But that's a whole different level from the sorts of things I'm sure Andrej and Marek do. But then again, what compares to being suspected of two murders and hunted down across Europe? I fail to see how whatever they're asking me to deliver can put me in much more shit than I'm already in at the moment.

Besides which, I don't know who else I can trust right now. There is no-one. When you're in a foreign country and you can't even go to the police, what options do you have? Who else can you trust? I really shouldn't be able to trust Andrej and Marek, either, but what reason do I have not to? After all, it was me who chose to come to Bratislava, me who chose to walk in that direction and me who chose to go into that bar. Andrej and Marek might not exactly be Mother Teresa and Princess Di, but I can also be pretty certain that they're not against me in this.

To people like them, business is business. It's purely a trading relationship of two very different sets of needs. I can help them, and they can help me. I'll help them out by doing their deliveries and they'll help me out by finding out who killed Lisa and Jess and who's trying to frame me. I don't know how they're going to do it, and to be honest I really don't care. I just want the truth. Everything else is irrelevant right now.

It seems like forever since I found Lisa's body in the hotel in Herne Bay. It feels almost like another lifetime. In such a short space of time, I've gone from being at work and having fun to walking through the streets of Slovakia trying to decide whether to become a drug runner for an Eastern European gang or try to get off two murder charges on my own. The dark humour isn't lost on me at all. The whole situation seems utterly ridiculous, as if I'm going to wake up and realise it was all a dream. A nightmare. But, deep down, I know that's not going to happen. I know that there's no getting away.

There's only so far one man can run. The world simply isn't big enough to keep running. I can't keep looking over my shoulder for the rest of my life, never knowing who I can trust and who I can't. I keep catching my reflection in shop windows and seeing how haggard and tired I look. I've aged years in a matter of days. What will I look like in a week's time? A month's time? Will I still be alive? All I know in this moment is that I can't do this alone. I need help.

I suddenly start to feel incredibly nauseous, and I dart off the street and into an alleyway, bracing myself between two huge bins as I retch and vomit onto the dirt-covered asphalt. The smell from the bins makes the feeling worse, but its effect on me is also a huge relief. It feels almost like I'm purging the bad feelings from within, spilling them out into the alleyway and ridding myself of the negativity.

And in this moment, my mindset changes. I realise I'm long past the point of no return and that I have no other option. I have the slightest possibility of an escape route – something I thought I'd had ever since I left Herne Bay, but which I now realise was always a false illusion. This is no longer about feeling sorry for myself. From now on, this is about the fight.

I stand up straight, wipe my mouth with the back of my hand and head back in the direction of Marek's bar.

49

The journey to the hospital was a blur. Driving wasn't an option – he'd had too much to drink the evening before. The taxi to the East Surrey Hospital was going to cost an arm and a leg, but that didn't matter. Money was just money. What concerned Dan right now was that he needed to get to Lisa's side.

Oddly, the news of her miscarriage wasn't the biggest shock to him: it was the fact that she'd been pregnant at all. They hadn't even been trying and the news that not only had they managed to create a child but it had then been taken away from them before they even knew about it was what hurt the most. He'd never get to enjoy any of the high points – taking the test, finding out the news, seeing the doctor, having the scans. All of that was lost before they even knew they'd had it.

Lisa's cycle had been less than regular over the years –

something which had been accentuated by the stress of her job – so she never had any real reason to suspect she might be pregnant. It wasn't something they'd ever even thought about, and the discussion about children had never happened. Dan always got the impression that Lisa wasn't interested, was too career driven, and if he was pushed to give an opinion either way, he'd probably have said he wasn't particularly keen on the idea of kids anyway. There always seemed to be an unspoken agreement that kids just weren't on the cards.

But the moment he took that phone call, that all changed.

Now the news hit him like a bullet, shattering all the hopes and dreams he never realised he'd had. And where had he been when Lisa was going through all this? Yet again he'd fucked up majorly without even realising he was doing it at the time.

The taxi driver was doing his best to get to the hospital quickly, which was a little easier than normal considering the time of night and the state he could see Dan was in. The whole journey seemed to take an age, blue motorway signs whizzing past in a blur, headlights searing through a film of tears as his whole mind turned numb. Eventually, they arrived, Dan thrusting his wallet at the taxi driver, who took out the money for the fare and returned the wallet to Dan, placing a friendly hand on his shoulder as he did so.

When he got into the hospital, Dan headed straight for reception, mumbling Lisa's name at the girl behind the desk when he got there. The girl tapped a few buttons on her computer, then told him that he needed the third floor. On getting there, he didn't need to ask again; the nurse on duty seemed to know who he was immediately, and took him to one side. Her words were a blur.

'As you can imagine,' she said, 'this has been quite traumatic for your wife. She's in quite a bit of shock.'

'Yeah, me too,' Dan replied.

'At the moment we're trying to stick to the cold, hard facts. That's probably the best way to come to terms with what's happened.'

'But I don't understand,' Dan said. 'We didn't even . . . I didn't even know she was pregnant.'

'Neither did she, by all accounts. It was quite a shock for her. We do have our bereavement counselling service to offer to you, but I think at this stage it would be good to be with Lisa and to comfort her.'

The word hit him like a ton of bricks. Bereavement. That's exactly what it was. A death. The death of his first, and possibly only, child. A birth and a death at once. A death without a birth. The death of a child he didn't know he had. A child he didn't have. Whichever way he looked at it, it was one huge mindfuck.

He followed the nurse through the corridor to the room at the end. As she pushed open the door gently, he could see Lisa lying in the bed, propped up with pillows under her back, her head leaning away from the doorway, looking out of the window into the blackness beyond.

'Lisa,' Dan said. The nurse stood respectfully at the door, not wanting to intrude. 'Lisa, it's me.'

Dan walked slowly over to the bed, hearing the door click closed behind him as the nurse made her way back down the corridor. Lisa kept looking out of the window, not even seeming to acknowledge his presence.

He sat down on the orange plastic chair next to the bed. It reminded him of the chairs they used to have in the class-rooms at school. He placed a hand on top of hers and squeezed.

Slowly, Lisa turned her head to face him. The look on her face was one he'd never seen before. It was a look of pure emptiness. Her eyes said everything and nothing at the same time.

She spoke just one word. 'Why?'

It was a question Dan had asked himself a thousand times since he received the phone call, but to which he still didn't have an answer. He knew he would never have an answer.

'I'm so sorry,' he said, choking back the tears. 'I should have been there.'

'You were working,' Lisa whispered, as if it were a world-known fact.

'I know.' How could he tell her that while his wife was having a miscarriage, while she was losing the baby she didn't even know she was carrying, he was in bed with a redhead he'd met at the wrap party earlier that evening? He doubted if that was something he'd ever be able to tell her, ever be able to come to terms with himself. In that instant, he *knew simultaneously that not only would he never forgive himself, but that his almost destructive hatred for himself meant he couldn't guarantee he'd never do it again, either. As far as he was concerned, this reinforced something he already knew: he was a serial fucker-upper.*

50

I really don't want to know too much. They say knowledge is power, but I've got a funny feeling that the less I know about Andrej and Marek, the safer I'm going to be.

Fortunately for me, they seem to believe my story. I told them everything about what happened in the hotel in Herne Bay. I told them about finding Lisa's body in the bathtub, about leaving with Jess and going to France and Switzerland. I told them about Claude and his farmhouse. I couldn't tell them anything much more than that, though. I never knew Claude's surname and I couldn't locate the farmhouse or the Swiss campsite right now if my life depended on it. Not from a map, anyway. The whole of Europe between East Grinstead and Bratislava is just one huge blur in my mind.

What shocks and surprises me is how casually they accept what I'm telling them. I think they can see that I'm telling them the truth, but surely any sane person in their right mind would at least raise their eyebrows if I told them what I'd been through over the past few days. Not Andrej and Marek, though. To me, that says far more about them and their lives than anything else.

They say they can help me. I don't know how, but I reckon they will. All I know is that they are potentially dangerous people. People who are wrapped up in what I can only presume is some sort of drug-dealing or smuggling operation. After I told them my story, Andrej asked me if there was anything I wanted to know about him. I shook my head and said there wasn't. Of course there was. There were a hundred and one things I wanted to ask him, but I daren't. Sometimes I think you're better off not knowing.

The fact of the matter is that, whoever these people are, they've probably got a far better chance of finding out who did this than I have. My only other two options are to go to the police and explain everything, which isn't an option as I have absolutely no confidence in the police, or try to take on the investigation myself, which is completely laughable considering my fugitive state.

They wanted to know absolutely everything about me. Things I've never told anyone. Even when I told Jess my life story I left some fairly important details out. I'm not sure why. A big part of me didn't want to rake over old ground, but I was also torn between my certainty that no-one from that far back would come back to haunt me, and that if they did I didn't want to know about it. I didn't want to face the facts and deal with what was going on. Story of my life.

I never even told Lisa absolutely everything about my childhood. A lot of stuff at the boys' home even I've probably forgotten or blocked out, but most of it was completely irrelevant. She didn't need to know about Mr Duggan, for example. No-one needed to know about that piece of shit. But I knew I had to tell Andrej and Marek everything. Every last detail. As great as Lisa was, she wouldn't have been able to do anything to help me. Jess could've, but I left it too late. Now these two Slovakian strangers are my only hope.

I try to forget about the whole blackmail thing, because I know they're right. They still haven't told me much about themselves and their set-up, but from the questions they're asking and the detail they want to know, I can only assume their influence stretches much further than Bratislava. For all I know, they could be part of some bigger network. I'm not sure whether that would be a good thing or not. It would certainly give me a much better chance of finding out what happened and who's after me, but it also scares me to think that I could potentially be involved with people like this.

This doesn't happen to normal, ordinary people. None of this does. But my life has never been normal and ordinary, and it definitely hasn't since I came back up to my hotel room in Herne Bay. Everything changed from that point on, and I know it won't ever go back to normal.

It makes me wonder what the point is. The easiest option – some might say the sensible option – would be to forget the whole thing, give up and end it. When I climbed up onto the roof of the hostel, burning the bag was only one of my intentions. As I stood on the edge of the building and looked out across Bratislava, I was acutely aware that I could take one step – just one step – and all of this would be over. But I didn't.

I've always been a fighter. I've never felt it right to give up in the face of injustice. I'd rather die fighting than give up. It's one of the reasons I reacted the way I did when I found out about Mr Duggan's death. That was sheer injustice at its highest level – a man who got to live his life the way he wanted without retribution, save for one night many years ago. And when it's an injustice I can't do anything about – like Mr Duggan getting off scot-free – it hurts a thousand times more.

Andrej goes off to make a few phone calls, and Marek offers me a drink. I tell him I'll have whisky. I figure they can at least let me have the rest of the day off from driving after pouring out my life history in front of them. A few minutes later, Andrej comes back.

'We have a job for you,' he says. I lift up my whisky glass in response, as if to show him I'm not going to be able to do anything right now. 'Tomorrow morning,' he replies.

51

It's all hazy at first. I'm flicking channels on the TV, and there's a couple I can't get. Channels 4 and 5, yet again. I blink, and the TV remote becomes my mobile phone. I've just finished sending a message, so I lock the screen and put the phone on my bedside table. It's dark, but I can still see perfectly. I can see everything. All of my senses are alive.

I can hear the footsteps treading softly on the carpet in the corridor outside, gradually getting louder until the adrenaline coursing through me turns the sound into a deafening roar which ends with a second's peaceful silence before the gentle knock on the door. I casually walk over to the door and open it, beckoning her inside. Her hair flows behind her as she walks, her whole appearance almost ethereal, a light, bright glow around her, shining like an aura.

'You said you wanted to see me?' she says, her pale skin glistening white, almost translucent. She's even more beautiful than I remember, and I have a distinct awareness of *remembering her far too fondly, almost like looking deep into the past with rose-tinted glasses.*

'Yes, come through,' I reply, beckoning her through the small side door to my left. The light is glowing inside, the whole room basking in the whitest white. 'Lie down,' I say. She smiles at me and steps over the side of the bath, swinging her other leg in behind her, before sitting down and resting her head back. It makes a small, gentle sound as her head makes contact with the cold, hard surface of the bath. I can see her muscles visibly relaxing in front of me. She looks happy, content.

'I understand,' she says, looking at me, her eyes conveying a lifetime of emotion. 'I understand.'

In that moment, I know things are changing. It's a moment of sheer beauty, of complete mutual human recognition. We both know, we both understand, and not a word needs to be said. It's serene. It's beautiful. It's what philosophers refer to as 'the numinous'. If I could savour the moment forever, I would – we both would – but we know it's not to be. We know what comes next.

The theme tune to Countdown is playing from the TV back inside the bedroom. I lean across the edge of the bath and put my hands around her throat, squeezing harder as she begins to gurgle. The music gets louder, my hands getting tighter around her throat. The blood tries to escape from her head, but it can't. She goes from pale white to pink, through red and on to deep purple, her lips turning blue. The Countdown music rolls into the final five-second sting as she begins to shake violently, her central nervous system putting up one last, final struggle for life as all signs of existence start to fade from her eyes. The final bong sounds from the TV at the same time as her body stops jerking, a beautiful, peaceful silence filling the room.

I rest her back against the porcelain, gently, taking care not to hurt her. I stand up, pull the shower curtain across and wash my hands before drying them on the towel. I glance into the mirror and check that my shirt is sitting comfortably and then I leave the room, my stomach starting to growl and rumble.

52

The next morning, my head is pounding. I don't recall drinking all that much, but it feels like I've got the hangover from hell. Logically, I know it's likely to be a combination of a bit of alcohol plus a fair amount of tiredness and a smattering of stress. I'm not quite sure what else I expected at the moment, but I don't feel in any state to go doing deliveries. Andrej and Marek have already been making phone calls, though, mostly in Slovak but with familiar words being interspersed through the conversations. *Daniel Cooper. Lisa Cooper. Jessica Walsh. Herne Bay. Claude. France. Innsbruck.*

They've both been very reassuring. Then again, they would be, wouldn't they? They want me to be the fall guy for their dodgy dealings. I tell myself not to take it personally, that they're my only hope. For them, this is pure business, I suppose. A large part of me is also hoping they're the sort of people who deal with so many crooks and villains that they'll be able to tell just by looking at me that I'm an honest sort of guy. Well, about as honest as I can be, anyway.

I get up, get dressed and make my way downstairs to the bar. When I get there, Marek is mopping the floor. The whole place smells of disinfectant with a faint undercurrent of stale lager. He looks at me, fires off a smile and goes back to mopping.

'Morning,' I say, trying to initiate some conversation.

'Good morning,' he says eventually, not looking up from the floor, his mop gliding across it with a light *swish-swoosh* in between dips into the bucket.

'Any news?'

Marek shakes his head almost immediately. 'No news. When we have news, we will tell.' I say nothing. 'Here,' he says, jiggling a small wicker basket on the bar. 'Eat.'

I look into the basket. It appears to be full of what looks like black bread or some sort of cake.

'What is it?' I ask.

'Breakfast,' Marek replies, beaming.

Not wanting to offend anyone, and starting to feel pretty hungry, I take a slice of the bread and start to eat. It's sweet, almost like cake, and very malty. It's not what I'd tend to associate with breakfast, but right now I'll eat anything. I somehow doubt there's going to be a local greasy spoon serving a full English fry-up.

'Did Andrej tell you any more about the job he wants me to do today?' I ask.

Marek says nothing in response, instead spending a few

more seconds mopping right up into the corner of the bar before he straightens up, plops the mop back in the bucket, dries his hands on his shirt and comes over to me.

'Bradley, you must not worry,' he says, placing his hands on my shoulders. His use of my pseudonym has the intended effect: it shows me that he's on my side, willing to play the game. 'The people you will see, our customers, they will not be trouble. My brother, Andrej, he is very well known here in Bratislava. Nobody will fuck with you.' Marek's usage of English swear words, oddly, makes me feel far more relaxed.

'I know. I trust you, Marek. I trust you both. But at the same time, whoever's trying to ruin my life has already killed my wife and chased me halfway across Europe to try to get to me. Saying "Don't worry" doesn't quite cut it.' I still haven't told him about what happened to Jess at the campsite. It doesn't seem important, somehow. She's dead, caught up in the crossfire. Part of me doesn't want Marek and Andrej to think that they're going to be next – that I'm some sort of jinx or liability.

At this stage, I don't know what's going to happen. I don't know how long I'm going to be here, what Marek and Andrej are doing or whether it'll work. Besides which, everyone who I thought would be able to help me is either dead or after me.

The worst thing is not knowing who's responsible. Knowing that the person could be around the next corner, or hiding in plain sight. I've got to admit, a part of me is even starting to doubt myself. Last night's dream seems to have blurred the lines between imagination and reality. Deep down, I know it's just my brain playing tricks on me, the paranoia seeping through. But that still doesn't change the fact that I *saw* it in my own mind's eye. I saw me killing Lisa. I know it can't be true, but I can't shake the horrible realisation that I don't actually remember going down to the restaurant that afternoon. I remember being in my room, and I remember being in the restaurant. Everything that happened afterwards is incredibly vivid, but before that it's all a bit of a blur. It doesn't explain how the hell Lisa would've got to the hotel – or how I knew she was coming – but it's still enough to give me cause for concern.

And then there's Jess. I remember being in the caravan with her, and I remember walking into town. The bit in the middle, though, is hazy. I don't remember anything between deciding to go into town, and actually going into town. I've got a lot of blank spots, but that's easily explained by tiredness and stress, I tell myself. I mean, seriously, look at what I've been through over the past few days. It's enough to give anyone some memory blanks. I'm amazed I'm still standing. I tell myself that I can't let my brain do this; I can't convince myself that I'm responsible for what's happened. If I do that, there's no going back. I need to stand tall and face the situation. Only then will I discover the truth.

Marek calls my name again. 'Bradley?' I realise I must have spaced out for a bit.

'Yeah, sorry, Marek. Miles away. So. Tell me about this job.'

53

My head still feels fuzzy as I start up the moped, the vibrations from the engine seeming to rattle my skull as I pull away from the back door of the bar. I've got a drop-off and a collection this time. I have one parcel to collect from a house on the outskirts of the city, which needs taking to a corner shop. From there, I have to collect another parcel and take it back to the house. There's a big pay packet for this one. I don't know how much, but I get the feeling that Marek and Andrej will see me good.

The journey to the house takes me alongside the Danube, and then up a steep hill which brings the speed of the moped down to a shade over 10mph at full throttle. I've half a feeling it'd be quicker to get off and push. When I finally get to the house, the first thing that strikes me is how peaceful it is. It's barely five minutes from the city centre, yet it seems much further. None of the noise of the city seems to travel up the hill.

The house is set back slightly from the road, raised a little, behind a large iron gate. I get off the moped and take off my helmet. There's an intercom system next to the gate, which I presume I'm going to have to use. I hope whoever's at the other end is expecting me and speaks English.

As I walk over and raise my arm to press the button, I hear a clunk and a click, and the gate whirrs as it begins to slide across, opening just enough to let me slip through before it closes behind me. I amble slowly up to the front door, the tall house looming over me.

When I get to the door, I look around for a doorbell, buzzer or knocker, but there's nothing. Just as I'm about to knock on the door with my fist, I notice a small brown parcel tucked behind a statue of an angel or cherub of some sort. It reminds me of the statue in the middle of Piccadilly Circus.

I bend down and pick up the package. It's been wrapped neatly in parcel paper and tied with string, yet it has no address or details on it. In the absence of any other information, and judging by the secretive nature of Marek and Andrej's deals so far, I can only assume this is what I'm meant to be collecting. I step back from the front door and make sure I'm in view of the house, so they can see it's this parcel I'm taking. That way, they'll be able to stop me if I've got the wrong one.

A few steps before I get back to the gate, it slides open – again, just enough to let me through – before closing behind me. I raise a hand in thanks to whoever's watching and operating the gate, before putting the parcel into the compartment under my seat and firing up the moped once again.

I take a quick look at the map that's been folded up in my pocket, double-checking to make sure I know where I'm going. Like most routes around this city, it seems easy enough. As with most cities, Bratislava is built around a few main streets, with small side roads linking them. As long as you know the general direction you're going in, you're pretty well covered.

From here, I'm heading north-east. The roads around this area seem to be a bit windy, but I don't envisage that'll be a problem. I came in from the south, by the river, which was more straightforward, so this is going to take a little more concentration. I pull away from the house, stuttering uphill at a ridiculously slow pace, before I reach the crest and start to accelerate downhill and around the bend, following the meandering road before I turn off in the direction I need to go in.

It's about ten minutes later that I realise I'm lost. The constant bends in the road have confused me as to which direction I'm pointing in. I was fairly sure I knew where I was, but if that was the case I should've met the main road a few minutes back. Right now, though, I'm on the side of a hill, and I can't even *see* the main road.

I try to figure out which way is north. Without sight of the river or any recognisable landmarks, that's nigh on impossible. The sun's starting to peer around the edge of a cloud to my right. If I knew what time of day it was, I could work out which way I was heading by the position of the sun. It's at times like this when I wish I had a watch. Mine, a Christmas present from Lisa, is still back at the hotel in Herne Bay, if not already bagged up and stored in an evidence cupboard somewhere. Since then, I've not really needed a watch. I've either been in a car with a clock, on a train with a clock, or floating around Europe without needing to give a damn what time it was. The thought tickles me somewhat.

I have a rough guess that it's somewhere around ten in the morning. If this was England, at this time of year, the sun should be somewhere towards the south-east. That means I'm currently heading north-west, rather than north-east. The only problem is, this isn't England and I'm not entirely sure the sun's position would be the same. I'm quite a long way east. It's all I've got to work with, though, so I head off again, trying to keep the sun on my right-hand side.

It's over half an hour before I finally manage to get my bearings and start heading down the main road. What I'm most amazed at is that this little moped still doesn't seem to need any fuel. You'd think that it'd be thirsty after struggling up those hills, but the needle's only dropped slightly below the full mark. One of the benefits of having such a small engine and no weight to carry.

Once I'm back on the main road, I'm happier. I'm a lot further up than I need to be, but that's fine – at least I have an idea of where I am. The traffic has started to build a little, but I'm making good progress – even if I am horrendously late.

When I finally get near the corner shop, I start to slow a

little, looking at the numbers on the front of the buildings. I see the shop in the distance and I head for it. As I get closer, I can see a man standing outside the front of the shop, smoking a cigarette. He's looking right at me.

I pull over to the side of the road, my eyes still fixed on him and his on me as I try to read his expression. I can imagine these are the sorts of people who don't like being fucked about, and me being late with the delivery clearly hasn't made him happy.

As I'm about to turn off the ignition and put on my best apologising face, I hear sirens. I stop for a moment, breaking eye contact with the man and cocking my head to try and gauge the direction they're coming from. I can't be certain, but what I can tell is that they're getting closer. And quickly.

I take a look back at the man. He's heard them, too.

54

My heart's thudding in my chest as I will the little moped to go faster. I speed off down the main road in the direction I was already facing, then swing right into a side road. The moped's never felt slower than it does now.

I can't hear the sirens any more, but that's only because of the noise of the moped at full throttle and the pulsing of the blood in my ears. When I get to the end of the side road, I meet another main road. I don't even stop to look, just bolt straight out across two lanes of traffic whilst veering to my left, car horns honking at me as I narrowly miss the front bonnet of a taxi.

I've got no time to stop and apologise, and I keep the throttle on maximum power as I lean forward, trying to will the machine to eke just an extra mile an hour out of its little engine. I make up another three hundred yards or so before I turn right again, onto another side street. At the end of this street I turn left again, onto another road.

As I round the corner, my tyres screeching as I try to get onto the right side of the road without letting go of the throttle, I see the face of a small boy looking at me as he and his mother step out to use the zebra crossing. I do all I can think to do, which is to shout 'MOVE!' just at the same moment the mother yanks her son back with one hand, her existing momentum leaving her other arm – laden with shopping bags – flying forward. I clip the bags and my scooter gives a worrying wobble, but my own momentum keeps me going in a more or less straight line. I glance into my wing mirror and see the debris strewn around the road, the woman's groceries bouncing and scattering across the tarmac.

The traffic is starting to thin a little, so I nip left across the light oncoming traffic and into an alleyway beside a hairdresser's salon. I slow, swerving around a couple of huge bins, before getting to the loading bay behind a few shops. I stop the moped, turn off the ignition, take off my helmet and sit for a moment. The sound of the sirens is gone.

I breathe a small sigh of relief, but I know I can't go anywhere just yet. I've attracted enough attention with my dreadful escape attempt just now, and I don't particularly want to be driving the moped around for a little bit. Not until I've had a walkabout to make sure the coast is clear. I know the police probably weren't after me, and that their presence probably had nothing to do with the corner shop, but I really didn't want to be anywhere near a police car. And, let's face it, I panicked.

I put my helmet down beside the moped and glance back at it. It seems stupid leaving the parcel here, in the compartment under the seat, but I definitely can't risk walking around the streets of Bratislava with it under my arm. I follow another alleyway to walk back in the direction of the corner shop, trying to look as casual as I can. Surprisingly, it's almost as if nothing ever happened. I'm now one street across from the woman who's no doubt picking up her groceries off the asphalt, and I've certainly got no intention of heading back in that particular direction again.

I cross the road, being careful to look this time, as I reckon I've probably exhausted my supply of good luck in that respect, and turn left, passing people going about their everyday business, walking in and out of shops, talking on their mobile phones, laughing and joking. As I pass a coffee shop, I decide to pop in. Everything seems normal, but it probably wouldn't hurt me to lie low for a bit, let the fuss die down – if there is any fuss.

The woman serving behind the counter in the coffee shop gives me what I can only describe as a weird look. I'm starting to think that this is just how people in Slovakia look at everyone, and that I'm probably being paranoid. 'Americano,' I say, pointing to the list of coffees above her head, as if she's not going to know what I mean. She says nothing, and simply turns towards the huge silver coffee machine to start preparing my drink.

I take five euros out of my pocket and hand it to her when she comes back with the cup, pointing to the charity collection tub next to the till to indicate that she can put my change in there. I figure I can at least do one bit of good today. Again, she says nothing, and the expression on her face doesn't change.

It doesn't take me long at all to drink my coffee, the scalding hot liquid making the tip of my tongue numb and sore. I always drink too quickly when I'm nervous – it's why I always used to fuck up first dates by getting plastered inside an hour and making a complete tit of myself. Fortunately for me, this is just coffee, and the worst that I'm going to get is a burnt tongue and a major caffeine rush. There's a small packet of biscuits on the saucer, so I pocket them and decide to have them later.

Once I've finished, I leave the coffee shop and walk casually back in the direction of the moped. I figure that most of the people who were in the vicinity last time I rode through will now have dispersed in their various directions, so I decide now's the time to head back to the corner shop and attempt to make the delivery.

When I get back to the moped, I take the packet of biscuits out of my pocket and lift the seat to put them inside.

I freeze.

The parcel's gone.

55

If I thought I'd panicked earlier when I heard the sirens, that's nothing compared to what I'm feeling now. I look all around me, trying to see if there's anyone around – the person who stole the parcel, someone who might have seen who did or someone who might have seen me come back to the moped. There's nothing. Plenty going on outside the loading area and the network of alleyways that come off of it, but nobody in the immediate vicinity.

I lean over and rest my hands on my knees, trying to steady my breathing. I don't know for sure what was in that parcel, but I've got a pretty good idea it was either a huge amount of drugs or an even huger amount of money. And bearing in mind the people I'm dealing with here, losing either of those things is far from ideal.

I look inside the compartment again, sure I must have missed something. I run my hands around the edge, just in case there's another compartment I've forgotten about. I check inside my helmet and I search the ground in case I somehow managed to drop it, even though I know deep down I did nothing of the sort.

My first instinct is to run. It always is. Story of my life. I can't do that, though. Everything I have is back in my room at the bar – my clothes, most of my money, my passport. Plus I've got the added problem that Marek and Andrej know all about me. They know who I am, where I come from and almost everything that's led up to this point. Even if they didn't know who I was, even if they still believed I was an Australian called Bradley, running away from these people still isn't something I'd risk, so what hope do I have now?

I stand there, still, silent, for what must be a good few minutes. The whole world seems to have closed in around me. Since I opened that compartment I've not heard a sound, had no concept of passing time. It's as though everything has just stopped and nothing has meaning any more, as though my brain has completely accepted its fate.

I haven't accepted anything, though. I'm not someone who ever likes to give up. Again, it's injustice. I didn't ask for the parcel to be stolen, for the police to rock up when I was about to do the drop-off, to get involved with Marek and Andrej, to find that bar on that day. I didn't ask for any of it.

The next thing I know, I'm crouching down on the ground, my arms clamped over my knees, my face buried in my arms, the sobs and wails overtaking me. I can feel my whole body bouncing as my chest heaves between breaths, releasing all of the tension and the sense of impending doom from inside me.

I need to go back to Marek.

Riding the moped feels wrong now, and the bar isn't far away from here, so I decide to push it back. The side of the footplate bashes against the side of my shins almost continuously the whole way back, but I can barely feel it. My whole body feels overcome with a numb acceptance. I know what this stage means. It means I've given up. It means I'm no longer able to fight, no longer able to find ways to deal with all of the shit that's being thrown at me. This is the end of the road. This is where I lose.

When I get back to the bar, Marek can tell immediately that I'm not coming with good news. Whether he already knows what's happened or not I don't know, but I imagine he can tell just from looking at me. I'd hazard a guess that I don't look wonderfully happy right now. He doesn't say a word, though, and just stands, watching me, waiting for me to speak. We hold eye contact. He doesn't look angry, more a calm sort of inquisitive.

'I fucked up,' I say, looking at him. 'The delivery. I did the pick-up, then I went to do the drop-off but the police came, so I sped off and parked up in an alleyway until things calmed down. I couldn't risk going back out on the scooter again just yet, so I walked back towards the shop to make sure everything was clear, and when I got back to the scooter the package was gone. I don't know how – I was only gone a few seconds. I don't know what to do.'

Marek says nothing for a good twenty seconds or so, his face unchanging the whole time. 'You left the package?' he says, finally.

I drop my head towards the floor and nod. 'Yeah. I know, it was stupid, but what other choice did I have? I couldn't exactly go walking towards the police cars with a parcel of . . . whatever that is . . . under my arm, can I?' I say, looking back at him and pleading.

'A parcel of what?' Marek asks.

'Well, you know. Whatever's in it.'

'Why would you not want to walk near police with this parcel? What do you think is in it?'

I swallow. 'Drugs.'

Marek pauses for a moment, and then lets out an enormous belly laugh, which bounces off the walls and reverberates around the bar like a gunshot. 'My friend,' he says eventually, 'you have a lot to learn.' I have no idea what he's talking about.

'What shall I tell Andrej?' I say.

Marek's face darkens immediately. 'You say nothing. I will speak to Andrej. Do you understand?'

'Yeah, I understand.'

'You do not tell him.'

'No, I won't,' I say. 'I won't tell him.' This all seems very strange. Why are they not cutting my fingers off with a meat cleaver? I'm now less sure than I've ever been as to what this is all about, and I'm not sure I want to know. I'm just grateful for the help, no matter how odd their take on help is.

Marek looks at me for a moment, nods a few times and steps outside to make a phone call. I suddenly feel very, very alone and very, very vulnerable.

56

I went to bed shortly after that incident yesterday. I felt as if the whole of my lifeblood had been sucked out of me, leaving me devoid of energy. I just wanted to curl up, so I did.

Marek woke me shortly after three o'clock in the afternoon to tell me that everything had been sorted and accounted for. I didn't know what he meant, and I couldn't understand why he was being so understanding. Whatever is in these parcels, they're worth enough to pay some serious cash to the courier, so I can't imagine some random British foreigner popping up and suddenly losing one is going to be absolutely fine with them. I get the feeling they're protecting me somehow, for some reason. That thought worries me. Call me paranoid, but Marek and Andrej have absolutely no reason to protect me. They don't know me. The only favour I've done them is making these deliveries for them, and I can't even manage to do those properly. It only leads me to believe that they have bigger plans for me.

You see it all the time in the movies. The hapless runner who keeps fucking up yet keeps getting taken under the wing of the gangland boss, who sees a very useful and very lucrative sign of potential somewhere in him. And he hones that potential, draws it out until he's got the perfect tool for the big heist he's been planning for years. I know my imagination is probably running away with me, but I can't think of any other reason why these two haven't at least thrown me out on the streets just yet.

Other than Marek waking me yesterday afternoon, I slept more or less straight through until this morning. I knew I'd been sleep-deprived recently, but even I didn't think it was possible for a human being to sleep for eighteen hours straight. I'm not sure I feel better for it, either. My head feels groggy and stuffed.

I get changed and head downstairs to the bar, unsure as to what I might find. Will Andrej be there, having waited for me to get up so he can speak to me about what happened yesterday? I hope not. Even though Marek said he'd square everything, I'm still slightly afraid of Andrej. And Marek, too, if I'm honest. But I'm completely tied in with them now. They know too much about me for me to do anything but stick it out. And, anyway, what's the alternative? Go back to England and face a trial for murder? No thanks.

The bar's quiet, empty. I'm sure it's usually open at this time, but the front door and the storm porch door are both shut – something I've not seen since I arrived here, and particularly not on a nice sunny day like today.

I go over to the door to give it a shove, see if it's locked, and it's then that I notice the envelope on the floor. It's addressed to *Daniel*. A few thoughts rush straight into my head. Is this a note from Marek? Perhaps he's just letting me know that he's had to nip out for a bit and he'll be back soon. If that's the case, why not leave a note on the bar or somewhere I'd be more likely to see it? He could've slipped it under my door upstairs, for instance. No, this looks as though it's been posted through the letterbox and landed inside. Why would Marek post a note through his own front door? Besides which, he never calls me Daniel. He always calls me Bradley, playing along with the charade in order to help protect my real identity.

Confused, I tear open the envelope and take out the paper from inside. It's a sheet of A5 writing paper, written on with a thick black marker. My heart lurches in my chest as I read the words in front of me:

> *You can run but you cannot hide. Mistakes must be paid for.*

That's all it says. I try the front door, but it won't budge. I jog over to the back door, which leads out into the alleyway and the motor scooter, but that's locked tight, too. There's nowhere I can go.

I feel my whole world closing in around me. I don't know who's sent this note, but there are very few possibilities. Who knows my real name and the fact that I'm in Bratislava? By my reckoning, only Marek and Andrej. So why did Marek tell me everything was going to be alright if they were then going to threaten me like this? No. It doesn't feel right. I can't quite put my finger on it, but I could tell from looking into Marek's eyes yesterday that there wasn't malice in them. Not malice directed at me, anyway. There was a strange sort of acceptance, as if this was a problem they were going to have to sort out, but sort out on behalf of me rather than punishing me for it.

But then that means this whole note makes no sense whatsoever. I feel as though eyes are on me, as though I'm being watched from all angles. It's a horrible sensation, and it's one I want to get rid of as quickly as possible. I fold the note and shove it back in the envelope before putting it in my pocket. I'm usually a fairly good judge of character and tend to be able to rely on my hunches, and my hunch is that Marek has popped out, locked the bar as I was asleep upstairs, and that this note is from someone completely different. There's menace in the words, almost as though the note itself holds the spirit and aura of the person who wrote it. And I'm now fairly sure that the person who wrote it is the same person who killed Lisa and Jess. And now they're here to kill me, too.

57

I went straight upstairs after receiving the note, and locked myself in my room. It's about the only place I can feel anything remotely related to safe. I locked the door and closed the curtains before hiding under the duvet. Out of sight, out of mind. I just want to curl up in a ball and die, letting all of this go. I want the whole thing to end and go back to how it was.

And that's what hurts most: the realisation that things will *never* go back to how they were. They can't. Lisa will always be dead. Jess will always be dead. And I will always be suspected – somewhere, by some people – of being a murderer. Things will never be the same. The best I can hope for is to clear my name and not have to live the rest of my life on the run. And, right now, that would be an enormous victory. But it's one I can feel falling away from me more and more quickly every day, slipping through my fingers like oil. All I need is a break. A chance to be able to prove the truth. But before that, I know I need to discover the truth. And that's where I'm going to struggle.

After about half an hour, I hear the door unlocking downstairs. I take a deep breath and head down, where I find Marek and Andrej taking off their jackets.

'Ah, Bradley. Good morning,' Marek says, in his usual jovial manner. I nod at them both, my eyes looking at Andrej, trying to judge his mood. I can only imagine Marek will have filled him in on the botched delivery yesterday, and I want to get an idea of just how angry he is. I can't tell a thing, though. Andrej's face remains as stoic and impassive as it always does. He has the perfect poker face and never gives anything away.

'Marek, do you know anything about a note?' I ask, getting straight to the point.

'Note?' he replies, as I spot the faintest raising of an eyebrow.

'Yeah. About half an hour ago I came downstairs and the bar was locked up—'

'Yes, we had to go out,' Marek says, interrupting me. 'I did not wish to wake you.' He says this almost as if it was a matter of duty rather than just being nice.

'No, that's fine. But when I came down I found a note by the door. I think it'd been posted through the letterbox. It was addressed to "Daniel".'

Marek stops what he's doing, and I see Andrej's eyes light up momentarily – a momentary slip of the guard –

before he retains his usual stoic look. They both look at each other briefly, not speaking a word but at the same time saying a thousand.

'This note,' Marek says. 'What did it say?'

I take the note out of my pocket and hand it to him. He takes it out of the envelope, spends a few seconds reading it and then hands it to Andrej.

They exchange a few words in Slovak, then Andrej speaks.

'Do you have any idea who sent this?'

'No, not a clue. No-one who knows my real name even knows I'm here. Except . . .' Marek's eyes meet mine. I can see they've already both taken the same leap of logic as I have. 'Not that I'm saying anything like that, of course,' I explain, back-pedalling. 'Just that someone's obviously either followed me here somehow or someone here has found out my real name.'

'We did not speak to anyone,' Andrej says. 'Not about who you really are. Not to anybody we cannot trust with our lives.' I'm not quite sure what he means by this, or how he knows he can trust anyone, or who he's told, but I'm in no position to question him right now. I'm just hoping they haven't told anyone who doesn't strictly need to know, because knowing who I can trust is my biggest problem right now. For a brief moment, I wish I hadn't told them anything. I wish I'd denied everything, claimed the passport was false. But then how would I have denied the news reports and press coverage?

Andrej exchanges a glance with Marek. 'We will deal with this.'

I stand for a moment, unsure what to say. 'What do you mean, you'll deal with it? How?' I fail to see how they'd be able to do anything, not to mention why I should trust them. Unless, of course, it's because they know something that I don't. That's a thought that both scares me and reassures me at the same time.

'Do not worry,' he replies. 'If somebody wanted to hurt you, they would not do it by writing a letter.'

I can't believe how casual he's being about this. Then again, it's not his life and his existence on the line. 'It's a warning,' I say. 'It clearly says so in the note.'

'People who mean business do not send warnings. They do not mess about with words and letters. Do not worry,' he repeats.

He sounds convincing, and he's doing his best to put me at ease, but I would be foolish if I said I wasn't still panicking. Andrej knows far more about the sorts of people who send threats than I do.

'So, what, you just want me to ignore it? I'm not being funny, but someone's already killed my wife and chased me halfway across Europe. How am I meant to feel safe when they know I'm here?' I purposely don't mention Jess.

'Bradley, trust us,' Andrej says, placing his hand on my shoulder. He gives me the impression of being more than one step ahead. I nod. 'Now, we have some deliveries for you. To make up for the incident yesterday.'

I can't argue with that. But it still doesn't shake the

feeling that my journey could very soon be at its end and that it won't be long before I'm face to face with the person who killed Lisa and Jess, and who's going to try to kill me.

'Sure. That's fine,' I say. 'But there's something I want you to do for me first.'

58

It was an odd request, particularly as I didn't want to tell them why I'd requested it, but fortunately for me Andrej acquiesced. Less than half an hour later, he was back at the bar, handing me a brand-new dictaphone.

Ever since this whole journey started, all I've wanted is the truth. All I've wanted is to know who killed Lisa and Jess, and why. I want to know why this mystery person has such an enormous grudge against me that they're willing to murder two people and completely ruin my life just to get to me. They're the sorts of answers I can't go without.

Not only do I not know this truth, but no-one else does, either, except the killer. I can't guarantee – not by a long shot – that I'm going to come out of this alive, so I need to know that my version of the truth is going to go out. I need to know that my story will be told, because I certainly can't guarantee that it'll ever be told by me.

The dictaphone's a fancy sort, with a dual-recording

mode. In short, it means the device will record both onto the device itself as well as onto a removable memory card. Once I've recorded my message, I'm going to leave the memory card with Marek and Andrej, keeping the dictaphone itself with me. Should anything happen to me, my hope is that someone will find the dictaphone. If it's the killer who finds it, at least I know that Marek and Andrej will have a copy. It feels bizarre trusting them with something so important, seeing as I barely know them, but who else do I have? There isn't anyone.

Having set the dictaphone up and inserted two batteries and the memory card, I set it to record. I haven't really planned what I'm going to say, but I think this is something that's best if it comes from the heart.

'I don't know who's going to find this,' I say, 'but my name is Daniel Cooper. There will be a lot being said about me, and it's important that the truth is told. Firstly, I *did not* kill my wife, Lisa Cooper. At the time she died, I was downstairs in the restaurant at the hotel. I wasn't even aware that my wife was at the hotel. When I came back up to my room, I found her body in my bathtub, but with no signs of forced entry to the room. This was the first time I'd seen my wife since I left our house the week before. When I saw the mobile phone in her hand, I looked at the screen and saw that there was a text message that appeared to come from me. I didn't send it. I'd never seen that message before, and there was no trace of it on my phone. At that point, I panicked. I freaked out. Finding your wife dead is one thing, but realising someone has tried to frame you for her murder is something completely different. I just wanted to get as far away from the situation as possible.

'I don't like confrontation, and I don't like injustice. But at the same time, I don't know how to handle either when they're thrust upon me. There was an incident in my past. The authorities will probably have found it on record by now. I don't know. I might be digging myself into a bigger hole by telling you about it. When I was young, I was in a children's home. A boys' home. It was run by nuns. There was a man who used to come to visit. He put a lot of money into the home, kept it running and all of the nuns thought he was practically a saint. Well, most of them. This man used to have . . . favourites. Out of the boys, I mean. One night, after he'd done it again, I lost my rag. My temper went and I flew into a rage. I battered the bloke black and blue. You've got to understand that wasn't because I'm a violent person. It's not. I'm not. It's because I don't know how to handle things. And that's why I ran from the hotel when I found my wife's body and realised I'd been set up. Because I couldn't handle the injustice.

'I didn't run on my own. When I got downstairs, Jessica saw me. She worked at the hotel, on reception. We'd . . .' I figure I might as well come out with it. It's not as if Lisa's ever going to know now. 'We'd been having a bit of a fling while I was staying at the hotel. I don't know why, but I agreed to let her come with me. I just wanted to get out of there as quickly as possible. She seemed to know what she was doing.

'We drew cash out of our accounts and headed for

Folkestone. We got on the Eurotunnel and went to France. We knew we needed to get as far away as possible, for two reasons. Firstly, to give ourselves some breathing space and time to work out what the hell we were going to do, and secondly to get away from the person who'd killed Lisa and would quite possibly try to kill me – if not make it their life's mission to make my existence a living hell. Jess knew a place in France. I don't remember the exact location, but it was a farmhouse near Locquignol. I reckon I could find it again if I was in the area, but right now that's the best I can do. A friend of her family lived there. A guy called Claude. He gave us cash, as well as a car. We left my car in his barn. The next morning, we drove down to Switzerland and hired a caravan on a campsite. That's when things started to get worse.

'I went into town one morning to get some bits, and when I came back Jess was dead. Murdered. I thought we'd managed to outrun the killer, but I knew in that instant that he knew exactly where I was and that he was trying to close in on me. So I ran. Again. I drove to Innsbruck and abandoned Claude's car in a petrol station. I went on foot to the main station and got on a train to Bratislava, which is where I've been ever since.

'I rented a room above a bar, run by a guy called Marek. His brother, Andrej, somehow managed to collar me into delivering parcels for him. I didn't know what the parcels were – I still don't, actually – but by the time I'd done one it was too late to back out. They found out my real identity. I'd told them I was called Bradley. They said if I left they'd turn me in, but if I stayed and worked for them they'd help me. Then I got a note through the door one day addressed to "Daniel" which said . . . Well, it was a threat. Let's just put it that way. That's when I knew I couldn't get away. From whoever is doing this. That's when I knew that wherever I ran, he'd be there. And that's why I'm recording this message. So that when I'm found – if I'm found – the truth is on record. My truth. Because only the truth matters. None of what anyone else is saying. I didn't kill Lisa. I didn't kill Jess. I've never killed anyone. This is the truth.'

My head spins as I click the 'Stop' button, and I feel like a weight has been lifted off my shoulders.

I take the memory card out of the dictaphone and put the device in my pocket. As long as I've always got this on me and Marek and Andrej have the other copy, I'm about as safe as I possibly can be. Which isn't very safe at all. I take the memory card downstairs and put it behind the bar, where Andrej said. Then I put on my jacket and step outside the back door, into the alleyway, and start up the moped. It's time to regain some trust.

59

I don't know if it's just the paranoia kicking in again, but I feel like I'm being followed. There's nothing tangible, nothing I can put my finger on, but it gives me a deep sense of unease. I don't take the most direct route to my pick-up point – far from it. I head off in the general direction of where I need to go before veering off into a side road to my right, then turning right at the end again, heading back the way I've just come, on a parallel road. I glance in my mirrors every couple of seconds, taking note of the cars behind me, getting to know each of them intimately.

None of them ever turn the same way as I do, but I still can't shake that feeling of being followed. Knowing that it's a paranoia coming from within me makes it even worse. I wouldn't wish this feeling on my worst enemy. After more twisting and turning I decide that I'm never going to feel completely comfortable, so I head for the pick-up point.

When I get there, I find out the shop I need to get to is

in a pedestrianised area of the city. I can see it – it's a jeweller's – but there's no way I'll be able to drive to it, so I park the scooter up round the corner and do the rest of the journey on foot. It's a pain in the arse, but my main worry is that I'm going to have to walk back through this pedestrianised area with the package under my arm. That doesn't exactly feel safe to me.

The woman working in the shop seems to know who I am straight away, and she beckons me over to the till. She bends down behind the counter and picks up a carrier bag. I can see inside – it's a large carriage clock. She smiles at me in that way people do when they're expecting you to go as quickly as possible.

As I walk back to the scooter, I can't help but wonder why the hell I'm transporting a carriage clock in a carrier bag. A few thoughts cross my mind – perhaps it's filled with drugs, maybe it's packed with explosives. Or maybe it's just a carriage clock being transported from a jeweller's shop. That last possibility doesn't seem so far-fetched – I imagine Marek and Andrej need to ensure some level of secrecy by giving me some perfectly innocent deliveries. From their point of view, it'd be a good test of my loyalties and reduce their risk of me flaking out, especially after the incident with the note.

When I get back to the scooter, I open the seat and go to put the carrier bag inside it. I catch sight of the folded piece of paper as it shifts in the breeze. I swallow, hard. I'm sure that wasn't there before, but I can't be certain. I didn't look in the compartment before I left the bar earlier.

My heart thumping in my chest, I delicately lower my hand towards the paper – as if dipping my hand into a pool of crocodiles to test the temperature of the water – and pull the paper out. Unfolding it, I see the words written on it in black pen:

Who are you buying jewellery for, Daniel?

Just seven words, but seven words that mean so much. They mean someone is here, watching me. There's now no doubt that the note was written and put here in the past couple of minutes, as even *I* didn't know I was going to a jewellery shop until I got here. But it's impossible – I know for a fact I wasn't tailed. The only people who knew I was here are Marek and Andrej. They sent me here. And they're the only people I can think of who might have a reason for terrorising me in this way, even though I have absolutely no idea what that reason might be.

My instincts kick in and in that moment a huge realisation dawns on me. It's all over. Whatever I do, I can't run. Whichever way I turn, the killer is there, tormenting me. And the worst part of it all is that he hasn't killed me, too. In many ways, that would be a relief, an escape. It would never clear my name, though, and that's something that means a lot to me. I can't live with injustice, but I can't resolve this one on my own, either.

Ten minutes later, I park the moped up outside the police station and walk slowly but confidently up to the door.

I've planned out the whole conversation in my head on the ride over here. I'll find an officer who speaks English and tell them everything. I'll tell them how I need someone to hear my case, that I've not committed any crimes (other than potentially getting involved in drug dealing, but I don't know that for certain, and in any case I can quite legitimately say I was blackmailed). It's my only option.

I know that I'll be arrested. I know that I'll be deported back to England, and I know that when I get there I'm going to be questioned at length about Lisa's death, but I'll get a good lawyer. The best. He'll be able to help me. After all, the truth is that I haven't done anything. I didn't kill Lisa and I didn't kill Jess.

But as I stand with my hand on the front door of the police station, I just can't shake that immovable feeling that I won't be able to find the truth this way. The British police are already hell-bent on the idea that I killed Lisa, and I don't have a thing – nothing – that can prove otherwise. Try as I might, how am I going to convince the people who are already convinced?

No. I need more. Much more. And I've only got one tiny glimmer of hope available to me.

60

I know what I need to do, but I also know that I have to complete this delivery first. Whatever happens, I need to either get rid of any incriminating evidence, or I need to ensure that Marek and Andrej don't have any more reasons to terrorise me – if it is them who are doing it.

I try to keep as calm as I can and make my way over to the drop-off point. I never quite know what I'm going to find until I get there, as I'm only ever given an address – never a name of a shop or any indication as to what the building is. When I get to my drop-off point, it's in a residential area. Not in quite the same league as the house I visited the other day, but pretty nice all the same. Certainly a nicer house than mine back home. If I'll ever be able to call it mine again. It's then that I realise I've referred to it as home. Is that just a force of habit, or am I starting to miss England? If I'm honest, I really don't know. My feelings are somewhat marred and blurred by everything that's happened recently.

I walk up the driveway of the address I've been given and I look for a doorbell. There isn't one, so I knock instead. A few seconds later, I hear someone approaching the door. When it opens, there's an elderly gentleman looking back at me, a television blaring out at full volume somewhere inside the house. The man can't be any younger than ninety, and he smiles genially as he sees me. As if he is expecting me. He doesn't say anything, and the best I can manage is, 'Delivery,' as I hold up the carrier bag, still not having bothered to learn a word of Slovak. The old man beams, takes the bag and pats me on the arm whilst saying something I don't understand a word of. I smile and wave as I walk back down his driveway and hear the door close behind me.

And that's when the idea occurs to me. I look back at his house, and then at the ones nearby. I'm looking for security cameras, but I can't see any. It strikes me as the sort of neighbourhood where crime just doesn't exist.

I make my way back up his driveway, but I keep to the side of it, walking in between his car and the fence. The car is a Hyundai hatchback – fairly new, by the looks of things, but not new or expensive enough that it's going to have a tracker installed. When I get to the end of the driveway, I'm level with the house. There's a gate in the fence that leads to the back garden, but it appears to be locked. In any case, I wouldn't be able to open the gate far, as the car's parked right up against it. I climb onto the bonnet of the car, my shoes clunking on the metalwork, then over the fence.

There's a patio the other side, and I drop down fairly noise-lessly onto it.

I can still hear the old man's TV from inside the house, and praise the gods for his dreadful hearing. I make my way round to the back of the house, ducking under each window, until I get to the back door. It's a wooden door with nine inset glass panes. I peer around and through one of the bottom panes, perched on my hands and knees like a dog. There's no sign of the old man in the kitchen, so I get up onto my feet and have a proper peer through. Just inside the door is a row of four hooks. On one is what looks like the key to his Hyundai.

I try the door handle. To my amazement and delight, it's open. I push the door gently, flinching and holding back as it starts to creak. After a few seconds there's still no sign of life from inside the house, so I push the door open just enough that I can get my arm inside, and I make a grab for the keys.

Just as I manage to hook my hand around them, the keys slip from my grasp and come clattering to the floor. I jerk my arm out and duck back down against the wall beside the door. I listen carefully for any movement. There's nothing. Back on my hands and knees, I push my arm through the gap in the door and grab the car key. Then I stand, pull the door to and make my way back around the side of the house.

When I get back to the fence, I realise there's no way of me being able to climb up. There's no handy car bonnet this side. I carefully check both of the windows along the side of the house – the old man's in neither of the rooms. Thanking my lucky stars, I clench his car key between my teeth, give myself a run-up and launch myself at the fence, my arms flailing upwards as I grasp for purchase on the top of it. I plant my feet against the fence and pull myself upwards, feeling my muscles burning before I hook my right elbow over the top and manage to pull the rest of my body up. Once I'm over the top, I step down onto the car bonnet and then duck down beside the car.

I wait a few seconds, just to make sure I've not been seen or heard, and then I press the button on the key fob. The car unlocks immediately, so I pull the handle and open the door as carefully and quietly as I can. With the door still slightly ajar, I quickly familiarise myself with the controls. I know that as soon as I start it up, I'm going to need to disappear very quickly. Once I'm happy that I know where everything is, I pull the door shut, start the engine up immediately and slip the stick into reverse. With a squeal of tyres, the car shoots back into the road. I push the stick into drive, and with another small squeal I'm accelerating off down the street.

61

In a heartbeat, I know exactly where I'm going. I've no idea how I'm going to get there, but I know it's going to take a long time. From my limited but slowly growing knowledge of Bratislava, I know which way is west. I head out of the city, being careful to stick to speed limits but at the same time not holding back where I can get away with it.

Yet again, my life has taken a bizarre twist and I'm driving through Slovakia in an old man's car, with only the clothes on my back. I've got the iPhone Jess gave me in my jacket pocket, having charged it fully last night. If Jess's body has been found by now, they'll have found her phone. I don't know how linked the phones are, but I'm certainly not going to risk using it.

A thought occurs to me. Can they track the phone just through it being on? I'm fairly sure I read somewhere that they can do that using the masts. Would it still be the case in Slovakia? I'm not about to risk it. Holding on to the steering wheel with one hand, I fish the phone out of my jacket pocket and hold down the button to switch it off. After what seems like an absolute age, the screen changes, and *Slide to power off* appears at the top. I do as it says, and the phone eventually shuts down. I put it back in my pocket – I still want the option of being able to use it if I should somehow get myself into some really deep trouble.

I do a quick mental calculation to work out how much money I've got on me. I reckon it's probably a couple of hundred euros. The fuel tank in the car's full to the brim, according to the dashboard, and I'm getting about 58mpg by the time I head out of town, which I reckon means I'll probably have to fill up the tank once more. Maybe twice. My journey's going to be about eight hundred miles, I esti-mate. I should be able to do that in eleven or twelve hours, depending on traffic, and I don't intend to stop for sleep. It'll be coffee that keeps me going. I have no time to lose.

A mile or so down the road, I pull over into a car park behind a gym. I'm pleased to find there's no CCTV that I can see, so I park up next to a row of vans. I can't read the writing on the side, but by my way of thinking they must be delivery vans for a local company as they're all sign-written identically. I crouch down behind one, and, using the key from the moped, I quickly but carefully unscrew the number plates from one of the vans. I do the same on the old man's car and swap them over. I figure that the people driving these vans aren't going to know the registration numbers off by heart – they're probably pool vehicles. That should give me a bit of breathing space. I get back into the car, complete with its new registration plates, and within three minutes of parking up I'm on the road again.

Before long I'm over the border into Austria, keeping the car on the main road as I carry on heading west. Once I'm past Vienna, I stop at a small service station and buy a couple of road maps. Using a pen, I trace my route. I know roughly the signs I'm looking out for: Linz, Nuremberg, Frankfurt, Bonn, Liege, Charleroi and Mons. Then I'll need to head south.

By the time I reach the outskirts of Frankfurt, the fuel in the car is getting low. I pull over, buy myself a few cans of energy drink and some sandwiches, and refuel the car. I think about doing another swap of registration plates, but I decide not to risk it. The whole journey will take me less than twelve hours in total, and it's unlikely anyone's going to realise the plates on the van have been changed within that time, and they're almost certainly not going to have the police in Germany looking out for the registration. I figure I'm as safe as I can be.

With the car – and myself – refuelled, I'm back on the road and I'm back on the A3, which has been my home for the past few hours and will be for a while yet. As I look in my rear-view mirror at the tarmac disappearing behind me, I know that I'm moving closer and closer towards finally being able to get some justice.

62

By the time I reach the French border it's past midnight. I've driven more or less non-stop, save for a couple of toilet stops and the refuelling outside Frankfurt. I don't have much fuel left now, but there aren't many miles to go, either. The lumbar area of my back hurts like hell. Every now and again I straighten up in my seat and push the bottom of my back forward, feeling the creaking and cracking as the vertebrae resettle into their proper positions. My knees are stiff, too, and my right ankle started to hurt about an hour ago. Stopping for a rest has never been an option, though. The only thing I can do is keep going, keep ploughing on.

About twenty minutes or so after I cross the border from Belgium into France, the roads start to look familiar. The memories come back, and it feels as though I've spent huge periods of my life here, whereas in reality I was only here for a few hours – most of them asleep.

There's a light on inside Claude's farmhouse as I pull the car up opposite, parking as far over on the gravel lay-by as I can. The road's so narrow that there wouldn't be room for a car to pass if I didn't. I silently apologise to the old man in Bratislava for scratching the side of his car.

I sit for a moment, taking in what's happened and what I'm about to do. It sounds bizarre, but even though I've just spent twelve hours driving here, I still don't know what I'm going to say to Claude. All I know is that if there's a chance anyone can help me, it'll be him. I've managed to get myself to the other side of Europe and back without being caught or killed – mainly thanks to a shave and a haircut and stealing other people's cars, but also partially thanks to Lisa and Jess's killer preferring to torment me rather than kill me.

I know for a fact I've not been followed here: you don't drive for twelve hours from one side of Europe to the other without realising someone's following you.

I think about what I'm going to say to Claude. I don't need to say anything. He'll know what to do. But I do need to tell him about Jess. I know they were close, I know he had been her salvation, and it pains me to think that I'm now going to have to tell him she's been killed. How do you even go about a thing like that? Straight to the point, I guess.

I unlock the car, open the door and step out into the cool night air. My legs feel like tree trunks holding my weakened torso somewhat upright, my neck cracking as I rotate my head and push my shoulder blades backwards. I close the car door and cross the narrow lane, before pushing open the creaking gate that leads to Claude's farmhouse.

When I get to the front of the house, I can hear a TV playing from inside. It reminds me of being back at the old man's house in Bratislava, and I feel a pang of guilt at what I did to him. The thought also crosses my mind that he's probably still sat there in front of the box, chuckling away at some late-night comedy programme, not having even realised his car's halfway across Europe.

I ring the doorbell, then knock on the door. After a few seconds, I hear nothing – just the sound of the TV. It sounds like a game show, or perhaps one of those late-night shopping channels. Without speaking a word of French, it's hard to tell. I ring the doorbell again, twice, and then knock louder. Still nothing.

There's no way Claude will have slept through that, so I can only presume he's not in the house. He can't be far, though, judging by the fact the TV's on. It's late, but the only other place he could be is in the barn. I doubt if he'll be out on the farm at this time.

I walk back down the path to the lane, then further up the road to the barn. As I get closer to it, I can see the large doors are slightly ajar. There's no light inside, but I quicken my pace as I approach the barn.

When I get there, I call Claude's name just before I get to the doors. Then I pause for a moment before pulling one of the large doors open a little further, calling inside.

'Claude?' My voice sounds croaky and weak.

I take a step inside, leaving the barn door open slightly

to allow some moonlight to stream in. It's the only light I've got.

I start to move around inside the barn, but I can't see or hear anything.

'Claude?' I call again, wondering how the hell he can't hear me. It's deathly silent apart from my voice, which rattles and echoes around inside this huge barn.

Something isn't right.

I turn to head back towards the open door, and it's at that moment I notice the moonlight softening as a figure walks across the doorway and stands stock-still, a shadow being cast across me and the floor of the barn.

It's not Claude. I know in an instant exactly who it is.

'Hello, Daniel.'

63

For the first time in my life, I'm lost for words. I can't even form a coherent thought, never mind speak.

'I can tell you didn't expect to find me here,' Jess says, not moving. After a couple of seconds I shake my head slowly. 'What's wrong, Daniel? Don't you believe in ghosts?' She walks towards me, then past me, sitting herself down on a bale of hay. 'Come. Sit with me.'

I'm struck dumb. I can't say or do anything. I can only presume I'm hallucinating. I saw her lying dead on the floor of that caravan. She was as dead as Lisa had been that day at the hotel. Or had I imagined the whole thing?

'Sit down, Daniel,' she says, as if she's speaking to a small child. Her tone of voice and the way she uses my full name takes me back to a time long before I met her, long before I met Lisa. It has the effect of jolting me awake, putting me right back into the here and now.

I walk over to her slowly, but don't sit down. I stand a good fifteen feet or so away from her, keeping my distance.

'Ghosts exist, Daniel. As you can see. Ghosts will always come back to haunt you.'

'You're dead,' I say, eventually.

She smiles with one corner of her mouth. 'In many ways. If you mean physically, then no.'

'But you're dead. I saw you. You were dead.'

'Did you? Did you really?' she says, taking a cigarette from her pocket and lighting it. She takes a huge drag and holds on to it before raising her chin and releasing the smoke into the barn. She does it with such ease, such grace, anyone would think she was a regular smoker. 'Or did you just see me lying on the floor, panic and run off like you always do?'

'No. You were dead. I felt your pulse.' I can't understand how this has happened.

'You felt the pulse on my wrists, Daniel. Because even by your own admission you're too feckless to find the pulse in the neck. Tennis balls under the armpits and squeeze. Oldest trick in the book. But then that's your specialist subject, isn't it? Always being one step behind everyone else.'

My head's spinning. 'Why?' I ask. It's all I can think to say.

She laughs. 'Seriously? *Why?* Are you actually asking me that?' I can see a flash of anger in her eyes. 'Do you have any idea how I've been treated throughout my life? By men?

Every man I've ever met has thought he can just use me for his own satisfaction. And it's not just me, either. You had a wife at home, Daniel. The perfect, happy life. And you threw that all away for a few moments of pleasure. With someone you thought would give you an easy ride. No worries, no responsibilities. Well let me tell you this, Daniel. There are always responsibilities. Even if you don't see them straight away. The moment you first took me up to your hotel room, you committed. You just didn't know what to.'

'This doesn't make any sense,' I say. 'I haven't done anything wrong.'

Jess laughs. 'And that's exactly your problem. You never think you've done anything wrong. It's always just down to the way the world works out, isn't it? It's always due to circumstance, to bad luck. You make your own luck in this world. And yours has run out.'

She takes another huge drag on the cigarette, which is now nearly burnt down. As I look at the glowing orb at the end of the cigarette, a thought ignites in my mind. I lift my hands slightly and place them on my hips, standing like a PE teacher at the side of a sports field. When I see her glance down at the floor, I manipulate my thumb and push it inside my jeans pocket, flicking the switch across on the dictaphone. I hope to God it's the switch that starts it recording. I've only used it once, so I can't be certain, but it's all I've got.

'How did you get here?' I ask her.

'There are such things as planes, Daniel.'

'But you couldn't get on a plane. You're wanted across Europe.'

'No, Jessica Walsh is wanted across Europe. If I'd used the British passport with Jessica Walsh in it, I'd be pretty stupid, wouldn't I?'

'You have two passports?' I ask.

'No, I have one. My French one. My parents were French. The British one isn't real, Daniel.' She says this in such a patronising manner, as if she's telling a thirty-year-old man that Santa Claus isn't real. 'That's where Claude comes in handy occasionally.'

'Claude? How do you mean?'

She shakes her head and looks up to the rafters of the barn. Her look is condescending, pitiful. 'He helps me. He always has. He understands me. Listen, he's got contacts. That's all you need to know.'

'You can't just rock up to an airport with a fake passport and expect it to work. They do scans and checks and all sorts of things,' I say.

'Don't be so naive, Daniel. There are ways and means,' she replies.

My mind jumps straight to some very weird places. 'But how did you get a job in the hotel without all the paper-work?' It's the first thing that comes to mind, as if my brain is completely blanking out the more obvious questions and reverting to the simple, straightforward, rules-based stuff. Because, right now, all of the rules have gone out of the window. In a world where a person can come back from the dead, I need to root myself in facts and logic.

'You're very sweet. Do you really think I can't get what I want without bending the rules a little? Really? After the past few days?'

I suppose she's got a point.

'How did you find me?' I ask.

She laughs again. 'I tracked you using the iPhone. I knew you wouldn't use it, but I also knew you wouldn't get rid of it. There's an app called Find My Friends. Sweet, isn't it? I saw you'd gone to Bratislava, so I went there, too. Why Bratislava, by the way?'

I can't answer that, so I just shrug.

'How odd. I had a lot of fun tracking you around, anyway. That's the beauty of technology – I never needed to keep you in sight, so you never saw me, either. I knew where you were at any time. When I tracked you through Bratislava and saw that you had started heading north, I had a pretty good idea where you were going. While you were doing twelve hours on the road, I had a two-hour flight from Bratislava to Charleroi. Much nicer. Food wasn't bad, either.'

'Where's Claude?' I ask. I can't see she would have harmed him, but I suddenly remember the TV blaring out and the lack of response from inside the farmhouse.

'Inside the house,' Jess replies. 'Yes, he's alive, and yes, he knows I'm here. I also asked him not to answer the door tonight and told him I'd be gone by morning. That's the good thing about Claude. He's trustworthy. And he trusts me. Strange what men do, isn't it?'

Then the thought, the realisation, hits my mind like a

bullet. My brain's finally made the connection, having dismissed it completely back at the caravan when I saw Jess lying on the floor, seemingly dead. 'You killed Lisa.'

Jess smiles. It's a funny smile, almost as if she's proud of me for having finally worked it out. She looks like a piano teacher who's just seen her youngest, poorest student finally manage to play 'Chopsticks' without fucking it up.

'Why?' I ask.

'I've told you why, Daniel,' she says, bending over and stubbing another cigarette out on the dirty floor. 'Because you're a serial abandoner. Because men like you deserve to be punished.'

'You wanted me as much as I wanted you,' I say, feeling almost like a fifteen-year-old schoolboy who's just been dumped by his girlfriend.

Jess shrugs. 'Call me a good actress. Call it whatever you like.'

There are tears forming in my eyes. I don't want to ask the question, but I know I need to. I need my own personal closure, and I need it for the dictaphone. 'How?'

She looks me in the eye. 'You want to know?' I nod slowly. 'You were in the bathroom one afternoon. After we'd . . . I got Lisa's number from your phone. I'd seen you tap the pin number in a couple of times, so it wasn't difficult. Early that afternoon, I called her. I told her I was working at the hotel where you were staying and that there'd been an incident and you'd asked her to come down. I knew it'd only take her just over an hour or so, and I knew what time you tended to go down for dinner. That's the problem when you make me part of your dirty little routine, Daniel. Why did you think I was so keen for you to get down to the restaurant?'

I blink rapidly. It's all starting to make sense.

'You left your phone in the room, as you always do. So while you were in the restaurant I sent a message to Lisa asking her to come up to your room. Then I deleted the sent message. I'm guessing you don't want to know the details of the next bit.'

I shake my head.

'Good. I'm not some sort of psychopath who gets kicks out of telling everyone how they killed someone. Let's just call it a means to an end, shall we? And before you ask, no, I felt nothing. Yes, she was just a pawn in the game. Get over it.'

I somehow get the feeling that killing Lisa affected Jess more than she thinks it did. There's emotion creeping into her voice.

'So you killed her because I cheated on her?' I ask. 'How does that make sense?'

'No. I killed her because you deserved to know what a lying, deceitful little shit you are. Because men like you hurt women. Because you need to lose the things you love before you even realise you loved them. It's all about power with men like you, isn't it? Power over women. Well I think we can safely say we turned that one on its head, don't you?'

Jess walks over to the large doors at the front of the barn and pushes them completely shut, before fastening the huge padlock across the two hasps. She's locked us in. She flicks a switch to turn on a small light up in the rafters, which gives off a soft orange glow.

'Do you think you're going to get away with this?' I ask, watching her as she moves behind some bales of hay.

'Define "getting away with it",' she calls. A few moments later, she appears back in view with a jerrycan in her arms. I know she's capable of doing some pretty extreme things. She has the same look on her face that she had before she stormed out of the caravan and savagely beat that dog. The look of determination, as if the red mist has descended and nothing on earth will stop her from doing what she's about to do.

'Jess, this is silly. Can we just talk about—'

'Talk?' she says, smiling. 'What do you think we've just been doing, Daniel? We've just been talking. What more do you want to know?' There's a couple of seconds of silence. I can't say anything. 'There we are. The time for talking is over, Daniel.' She unscrews the cap of the jerrycan and begins sloshing the liquid around the barn. It smells strong, the stench of petrol filling my nostrils as I fight for a clean breath.

'Jess, stop. You don't know what you're doing,' I say, moving towards her.

She throws the jerrycan to the ground, the petrol still gulping and glugging out of the neck of the can as she puts a hand out in front of her to stop me. With the other, she dips into her pocket and pulls out a lighter. It's a cheap plastic one – not one she can just throw to the ground at any moment, which provides me some small semblance of relief.

That relief doesn't last long, though. Before I can even process what she's doing, Jess has knelt down next to a bale of hay, flicked the lighter on, and the blue flame has caught the dry grass, turning it a bright, glowing orange.

64

The dry hay starts to fill the barn with smoke incredibly quickly. It's a deep, insipid grey with a touch of green. It almost mesmerises me for a few moments. I can't believe how fast the whole place has taken light. There's a thick black fog being provided by the burning petrol, too, and I'm disorientated. I haven't moved, but I still don't know for sure which way I'm facing. The smoke seeps into my lungs, tickling at my throat and making my chest flutter and heave.

The barn is lit up bright, but I still can't see anything. My eyes burn, and I blink rapidly as I try to wash the smoke from them. The heat starts to affect them, too, and I feel myself pulling my eyes closed to protect them. The whole barn moves and shimmers in a haze of heat, the waves of smoke hitting me every couple of seconds as I flit between trying to stop the pain and fighting to keep my eyes open, fighting to see where I am.

I can't see Jess, either. I don't know whether she's

somehow got herself an escape route or whether she intends to go up in flames with me and the barn. Either way, she seemed very confident and sure of herself. She knew exactly what she was going to do. She will have planned this long ago. And poor old trusting Claude is sat in the farmhouse, completely oblivious to what she's doing. By the time he works it out, it'll be too late. The barn will have burned to the ground, and he won't be able to do a thing about it. There won't be anything he can do by now anyway. The whole place is alight and the flames are growing by the second.

I stagger around, trying to keep heading in a straight line. The only problem is I have no idea if I'm succeeding or not. I can't see a thing. I figure that if I can reach one of the walls, I can feel along for the barn doors, one of the two sets, and somehow kick them in. I don't know how I think I'm going to do that, but it's the only hope I've got. Walking in a straight line is far more difficult than it sounds, though. I have no sense of direction, and my mind is filling with fear and panic as my lungs fill with acrid smoke.

I want to take a deep breath and yell, scream and shout at the top of my lungs in the hope that someone, someone out here in this vast French wilderness, will somehow hear me. I know there's no chance of that happening, but it's completely irrelevant as I'm barely able to breathe, let alone take in a lungful of air.

The darkness builds and I can scarcely see the flames for the smoke. It billows and rolls as the fire crackles. I hear a sound like a gunshot, the sound of part of the roof giving way overhead, and I instinctively cover my head with my arms as I hear it come crashing to the ground not far from me.

I remember something I read in a book once, and I drop to my knees, crawling around on the floor, trying to gulp down the remaining oxygen that sinks to the ground during a fire. The air down here is cooler, a draught rushes across my face as I slug at the air, trying to force it down into my lungs, replacing the thick black smoke I've inhaled. It's not helping me much, as I'm moving more slowly, the fire slowly engulfing the entire barn. I look up into the heat haze and see the flames licking around the rooftop, just as another piece of wood cracks and lands a few feet away from me, a hole appearing in the roof as the flames soar upwards, reaching towards their freedom.

Crawling forwards, trying to regain some sort of traction and keep heading in a direction – any direction – I cough and splutter as the smoke and ash fill my lungs.

I see stars in front of my eyes and feel my chest burning, heaving with the lack of oxygen. There's a ringing in my ears, and my limbs start to feel numb, heavy. I feel the heat burning at the surfaces of my eyes as I put my head down on the dirty floor and let the smoke envelop me.

65

I'm jolted back to reality by the convulsions of my body and the cracking of two of my ribs, my lungs burning as though they've been filled with acid. I cough; a deep, throaty cough which rattles and lingers as I spit blackened saliva onto the ground beside me.

I try to focus my eyes, but they sting as I fight to stop blinking, my eyes reacting to having been severely irritated by the smoke. As I roll my head from side to side, through the milky film I can see the vague outline of a big man with a big moustache.

'Claude,' I rasp, my throat immediately feeling as though it's lined with rusty nails.

'You are okay,' he says, placing a hand on my shoulder. 'The ambulance is on its way.'

'But Jess,' I say, forcing the sounds out through the pain.

'It is okay. Do not speak,' Claude replies. As I get used to my tear-stained vision, I can start to see the look on his face. It looks pained, emotional. But I don't know him enough to know what this means. I can only assume it means that Jess didn't make it out of the barn.

Behind me, I can hear the barn crackling as the sounds begin to permeate my consciousness, and I roll my head sideways to look at it. The flames are lapping out through gaps in the wooden cladding, which they've pushed wider apart, reaching up to the freedom of the skies. What's left of the barn is completely blackened, much of the roof caved in as the exposed rafters begin to peek through into the night sky, lit up by the orange glow of the flames. Unless Jess managed to escape before I got out – and I'm fairly sure she didn't – I can't see any way that anyone could have survived this.

I'm not sure how that makes me feel. My first instinct is sadness, sorrow and regret. That doesn't last for long, though, as I begin to come to terms with the fact that Jess killed Lisa and then tried to kill me. I knew from the beginning that she was disturbed somehow, but I'd always managed to view her as the victim. Perhaps she still is, in some way. Perhaps she's the victim of her own disturbed mind.

A thought, a realisation, bursts into my mind like a lightning bolt. I hear myself gasp and I snap my head round as quickly as it'll turn – which isn't very quickly at all – to look at Claude.

'Jess's parents. The fire. The holiday home,' I say. I can see by the look in his eyes that he doesn't need any more explanation to know what I'm talking about.

He looks up at his barn, the flames licking around it, and swallows, a tear falling from his eye.

'She did that, too, didn't she?' I whisper, forcing Claude to admit the truth.

He nods, silently, closing his eyes and bowing his head.

'She told me it was you,' I say, bending the truth slightly.

He looks at me, no sign of emotion on his face. He doesn't seem surprised in the slightest. 'I tried to help her. I protected her. I always tried to protect her. What she did not know is that I was protecting her from herself.'

'From herself?' I ask. They're the only two words my mouth can form, the bitter smoke constricting my throat and making my voice rasp. I have a million questions for him, and I can see that he knows that.

'Sometimes . . . sometimes I think Jessica is toxic,' he says, looking deep into my eyes, a seriousness burning through the painful sorrow etched on his face. His English is even better than I realised. I wonder if he was holding back on that before so I wouldn't ask him more questions.

'What do you mean, toxic?' I ask.

Claude is silent for a few moments. 'Do you ever believe that people are born bad?'

I find myself shaking my head. 'You can't just write it off as being born bad. There has to be a reason. There has to be. There's a reason for everything.'

'She would have told you herself she was evil,' Claude says. 'Her parents. Her stepfather. He—'

'I know,' I say, not wanting to put Claude through the pain of having to tell me. He looks surprised.

'She never forgave herself for what they did to her.'

'Forgave herself?' I say. 'What did she need to forgive herself for? She didn't do anything.'

'She saw it differently,' Claude replies. 'She thought she had evil blood. The bad things she did, she blamed it on them. She said she was born evil to evil parents.'

'Christ.'

'Before she went to England,' Claude says, stopping to swallow and compose his thoughts, 'she asked me to do something.' I can see the pained look on his face as his brow furrows. He raises his head and looks me in the eye. 'She was scared, Daniel. She was petrified. Petrified of that evil spreading further. She wanted me to help her be sterilised.'

I don't know what to say to this. 'Sterilised?' I ask. 'How old was she?'

'Far too young,' Claude replies, shaking his head. 'Far too young. But I could see it in her eyes. The evil she spoke about. We found a doctor in a local village who agreed to carry out the operation. It cost a lot of money, but afterwards she seemed . . . more at peace.'

'Happier?' I ask, thinking back to the faint scar I noticed below her belly button.

'No. Just more at peace.'

'Why did you help her?' I ask. 'I mean, if you thought she was born tainted or had bad blood or whatever. Why didn't you just get as far away from her as you could?'

Claude makes a noise that almost sounds like a laugh.

'You can't get away from that girl. You'll never get away from her.' *Better the devil you know,* I think to myself. 'And I thought it might help. A young girl burns down a house and murders her parents. And she was just so calm. It was like she had just got back from taking the dog for a walk.'

'Believe me, I know exactly what you mean,' I say. 'What happened after the fire?' I ask, tasting the acrid smoke and blood in my throat.

'She went to England.'

'With her new passport?'

Claude looks momentarily guilty. 'Yes.'

'Jess isn't her real name, is it?' I ask.

Claude shakes his head.

'What's her real name?'

Claude looks up at the road as he hears the sirens of the ambulance approaching.

'Come. The ambulance is here.'

66

It feels strange being in my house. The sights, the smells, the familiar sound of the radiators knocking and humming – it all takes me back to a time when things were very different. I keep expecting Lisa to walk out of the kitchen at any minute and ask me if I want a cup of tea. It feels like years since I've been here. It's difficult to believe we're still in the same month.

The living room is darker than usual, mainly due to the curtains' having been pulled shut. Some daylight seeps around the edges, bleeding across the wallpaper, but at least I'm sheltered from the flashbulbs of the press photographers who are being kept at bay at the end of the driveway by the police. Percy, the stuffed bear, sits solemnly on the wall unit, wedged gracefully between two shelves. I look at him for a moment, and smile.

DCI Kelman, a man who can barely be pushing fifty but who's sporting a cropped head of grey hair and an athletic look that'd make most men twenty years younger than him jealous, moves his lower jaw around in circles. I can hear the occasional click and crunch.

'Best thing to do is keep away from the front of the house, if you can. They'll get bored pretty quickly. I'm going to give them a statement in a moment. Anything you'd like me to say?'

I think for a couple of seconds.

'I dunno. Just that I didn't do it.'

Kelman smiles. 'I think I'll probably remember to mention that at some point, don't worry. I meant more about your own personal feelings. For your wife.'

How am I ever meant to put that into words? I don't want to tell Kelman this, but I've barely had a moment to think about life without Lisa. My overriding feeling is of guilt. After all, I'm the reason she died. Kelman tells me I can't blame myself, that Jess admitted to Lisa's murder.

I thought I'd have a tougher time convincing the police of my innocence, but the recording on the dictaphone seemed to go a long way. Having Claude's statement about Jess was vital. We didn't mention the false passport stuff, or the burning down of her parents' holiday home all those years ago. That's stuff they'll find out on their own. All I needed was someone else to testify that Jess existed, and that she was responsible for what happened.

Even before I'd got back to East Grinstead, the British and French police had liaised with each other, the French police taking DNA samples from Claude's farmhouse and matching them to a stray hair found in the bathroom at the hotel in Herne Bay. As far as a court of law would go, that wouldn't prove anything. Her hair had every right to be in the hotel in which she worked, particularly as I'd already admitted having an affair with her in that room. My main advantage was that the police seemed to believe me, and any evidence to the contrary would be purely circumstantial and wouldn't stand up in court.

A younger officer enters the living room, dressed in a sharp suit.

'Sir, the Austrian police have confirmed that they've found the Citroën. It was left in a petrol station just outside Innsbruck a few days ago. Registered in France to a Monsieur Claude Robert. Apparently they passed it over to the French police to follow up, but it fell somewhere down their list of priorities.'

'Why doesn't that surprise me?' Kelman replies, raising his eyebrows. 'Have they done DNA swabs?'

'Not yet, but we've got them on the case.'

Kelman nods, a confident look in his eye. 'I presume we'll find Jessica's DNA in it, will we, Daniel?'

'I should imagine so,' I reply. 'But all that'll tell you is that she was in the car. It doesn't prove that she killed Lisa, does it?'

'No, but the circumstantial evidence would lead to that. Not enough to stand up in court, but the crucial thing is there'd be even less pointing in your direction.'

I'm comfortable that Kelman believes my side of the story. I could see from the look on his face when he listened to the dictaphone recording that he personally wouldn't need much more.

The police had only got as far as France in terms of looking for me. That surprised me. I was sure they would've at least managed to track us to Claude's farmhouse and that CCTV between Claude's and the Swiss campsite would have picked us up at some point. The cameras lost us as we turned off the motorway a good few miles away from Claude's place, and my car never reappeared again. The next day, we were on the road in Claude's old Citroën. In many ways, I wish I'd known this from the start and hadn't had to risk my life in Bratislava.

I gasp, a sudden thought entering my mind.

'What about Slovakia? What about Marek and Andrej?' The twists and turns of the past few days have left enormous gaps in my reasoning.

'The guys who owned the bar? The drug dealers?'

'We don't know they were drug dealers,' I say, almost as if I'm trying to defend them.

Kelman shrugs. 'What do you reckon? I don't mean to sound rude, but if what you've told us is true, firstly it doesn't concern us, and secondly I don't see why they'd give a tuppenny toss. They've got bigger things to worry about than some foreign bloke ditching their moped halfway across town.'

'But they know who I am. They know where I live,' I say. 'They're dangerous people.'

Kelman forces a smile. 'We've got officers stationed outside your house, Daniel. I'm not being funny, but we're hardly going to just disappear and leave you on your own. There's even a few of our own who still think you're guilty, and that's before you start dealing with those bastards from the press out there. Which reminds me, do you want me to get them to piss off?'

I shake my head. 'Nah, I reckon I can deal with a few photographers after what I've been through recently.'

'We can have you put up in a hotel if you like. We won't be paying for it, but it'll be a reduced rate.'

I laugh. It's the natural, instinctive reaction. 'No. I think I'll be staying away from hotels for a while.'

67

The press had given up the ghost within forty-eight hours. There were newer, juicier stories for them to get their teeth stuck into. A new innocent victim for the baying pack to latch on to. After the police announced that they would not be pressing charges against me and that they had reason to believe the person responsible had died in a fire in France, the press seemed to ease off a bit.

The fact was that almost nothing remained of the inside of Claude's barn. The French authorities were still combing it, trying to find evidence that Jess had indeed perished. It would take some time, they said, but they had no reason to believe anything else had happened. Claude's testimony was that he'd managed to pull me out of the barn just as he saw me losing consciousness, and that he hadn't seen Jess at all. She had been further into the barn than I was at that point, and judging by the look on her face and the things she was saying, she had no intention of living anyway.

The police told me they wouldn't be able to give me any sort of ongoing protection. They'd offered to put me up in a hotel and suggested that I go and stay with family or friends, but none of those ideas seemed particularly attractive. I've got used to being on my own recently.

I'm going to take a few days to take stock and let life resume its normal rhythms before I decide what I want to do. I'm still flitting between returning to normality and embracing the chance to start again, build myself a new life in a new place. Perhaps not abroad, though. And preferably away from any hotels.

The doorbell rings, and I poke my head around the lounge door and squint as I look at the frosted glass panel in the upper half of the front door. I can see the reflective colours of the postman's waterproof jacket, so I unlock the door. He's standing there with a large cardboard box.

'Delivery for Mr Cooper?' he says, thrusting the box at me. 'Sign here, please.' He eyes me carefully, no doubt having heard my name and seen my photograph, as has most of Europe by now.

I avoid eye contact with him, sign his PDA with a random squiggle and close the door. I hold the cardboard box in my hand for a few moments, feeling the weight. I'm not expecting anything. I put the box down on my kitchen table and look more closely at the address, which has been written in black marker pen. In the upper-right corner is a selection of stamps, postmarked with a picture of two ice skaters and some words I don't understand. One stands, out, though: *Bratislava*.

I instinctively think about calling the police, worried about what might be inside. Something stills me, though. It's something in the way my name and address have been written on the front of the box. Calmly, almost with kindness. I'm not the sort of person who thinks inanimate objects carry an aura, but I'm definitely starting to trust my instincts much more after recent events.

I take a small paring knife from the block and cut through the tape that holds the box shut. Carefully, I lift open the flaps to find my rucksack, wrapped in two thick layers of bubble wrap. Sellotaped to the outside of the bubble wrap is a note, written in the same black marker pen as was used to write the name and address on the front:

For Bradley. From Bratislava.

68

Martin da Silva turns down the volume on his Audi's stereo as he always does just before turning off the engine. It was a force of habit, and he knew it, but it still didn't stop him.

He opens the door and steps out into the cold, damp night air. It was much as he expected from a November night in Carlisle, but at least he'd go home tomorrow afternoon with a ten-grand Christmas bonus if he managed to complete the Granex deal at tomorrow's meeting. He knew he would. He always managed to complete deals, and this one was a dead cert.

He'd get himself a new suit with the cash, he told himself. The Armani number he was wearing right now was at least two years old, and it was about time he treated himself. Thanks to inheriting his father's Hispanic good looks, a smart designer suit was almost mandatory in completing his image.

He certainly wouldn't tell Katrina about the bonus, he

told himself. She'd only blow it on more Louis Vuitton shoes or handbags. A nice suit was one thing – he needed that for his professional image, and for other stuff besides – but what could his wife possibly do with twenty handbags?

Martin lifted his chin, exuding confidence as he walked towards the reception of the hotel, his leather-soled shoes clip-clopping across the tarmac as he swung his overnight bag beside him.

The automatic doors slid open as the warm air from the reception area rushed to meet him. Safely inside, the doors closed behind him and he approached the reception desk, waiting for a moment before pressing the buzzer.

A few seconds later, a young, slim woman appeared through a doorway. She can't have been more than twenty-five, but it was always difficult to tell some women's ages. Martin couldn't help but raise one corner of his mouth in a suggestive smile as he watched her walk behind the desk, her eyes full of sparkle and youthful exuberance. She looked at him for a moment before speaking, glancing down at his wedding ring.

'Can I help you, sir?'

Martin moved his right hand over his left, covering his wedding ring.

'Yes, I've got a reservation for tonight. Martin da Silva.'

The girl smiled and glanced over at her computer screen.

'Ah yes. Here you are. Let's just see what room you're in . . .'

Martin gulped and swallowed as she leaned forward to

get a better look at the screen, simultaneously giving him a better look down her blouse.

'Right. We've got room 202. That's up on the second floor. The only thing is, the TV's on the blink. Doesn't get Channels 4 or 5. But I presume that won't be a problem if you're only staying the one night . . . ?'

Martin smiled seductively. 'Oh, I'm certainly hoping not.'

ACKNOWLEDGMENTS

I spent a lot of the second half of 2015 in hotels all around Britain. In between trying to grab snatches of time to continue working on my books, a few things struck me as being really odd about the whole situation. Being quite a private person, the fact that I was sleeping in a bed someone else had been in only hours earlier, just inches away from a complete stranger who's separated from me only by eight inches of brick, was quite bizarre.

When you wake up in the room of a chain hotel which looks the same as every hotel room you've slept in for the past couple of months, it takes you a few minutes to even realise which part of the country you're in. Everything's the same, but somehow different. It's quite an odd and depersonalising thing.

I'm always on the lookout for new book ideas and like to try and throw the 'What if?' line into everyday situations and see where my mind takes me. One evening, whilst I was getting ready for bed in my identikit hotel room in Glasgow (or was it Edinburgh? Or Harrogate? Or Stourbridge?) I threw a new 'What if?' into the mix. What if I turned around and there was a dead body in the bath? That was the spark that led to the plot for this book.

That's perhaps the most exciting moment in the process of writing a new book – that spark that sets it all off and leaves you with a big beaming smile as you realise you've got the golden nugget at the heart of a new book. And that's when the hard work begins!

I should just add a small caveat: my protagonist staying in a hotel is where the inspiration from real life starts and ends. I should just point out that we have no other similarities. Especially as my wife is reading this.

I hope you enjoyed reading the book as much as I enjoyed writing it. My psychological thrillers are proving extremely popular (especially since *Her Last Tomorrow* flew up the Amazon charts and became a bestseller), and I absolutely love writing them and coming up with new, horrifying scenarios for perfectly ordinary people.

If you've read *Her Last Tomorrow*, you might've spotted a couple of familiar characters popping up in the shop in Switzerland. Sorry. I couldn't resist it.

If you know France, Switzerland, Austria or Slovakia at all, you've probably noticed that I don't. Although I've based every location in this book on real locations, I must admit to some artistic licence where necessary and hope you'll forgive me for it.

My thanks go to Österreichische Bundesbahnen, the

Austrian train operator, for the information on travel between Innsbruck and Bratislava. Thanks also to the residents of Innsbruck for unwittingly allowing me to invent a petrol station and flyover.

I must also thank Lucy Hayward, for her eagle eye and pointing out a few daft errors in the manuscript before they got too far.

And last but certainly not least, the biggest thanks must go to my readers and members of my VIP Club, who are the whole reason I keep doing this. You guys rock.

MORE BOOKS BY ADAM CROFT

RUTLAND CRIME SERIES

1. What Lies Beneath
2. On Borrowed Time
3. In Cold Blood

KNIGHT & CULVERHOUSE CRIME THRILLERS

1. Too Close for Comfort
2. Guilty as Sin
3. Jack Be Nimble
4. Rough Justice
5. In Too Deep
6. In The Name of the Father
7. With A Vengeance
8. Dead & Buried
9. In Too Deep
10. Snakes & Ladders

PSYCHOLOGICAL THRILLERS

- Her Last Tomorrow

- Only The Truth
- In Her Image
- Tell Me I'm Wrong
- The Perfect Lie
- Closer To You

KEMPSTON HARDWICK MYSTERIES

1. Exit Stage Left
2. The Westerlea House Mystery
3. Death Under the Sun
4. The Thirteenth Room
5. The Wrong Man

All titles are available to order from all good book shops.

Signed and personalised books available at adamcroft.net/shop

EBOOK-ONLY SHORT STORIES

- Gone
- The Harder They Fall
- Love You To Death
- The Defender

To find out more, visit adamcroft.net

GET MORE OF MY BOOKS FREE!

Thank you for reading *Only The Truth*. I hope it was as much fun for you as it was for me writing it.

To say thank you, I'd like to give you some of my books and short stories for FREE. Read on to get yours...

If you enjoyed the book, please do leave a review online. Reviews mean an awful lot to writers and they help us to find new readers more than almost anything else. It would be very much appreciated.

I love hearing from my readers, too, so please do feel free to get in touch with me. You can contact me via my website, on Twitter @adamcroft and you can join my Facebook Readers Group at http://www.facebook.com/groups/adamcroft.

Last of all, but certainly not least, I'd like to let you know that members of my email club have access to FREE, exclusive books and short

stories which aren't available anywhere else. There's a whole lot more, too, so please join the club (for free!) at https://www. adamcroft.net/vip-club

For more information, visit my website: adamcroft.net